What People Are Saying about Penny Zeller and *McKenzie*...

Penny Zeller writes with wit, brilliance, descriptive clarity, and gentle, inspirational prose. She provides a plentiful supply of intrigue, romance, and drama, truly enough to keep anyone reading during every spare moment. I am eager to watch the impact this book will make on Christian fiction as a whole, but especially on individual readers, as they clearly find a well-defined yet never preachy message of God's unchanging, never-failing, ever-forgiving gospel. This book is intended for your keeper library shelf, with its beautiful cover, endearing story line, and gripping characters who will stay with you. Don't delay in adding it to your to-be-read pile. Matter of fact, lay it on the top!

—*Sharlene MacLaren*
Award-winning, best-selling author,
the Little Hickman Creek and The Daughters of Jacob
Kane series, *Through Every Storm*, and *Long Journey Home*

Penny Zeller's *McKenzie* is a moving, compelling story that's rich with panoramic beauty and characters you'll identify with. You will laugh, you will weep, you will wish you had taken speed-reading in school so you could find out even faster what happens next! I'm definitely adding this one to my keepers list!

—*Loree Lough*
Award-winning author of seventy-five novels, including
Beautiful Bandit (book one in the Lone Star Legends series)

McKenzie is a captivating tale weaved together masterfully with characters that quickly steal the reader's heart. They certainly did mine.

—*Shirley Kiger Connolly*
Author, *Flame from Within* and the *I See God* series

McKenzie is a sweet love story that transcends the pages of time and brings a fresh, new voice to the historical genre.

—*Bonnie Calhoun*
Publisher, *Christian Fiction Online Magazine*
GPCWC Writer of the Year, 2009

With a gentle touch and warm style, Zeller pens a story that looks deep into the heart of love—the kind between sisters that her heroine would do anything to honor, and the unexpected romance that springs up in its pursuit. *McKenzie* is a novel that will lead you on an adventure along with the title character and touch your heart as Zach touches hers.

—*Roseanna M. White*
Author, *A Stray Drop of Blood*
Senior Reviewer, *The Christian Review of Books*

McKenzie

McKenzie

Penny ZELLER

WHITAKER
HOUSE

Publisher's Note:
This novel is a work of fiction. References to real events, organizations, or places are used in a fictional context. Any resemblances to actual persons, living or dead, are entirely coincidental.

All Scripture quotations are taken from the King James Version of the Holy Bible. Scripture quotation in the Acknowledgments marked (NIV) is from the *Holy Bible, New International Version*®, NIV®, © 1973, 1978, 1984 by the International Bible Society. Used by permission of Zondervan. All rights reserved.

McKenzie
Book One in the Montana Skies Series

Penny Zeller
www.pennyzeller.com

ISBN: 978-1-60374-216-0
Printed in the United States of America
© 2010 by Penny Zeller

Whitaker House
1030 Hunt Valley Circle
New Kensington, PA 15068
www.whitakerhouse.com

Library of Congress Cataloging-in-Publication Data

Zeller, Penny, 1973–
McKenzie / by Penny Zeller.
    p. cm. — (Montana skies ; bk. 1)
    Summary: "McKenzie Worthington heads west as a mail-order bride with plans to return to Boston as soon as she finds and rescues her sister, Kaydie, from an abusive marriage. What she didn't count on was falling in love with her husband, a handsome, godly rancher named Zach Sawyer"—Provided by publisher.
    ISBN 978-1-60374-216-0 (trade pbk.)
    1. Single women—Fiction. 2. Sisters—Fiction. 3. Abused wives—Fiction
4. Adultery—Fiction. 5. Montana—Fiction. I. Title.
PS3626.E3565M33 2010
813'.6—dc22
                                        2010019273

1 2 3 4 5 6 7 8 9 10 **WH** 16 15 14 13 12 11 10

Acknowledgments

A special thanks to the following:

Jesus Christ, my Lord and Savior—May my writing always glorify You and bring others to a knowledge of Your saving grace.

My husband, Lon—Thank you for your encouragement and support. This wouldn't have been possible without you!

My children—You are such blessings in my life! I love you and thank God for you daily.

My grandmother, Ruth Brown—Thank you for your enthusiasm in reading each new manuscript I send your way.

Barbara Dafoe—Thank you for your wisdom, insight, and inspiration.

Fellow author, Sharlene MacLaren—Thank you for your encouragement. I want to be just like you when I grow up!

My editor at Whitaker House, Courtney Hartzel—You have been awesome to work with. Thank you for all you do.

Christine Whitaker and the staff at Whitaker House—What a blessing and a privilege to work with such an outstanding company!

My readers—May God bless you as you grow daily in your walk with Him.

—*Penny Zeller*

May the words of my mouth and the meditation of my heart be pleasing in your sight, O LORD, my Rock and my Redeemer.

—Psalm 19:14 (NIV)

To Madi

CHAPTER ONE

*C*lutching the envelope that had just been delivered to her home, McKenzie Worthington walked into the parlor and closed the doors behind her. Sitting down, she ran her finger over the familiar, hasty penmanship on the outside of the envelope. There was no return address, but McKenzie already knew who had sent the letter. Bracing herself for the words on the pages within, she carefully opened the seal and unfolded the tattered, soiled piece of stationery.

My dearest sister McKenzie,

I write this letter with a heavy heart and a fearful spirit. I am convinced that Darius is not the man I thought him to be when I married him. He drinks almost continually, and when there is no more money to purchase his whiskey, he places the blame on me. He used all the money in my trousseau long ago, and we are constantly on the run to avoid the law. His threats are many if I dare turn him in to the local sheriff.

We are without food much of the time, but Darius always finds funds for his alcohol. All the money sent to me in the past, he has found a way to spend. I wish more than anything that I could find a way to leave this place and return home. However, he has threatened my life if I leave and has arranged for several of his friends at the saloon to keep an eye on me. One of his friends, Bulldog, lives nearby and watches my every move. He scares me to death, McKenzie.

Please, help me get away from my husband. He is such a mean man with a horrid temper. I fear for my life, at times. If he knew I was writing to you, I know he would kill me. I ask again that you please not tell Mother and Father the seriousness of my situation, since they will surely say that I deserve it for running away with Darius. But please come, and come quickly.

With much love,
Kaydie

When she had finished reading the letter, McKenzie clutched it to her chest. She could feel a tear threatening to fall, and she diverted her attention to the mantel above the fireplace. A large, three-foot-square oil painting hung proudly in the same place it had for the past ten years. McKenzie stared at the three people in the portrait and suddenly yearned for things to be as they had been then. Time had passed so quickly; the years of her childhood seemed barely a whisper in the conversation of life.

On the left-hand side of the painting, McKenzie's younger sister, Kaydie, posed in her pink satin gown. Her long, blonde hair flowed over her shoulders, and her brown eyes seemed to hold a sparkle that McKenzie knew was long gone due to Kaydie's present circumstances.

Sitting on a higher stool in the middle, McKenzie's older sister, Peyton, emphasized her role as the eldest and most favored Worthington daughter. Beneath her dark, rolling locks, her large, green eyes held the look of arrogance and superiority that she continually flaunted over her less-preferred sisters.

On the right-hand side, her head tilted toward Kaydie's, sat McKenzie, then fourteen years old. Her long, strawberry blonde hair was pinned up at the sides, and she wore her favorite turquoise gown. The smirk on McKenzie's face had caused her mother great disturbance. "Proper ladies never smile in a portrait. Your father will be so disappointed," her mother had scolded her. "We shall have to insist the painting be redone."

The artist had been paid a reduced fee for failing to change McKenzie's smile to a look of solemnity and had never been asked to paint any further portraits for the Worthington family. So, the portrait of Arthur and Florence Worthington's daughters had never been repainted.

Once the servants had hung it above the mantel, there it had remained, serving as a memory in different ways to the different members of the Worthington household. To Peyton, it was a reminder that she was the eldest and the most obedient. To McKenzie and Kaydie, it was a reminder of enjoyable days past, when they would secretly embark on adventures that were considered unbecoming for young women from families of prestige and wealth. To McKenzie's mother, the portrait was a disgrace because of McKenzie's smirk, and to her father, it was the observance of a costly tradition that had been carried on from generation to generation.

McKenzie scanned the portrait again, her focus stopping on Kaydie's face. *Hang on, my dear Kaydie. I promise I will figure out a way to save you from Darius. Please don't give up hope*, she silently begged her sister. *I don't know how I will do it or when, only that I will. This much I promise you.*

McKenzie sat for a moment longer in the quietness of the parlor. She recalled her parents' disturbance when their youngest daughter had eloped with Darius Kraemer and moved West with him.

McKenzie's mother had covered her mouth with her left hand and fanned herself with her right, clearly indicating her dismay at the situation. "I am so distraught by Kaydie's marriage that I can barely manage day-to-day living," she'd lamented.

"She never should have married a man so far beneath her. Now we'll likely never hear from her again," Peyton had said, sipping her tea. "Of course, Kaydie was always the one who thought she could do whatever she pleased and face the consequences later." Peyton's voice had done little to hide her smugness. "I would never do such a thing. Not only was it an unwise decision to marry someone without a pedigree and move far from civilization, but it has brought nothing but shame to the Worthington family. I can't begin to count the number of times I've had to make up stories to explain her absence in order to preserve our family's impeccable reputation."

McKenzie had glared at her older sister. "Now, Peyton, not everyone can marry such a fine gentleman as Maxwell Adams," she'd said with more than a hint of sarcasm, thinking of how grateful she was that she herself hadn't married Maxwell, or anyone like him. While he was polite and treated Peyton well, he was also stuffy and prudish, and he seemed incapable of doing anything for himself. It had been Peyton who had secured his position at their father's law office.

Maxwell hadn't even been able to apply for the job himself. In McKenzie's opinion, Maxwell was a helpless, spineless, sorry excuse for a man.

"At least I am married," Peyton had said, glaring at her sister, "unlike some people I know." Peyton never missed an opportunity to rub in the fact that McKenzie, as an unmarried woman, was an oddity in a society that held marriage as the highest priority for women—marriage to a man from a wealthy family and with a thriving career, of course. The fact that Peyton had been successful on both accounts gave her an edge over a sister who in most other respects won the competition war.

"Now, girls, please. This bickering between the two of you must stop," their mother had said, wringing her hands.

"You're right, Mother. It is a shame that McKenzie doesn't conduct herself in a manner more in line with our upbringing," Peyton had said, smiling smugly at her mother.

McKenzie shook her head now and pictured her mother. With the exception of her long, gray-blonde hair and the age difference, she and Peyton could be twins. Her mother's large, emerald eyes made her look as though she were in a constant state of surprise. Her pert, upturned nose further conveyed the air about her that she knew she was from one of the wealthier families in the Boston area, both by birth and by marriage.

"Marry a man of wealth, have children, attend social gatherings, and busy yourself with acceptable volunteer work" were the maxims McKenzie's mother sought to instill in her daughters. Kaydie had managed to fulfill one of those wishes—she'd married. Yet, it had been in defiance of her parents' desire, for Darius was hardly wealthy. Yes, they had met while doing volunteer work, but, based on what McKenzie knew now, it had probably been a ruse.

The chiming of the tall, mahogany clock in the corner brought McKenzie back to the present, and she again focused her attention on Kaydie's predicament. She knew that mailing money to Kaydie to secure her fare to Boston would be impossible, as she had no access to any funds; the money in her dowry would be passed to her husband alone.

Poor Kaydie had thought her normally calm and complacent life would be so full of adventure when she'd agreed to marry the wayward Darius. He'd captured her heart and taken her from security and wealth to the dangerous, uncivilized Wild West. Granted, he was an attractive man with allure brimming in his erratic personality. He'd even said all the things Kaydie had longed to hear, making the men of Boston pale in comparison. Only after it was too late had Kaydie discovered that Darius made his living by swindling and robbing. When things didn't go according to plan, he took out his fury, both verbal and physical, on Kaydie, essentially holding her hostage in her own marriage.

Now, Kaydie was suffering because she'd fallen in love with what had turned out to be a mere façade. Her dowry, which Darius had been after from the beginning, had been spent while Kaydie had been blinded by the love she'd thought she had found.

McKenzie had always been closest to Kaydie and knew that there must be a way to help her. Besides, she knew Kaydie would do the same if the situation were reversed. She reached up to twirl one of her tendrils between her finger and her thumb, as she habitually did when she was in deep thought. Not one to allow discouragement to defeat her, McKenzie knew she had to be the one to concoct a plan to rescue her sister. Kaydie's life depended on it. No one else knew of the four letters Kaydie had mailed intermittently to McKenzie.

McKenzie had been sworn to secrecy regarding Kaydie's pre-dicament, and, besides, her parents would no doubt have no shortage of words regarding their judgment of their youngest daughter's poor choice. No one else knew the way her life had taken a turn for the worse. No one else knew of Kaydie's des-peration. McKenzie was the only one who knew and the only one who could help. But how would she afford the trip west? And, once she got there, where would she stay? Who would protect her while she searched potentially dangerous towns for her sister?

Just then, it came to her—an idea so crazy, she thought that it just might work.

CHAPTER TWO

"*I* would love to help you write an advertisement," said Lucille Granger, her eyes holding a twinkle.

Zach looked at Lucille, with her gray hair swooped in a tight bun on her head, pulled back so tightly that it made her eyes turn up at the outer corners. Her plump fingers awaited the go-ahead to assist Zach with the task he anticipated yet dreaded. He'd known Lucille for over a decade. She and her husband, Fred, had been more than kind to Zach when he'd first moved to Pine Haven with little more than a bedroll. They'd given him a job at Granter Mercantile, the store they owned and operated, and had become a surrogate aunt and uncle to him.

Surely, Lucille would be able to carry out the task she so eagerly awaited. After all, Zach reasoned, Lucille had an education and was very creative. She would have just the talent Zach needed to help him land a wife for himself and a mother for Davey. Yet, she did have one negative aspect of her personality—a penchant for gossip. It wasn't that she was malicious or desired to cause trouble, but she simply struggled with keeping interesting information to herself. It was like her delicious, homemade honey bread, which was famous for a twenty-five-mile radius—she couldn't wait to share it. Once someone took the chance of telling Lucille any news, it wasn't long before the entire town knew.

"All right, Lucille, but you have to promise me you'll take this seriously, not tell anyone, and do your best in the advertisement to make me sound like a decent man."

"That won't be hard, Zach. You are a very decent man, and I will take it seriously," Lucille said. He didn't miss her neglect to mention his other request. Still, he figured finding a wife would be worth the risk of having Lucille spill juicy gossip all over town.

Lucille reached for a pencil and tapped it on the counter. "I'm going to think on this in between customers, and we'll meet again tomorrow. How does that sound?"

"That would be fine, Lucille," Zach said. He picked up the bag of flour he'd purchased and turned to exit the store.

"By the way, Zach, would you like for me to mention Davey in the ad?"

Zach thought for a moment. "Not right at first, Lucille. I'll reply with that information if someone is interested."

"I should think you'd have a lot of women interested," said Lucille with a giggle that made her sound like a silly schoolgirl. "If I'd had a daughter instead of three sons, I would have wanted her to marry you."

"Thank you, Lucille," Zach said and blushed. In a way, he wished Lucille had a daughter. Even though she probably would have been several years older than Zach, at least it would have saved him the time, hassle, and embarrassment of advertising for a wife. As it was, there were few unmarried women in Pine Haven, and absolutely none with whom he was interested in spending the rest of his life.

"You're welcome, Zach. Now tell Davey, Rosemary, and everyone else hello for me, and I'll see you tomorrow, bright and early."

Zach nodded and stepped out the door, then made his way to his wagon, into which he loaded the sack of flour. If this harebrained idea ever worked, he would be amazed. Still, he'd spent much time praying to God for wisdom, discernment, and guidance on this issue. One item was of chief importance: Davey needed a mother. If God led Zach to a woman, she would be the right one—of that, Zach was certain.

"Well, what do you think?" Lucille asked Zach the next morning when he finished reading the advertisement she'd written.

Zach rolled his shoulders in an upward manner, as he always did when he was nervous, and read the handwritten words again:

Twenty-five-year-old rancher in Montana Territory looking for possible matrimony. Man of integrity with dark brown hair, blue eyes, and shy demeanor seeks a kind, educated, hardworking, Christian woman with good disposition with whom to share his life. Must be willing to relocate. Please correspond by mail to Mr. Zach Sawyer, Pine Haven, Montana Territory.

"I don't know, Lucille."

"I think it sounds great," said Lucille. "You know, my writing expertise would draw a fair wage in some parts of the country."

She stared at him for a moment before speaking again. "I've mentioned your age and appearance, and what you're after—possible matrimony. By saying 'possible,' you give yourself the option to decline, should the replies prove unsatisfactory. Second, I've written what you are looking for in a woman." Lucille grinned and leaned closer to him. "Was I not right in what you desire in a wife? I believe the only thing I failed to mention, and I can easily add, is that you desire someone beautiful."

"Don't add that, Lucille. A woman might not find herself beautiful, even though I might, and then she wouldn't respond. I reckon you could leave it as is."

"You don't sound too pleased. I'll have you know, Zachary Sawyer, I stayed up half the night to write this. I changed the wording no fewer than fifteen times, and I made you to sound like a highly educated man." Her voice rose to the pitch it always had when she'd scolded her sons for eating one too many cookies before supper.

"Thank you, Lucille. I appreciate all the time and work you've put into this. By the way, I'm not uneducated. I went to a fine city school before my parents died, and the orphanage where I grew up did offer more than sufficient lessons."

"Oh, I know that. I didn't mean to make it sound as though you weren't intelligent; I just wanted the women reading the advertisement to realize you were educated to some degree. You see, some women might see the words 'Montana Territory' and think you are a backwards fellow without much schooling. We want to prevent anyone from drawing conclusions of that sort." Lucille patted him on the arm. "Now, you take this and mail it today." She pointed at the post office a few buildings down, as if Zach was ignorant of its location, even after all the years he'd lived in Pine Haven.

"All right, Lucille. Thank you again."

"Now, you promise me, Zach, that you'll go right over and have Mr. Victor mail it right away. As you can see, I have copied it over five times—no quick task, I might add—so that you can mail it to the five newspapers on this list. These are some of the finest newspapers in the East, including *Marriage Times* and the *Boston Herald*." Lucille grabbed the stack of copies from Zach and added the listing of newspapers to it. Then, she tapped them on the counter several times to line them up in perfect order before handing them back to Zach.

"I don't know, Lucille. Maybe it's not the right thing to do. I mean, Davey does have Rosemary...."

"Rosemary is one of my closest friends, and she's a grand influence on Davey, but he needs a ma. Plus, you need a wife. Now go, Zach, and mail the advertisement. Then, come back over and have a piece of my world-famous, homemade honey bread." Lucille adjusted her thick glasses on her nose and gestured with her right hand toward the door.

"All right, Lucille, I'll do it."

Zach sighed as he headed for the post office. *Lord, please let this be the right thing to do*, he silently prayed. *The last thing I want to do is make an error, because there's so much at stake.* The last thing Zach wanted to do was receive an answer from a woman who had no desire to be a mother and who lacked love for the little boy who'd joined his life and had planted seeds of untold love in his heart.

CHAPTER THREE

*M*cKenzie thumbed through the pages of the *Boston Herald* until she came to the section of listings written by men seeking women to travel west to become their brides. What they had to offer was just what she would need during her rescue mission: money for the trip and a place to stay, as well as the help of a man in finding Kaydie and taking her away from her husband once she'd been found. Becoming a mail-order bride seemed like a viable way of fulfilling these needs.

McKenzie sighed as she gazed at the overwhelming list, spaced in perfect columns. Her eyes had a difficult time focusing on the endless calls for brides. When she realized there was more than one page of listings to peruse, she fought the dizziness threatening to overwhelm her. Was she really succumbing to this? She felt momentarily sick at the thought. *It will all be worth it to have Kaydie back*, she reassured herself. Having a place to stay while she searched for her sister was crucial. There weren't hotels in many of the towns in Montana

Territory, and there was no telling how long it might take her to find Kaydie.

As her eyes searched the newspaper print, McKenzie mentally dismissed all the advertisements posted by lonely miners in California. The thought of being wed to a gold-grubbing man disgusted her. She could only imagine the filthy lifestyle she'd be forced to endure. Besides, most of those men were likely twice her age, and the idea of marrying a man old enough to be her father was repulsive. Yes, she had limits, even when it came to saving her sister. There was only so much sacrificing she could and would do. There was only so much she would force herself to endure, even if it was to be temporary.

With a pencil, she continued to cross out advertise-ments in states and territories other than Montana. She only needed to find an offer in the Montana Territory, perhaps the Wyoming Territory, if she was desperate. Judging from the map, the two weren't too far apart.

When she had finished round one of her search, McKenzie flipped to the second page. Tapping her pencil in frustration on her mahogany desk, she thought of the work this endeavor was producing—and she hadn't even begun the difficult part. What if she were really searching for a husband? Thankfully, that was not the case. Yet, she knew of women who were that desperate. At twenty-four, she was anxiously nearing the point when many women become bound for spinsterhood. Her own family refused to let her forget for a moment that she was the only unmarried Worthington sister and that she wasn't getting any younger. Still, McKenzie wasn't so desperate that she would seek a stranger thousands of miles away with whom to spend her life. Surely, a fine, upstanding Boston man would be proud to have her as his wife. Yet, none had stepped forward to ask for her hand. McKenzie returned her thoughts to the newspaper. Yes, she would do just about anything, including marry a stranger, if only to bring her beloved sister back to Boston.

Advertisement after advertisement yielded no hope, and McKenzie was about to give up when she spied, in the bottommost box, an advertisement written in a smaller font than the rest, as if the newspaper had suddenly decided to conserve ink.

Twenty-five-year-old rancher in Montana Territory looking for possible matrimony. Man of integrity with dark brown hair, blue eyes, and shy demeanor seeks a kind, educated, hardworking, Christian woman with good disposition with whom to share his life. Must be willing to relocate. Please correspond by mail to Mr. Zach Sawyer, Pine Haven, Montana Territory.

McKenzie's eyes widened. The words "Montana Territory" jumped out at her, and she read them three times to be sure her eyes weren't deceiving her. *Maybe this won't be such a horrendous task after all*, she thought. At least this Mr. Sawyer was only a year older than she, and the combination of blue eyes and dark brown hair did sound somewhat appealing. Besides, she recognized the name of the town of Pine Haven from when she'd studied a map of the Montana Territory at the library.

McKenzie could only hope that Pine Haven was close to the area where Kaydie had been when she'd penned her last letter.

CHAPTER FOUR

I suppose no woman in her right mind would want to move from the modern conveniences of the East to the unknown West," Zach sighed as he finished his daily work in the barn.

"So, I take it there have been no responses to your advertisement?" Asa, one of his hired hands, asked.

"Not yet. I placed the advertisement in five different newspapers over a month ago. Surely, I should have heard by now. Of course, it was probably the silliest idea I've ever agreed to in my life. That Lucille can be pretty convincing. When she first mentioned the plan, I thought it might all work out. Then, when she offered to help me write the advertisement, I was even more convinced."

"Ah, I wouldn't let it get you down—not yet, anyway," Asa said in his characteristic Irish accent. He walked over and patted Zach on the shoulder. "These things take time. Be patient, my friend."

Zach sighed. "I've prayed about it every night, so I guess it must not be in the Lord's will for me to receive a reply."

"Ah, you give up too soon. The Lord has great plans for you, Zach. He knows the woman you are meant to marry. Leave it in His hands."

"Believe me, Asa, I'm trying, but it's hard to be patient, especially since every time I go into town, I'm asked by at least a dozen people if I've received a reply."

"Well, that's the nosy townsfolk for you. I do think that many of them do have your best interests at heart. Unfortunately, I think Lucille had a hand in sharing the news with those who shop at the mercantile, which is just about everyone. Still, waiting is never easy, especially when it comes to matters of the heart."

Zach nodded and looked at the man before him. Asa had a reputation for being wise, and his advice had always confirmed that fact. He stood five feet eight inches tall and had a stocky build with graying brown hair and eyes that nearly disappeared when he laughed. He'd been married to Rosemary for almost thirty years and had dedicated his life not only to his wife, but also to his Creator. "I know you're right, Asa. It's just that when I promised to adopt Davey, I had hoped that the Lord would someday give me the blessing of a wife to be his mother."

"Is having a mother for Davey your top reason for wanting a wife?" Asa asked.

Zach was thoughtful for a moment. "I suppose that is a big part of it. But I would like to marry and share my life with the woman God has planned for me."

"Good. I'm glad a mother for Davey is not your top reason. That's not a good foundation on which to build a marriage. I believe God has just the woman for you, not only to be your wife, but also to be Davey's mother. Let's wait on His perfect timing, shall we?"

Zach nodded, knowing that Asa was right. "Maybe God is working some patience into me," he chuckled, knowing that patience had never been a virtue he possessed. "So, how did you and Rosemary meet?" he asked, changing the subject. Of all the years he'd known the couple, he'd never heard the story of their courtship.

"Ah, my sweet Rosemary, the love of my life...." Asa's face lit up. "I lived at her parents' boarding house."

"Really?" Zach asked.

"Yes. I know some people don't believe it, but for me, seeing Rosemary was...well, it was love at first sight. I just knew that someday she would be my wife."

"You knew that quickly?"

"Something inside me just knew. Of course, her pa had other plans for her. He didn't want her marrying some Irish drifter."

"Who wouldn't like you, Asa?" The thought of someone finding Asa less than agreeable was shocking to Zach.

"Ah, there are some I am sure don't like me. I think, for Rosemary's pa, it was that he didn't approve of me. After all, I had come to work in the mines and had not a penny to my name. I was a scrawny lad back then with a quick wit—which, at times, got me into some trouble. Rosemary's pa and I started off on the wrong foot, so that didn't help matters. Besides, there was this fellow by the name of Charles, whom Rosemary's pa wanted her to marry. His parents owned the mercantile to the right of the boarding house, and he was an upstanding citizen with a lot of potential." Asa chuckled. "See, when you get me started on a story, it's always a long one."

"I love hearing your stories, Asa. Please, go on."

"Well, you see, Rosemary and Charles had courted briefly, but it seemed that while Charles would make a suitable husband, Rosemary had no feelings for him. She'd known him all her life and thought of him more as a brother." Asa's eyes twinkled. "I think Rosemary found me an exciting alternative to the rather bland Charles, but you'd have to ask her that, yourself. Anyhow, I think she tried to love Charles and conjure the feelings of affection he carried for her, but it wasn't meant to be. I asked her pa after five months of knowing him if I could be allowed the privilege of courting his daughter. By this time, Rosemary's ma—she was a great woman—had spoken to her husband about their daughter's lack of interest in Charles, so I believe he was more open to the idea of his daughter's being courted by me. To make a long story short, Rosemary and I fell in love, and I asked for her hand in marriage three months later. I thank God every night that He gave me Rosemary. She is the best thing that has ever happened to me."

Zach smiled at his friend and hoped that, someday, he'd be able to say that about a woman God had chosen for him.

"You know, Zach, it never mattered to us too much that we never were able to have children," Asa continued. "Rosemary had seven younger brothers and sisters, so she'd felt like she'd already raised a family. Plus, it's allowed us to step into the role of parents to those who needed us."

"You both sure have been a blessing to me," Zach said.

"Ah, and likewise, Zach. We were so thankful you offered us this job. With my back, not many folks are eager to hire me anymore."

"It was actually because of Rosemary's fine cooking that I hired you both," Zach joked, jabbing Asa playfully in the ribs.

"Ah, I see how it is. Have a serious conversation, and the truth comes out!" Asa jabbed him back, and they both laughed. "Why don't we go in and see what that sweet Rosemary has made us for dinner tonight?"

"I agree. Thanks, Asa, for your advice."

"Anytime, my friend. I offer it free of charge."

CHAPTER FIVE

McKenzie sat down at her desk to pen a letter in response to the advertisement. Making her penmanship even more precise than usual, she took pains to be sure her writing accentuated her education and her life of privilege. Starting to the left of her monogrammed stationery, she wrote:

September 20, 1881

Dear Mr. Sawyer,

This letter is in response to your advertisement in the Boston Herald *regarding a mail-order bride. I believe I meet the qualifications you specified in your advertisement.*

My name is McKenzie L. Worthington. I am a Boston native, twenty-four years of age, possess an outgoing demeanor, and am well educated. I am the middle child of three daughters born to Arthur and Florence Worthington, and, for generations, our family has attended Fourth Street Presbyterian Church.

I look forward to receiving your response.

Most sincerely,

McKenzie L. Worthington
1589 Wild Willow Avenue
Boston, Massachusetts

McKenzie read the letter, crumpled it up, pulled out a fresh piece of stationery, and rewrote it. She had to make her first impression her best, and, by all appearances, her script needed improvement. She could hear the words of her fourth grade teacher, Miss Webstell, in her mind as if they had been said just yesterday: *"Now, McKenzie Worthington, I expect each of those letters to rest comfortably and conveniently on the lines of the paper. What you have handed in as your assignment will never do. Please rewrite the first seven lines, and, when you feel they would meet my scrutiny, you may turn your paper in to me."*

Satisfied that her letter would have met Miss Webstell's approval, McKenzie folded it carefully and placed it in the lilac-colored envelope, which she sealed. As she affixed a stamp in the upper right-hand corner, she willed the anxious feeling in her stomach to flee. After all, she wasn't really searching for a husband. Why, then, did she feel as though something exciting was about to happen?

As Zach approached the post office, he saw Lucille Granger leaning out the window of the mercantile, her head craned to the right, as if on the lookout for him. When he stopped his wagon in front of the post office, she rushed outside and onto the porch. "Zach! Did you hear the news?"

Lucille's short, squatty legs carried her down the stairs, and her boxy frame waddled across the dusty street, her bonnet flying behind her. She struggled to keep her pink calico dress from tripping her, using one hand to hold up her dress while waving wildly with the other.

Zach climbed down from the wagon and waved casually at Lucille. He tried to ignore the group of people who had stopped to observe the commotion Lucille was causing and envied Lucille, who seemed oblivious without effort.

"What is it, Lucille? Is everything all right?" His first thought was that Lucille's husband, Fred, was injured or sick. Why else would Lucille be in such a panic? He was very fond of the Grangers and prayed that nothing bad had happened.

"Zach! I thought I would never get your attention." Lucille's breath came out in puffs from a combination of her excitement and the mini-marathon she'd just run.

Zach held out his hands and let Lucille support herself as she caught her breath. "Is Fred all right?" he asked.

"Pardon?"

"Your husband, Fred—is he all right?"

"Fred? Oh my, yes, he's fine, just fine." Lucille pursed her lips. Whatever she was about to say, it looked as if she might burst if she had to keep it a secret for a mere second longer.

"Then, what is it, Lucille?" Zach glanced around at the townsfolk gathered nearby. If Lucille was causing a stir, it must be something important. After all, after the one-page newspaper, Lucille was the best carrier of news in Pine Haven, whether she realized it or not.

"Zach, you received not one but *two* responses to your advertisement! Can you believe it? You received two in one day!" Lucille exclaimed between dramatic gasps.

"Slow down, Lucille. Two responses?"

"Yes! You see, I was checking to see if there was any mail for Fred and me when I saw there on the counter two letters addressed to you." Lucille puffed out her chest like a proud rooster.

"Lucille, United States mail is supposed to be for the recipient only," Zach teased.

"Oh, dear me. I wasn't looking or anything, mind you. You see, the letters were just there, plain as day, begging my eyes to take a tiny peek. It wasn't Mr. Victor's fault or anything, I assure of you that." Lucille paused for a moment. "Not only did I see that they were addressed to you, but I also noticed that the return addresses were from women. And, Zach, one of the letters is in the most beautiful, purple-colored envelope I ever did see. Now, march yourself into the post office and retrieve those letters! You know we are all dying to hear what they wrote!" Lucille beamed at him.

Zach smiled back at her and shook his head. He could hardly be mad at Lucille for acting so presumptuously. She didn't mean to be bossy or nosy; it was just in her character, and he, as well as the rest of the residents of Pine Haven, had come to accept it. "I'm thankful Fred is fine. I'll go in right now and get those letters, Lucille, but I will read them first in private and then decide whether or not to share them with you and the rest of Pine Haven, all right?"

"Oh, if you insist. But do hurry. I know I'm not the only one who wants to know all about the future Mrs. Sawyer!"

CHAPTER SIX

*Z*ach avoided the temptation to rip open the letters immediately and finished his errands in town first. Then, on his way home from Pine Haven, he pulled to the side of the road and stopped the wagon. *Lord, help me to know which one, if either, or possibly both, that I should respond to,* he prayed before carefully opening the first envelope.

With his hands shaking from nervousness, though he figured he'd blame the chilly, fall weather, Zach unfolded the letter in the white envelope and read it:

Dear *Mr. Sawyer,*

I hope this letter finds you well. I am responding to your advertisement for a mail-order bride in the *Marriage Times.*

I am an extremely handsome woman of twenty-two years of age with long, ebony hair, brown eyes, and a shapely build. My extraordinary personality has been considered one of the finest by those who know me best. As I have been told many times, I am surely without fault. My education is far superior to that of most other women in the region, and I come from one of the finest, wealthiest families in the Baltimore area.

I desire to marry a well-to-do husband in the West with whom I can maintain the lifestyle to which I have grown accustomed. (The West holds a great deal of intrigue for me, as one of my ancestors was a French fur trader who traveled throughout your area.)

I have mailed a copy of this letter to each of the potentially suitable men in the *Marriage Times* advertisement listings. Consider yourself privileged to be among them. When the responses return to me, I will take my time to determine which advertisements are worthy of continued correspondence.

It would be in your best interests to respond as quickly as possible, as I imagine the competition for my hand in marriage will be fierce. Only those men with significant wealth, high social standing, excellent dispositions, and above-average appearances will be considered as candidates for matrimony.

> Yours truly,
> Dovie Patrick
> 126 12th Avenue
> Baltimore, Maryland

Zach sat motionless for a moment, staring at the letter he had just read. Did this Dovie Patrick honestly believe men would respond to someone who had sent out the same letter, with the exception of the salutation, to multiple men? It appeared she was in search of the best offer and would reject anyone who did not meet her strict criteria. *I waited two months for a response like this?* Zach thought. Hesitant to bother reading the second letter, he sat in silence pondering if wealth and prominence were the only items on the mind of every woman who answered an advertisement.

"I knew this was a crazy idea," he said with a sigh. He recalled the day Lucille had talked him into the plan just two months ago....

<hr>

"*You know, Zach, I've been thinking,*" *Lucille said as she filled his order.* "*There aren't many eligible women in Pine Haven, and you're not getting any younger. Have you ever thought of finding a wife?*"

Zach laughed. "*You know, Lucille, come to think of it, I have given that some thought in recent days. But, as you say, the pickings are slim in our town.*" *He paused.* "*Plus, you were already taken,*" *he teased.*

Lucille blushed. "*Now, Zach Sawyer, if I was thirty instead of fifty, I might consider you. But as it is, I am a happily married woman and far too old for you,*" *she teased him back. She cleared her throat.* "*Let's get serious. We shouldn't let the fact that there aren't many women in Pine Haven stop you from finding a wife. Have you ever thought of looking elsewhere for a bride?*"

Zach eyed the woman with suspicion. "*What do you mean, Lucille?*"

Lucille looked around the mercantile, as if to be sure no one would hear the words she was about to speak. When she was confident it would be a private conversation, she continued. "*Remember when my sister, Laverne, came to visit from Kansas City a few months back?*"

"Yes." Zach recalled the day well. It was the day that he discovered Lucille had a twin sister who was the same as Lucille in every way, except that Lucille was married to Fred, and Laverne was married to a man named Theo. It was almost eerie when the two of them were together, with the same appearance, the same laugh, and the same, mischievous personality.

Lucille leaned in closer and whispered, "One night, I was unable to sleep, so I came downstairs and saw that Laverne had left the newspaper she'd brought from Kansas City on the counter. I decided to sit a spell and read it. After all, it had been so long since I'd read a real newspaper. On the very last page was a section that advertised for mail-order brides."

Suddenly, as if he'd been awakened from a deep sleep, Zach knew what Lucille's suggestion would be, and he prepared his defense. "Now, Lucille—"

"Now, you wait just a second here, Zach. I know what you're going to say." Zach found Lucille's short finger inches from his nose. "I am not finished. As I was saying, I saw on the last page a section that advertised for mail-order brides. I read through the list and thought, Now, that would be interesting. I wondered for a minute how it would have been if I had been a mail-order bride and Fred had advertised and we'd met that way. It would have been so romantic. I can see it now...I would step from the stagecoach, and our eyes would meet. Nothing around us would matter, only the blossoming of new love." Lucille held her hand to her heart and closed her eyes, as if to live the tale she had fabricated in her mind. After a short time, she opened her eyes, rolled them in exaggeration, and continued, "As it is, we met at a church potluck, so it was nothing exciting. Besides, it took me some time to fall in love with him. But this? This is exciting. I read through each advertisement and thought, Now, I know there is someone who could find a bride this way. Please forgive me, but I thought *of Mr. Victor first, seeing as how he's getting up in years and has never been married, the poor man. But then, just the other day, I thought of you."*

"Lucille, I know you have the best of intentions, but that's not how I want to meet my future wife. It seems so impersonal."

"Now, Zach. It is nothing of the sort. You correspond back and forth, and when you are convinced that she is the one, you send for her. When she arrives, if you are adamantly opposed—if she has lied in her correspondence, for instance—then you are under no obligation to marry her. But if you do choose to make her your wife, think of how nice it will be for Davey to have a mother again. That poor little boy...." Lucille shook her head ruefully. "No little boy should ever be without a ma," she continued, reaching for her handkerchief and dabbing at the corner of her left eye.

Zach sighed and suddenly felt sorry for Fred. He wondered if the man had ever won a debate with his wife. Considering the present situation, it was unlikely he had. "Lucille, God will provide me with a wife if it is His will, when His timing is right. Until then, I'll just have to be patient."

"Oh, I agree God will provide you with a wife, all right, but what if it's the good Lord's will that you find one by advertising in a newspaper? After all, are you just going to sit there waiting for one to show up all on her own in Pine Haven, of all places? This isn't exactly the New York City of the West."

Zach had to agree with Lucille that Pine Haven had little to draw women there of their own accord. "I don't think so, Lucille, but thank you for thinking of me."

Just then, a customer entered the mercantile. "Lucille, I have a list of supplies I'll be needin'."

Lucille looked up at the customer. "It'll be about five minutes, Mr. Johnson. I have a critical conversation with Mr. Sawyer to *finish. So, take your time and look around, if you wish. Otherwise, you may want to come back later."*

Mr. Johnson nodded. *"I'll walk over to the post office and see if there's any mail while I'm waitin.'"*

"Fine idea. You run along, then." Lucille again leaned forward toward Zach. *"As I was saying, this is an excellent idea, and one I don't think you can afford to pass up. Do you want to be a bachelor all of your life? That sounds like a lonely existence to me. Besides, you have more than just yourself to think about—you have Davey to consider. Please, Zach, don't let this opportunity pass you by. I know it's the true desire of your heart that you find a woman to love."*

"Lucille, I wouldn't even know what to write."

"I would be happy to help you with that, but we can talk more about it later. There then," Lucille patted his hand. *"It's all settled. I'll find some names of some newspapers in the East, and we'll get started on this plan."*

❦

The sound of his horse whinnying brought Zach back to the present. After reading the letter from Dovie, he realized again that he never should have allowed Lucille to talk him into her silly plan. "I might as well open the other letter," he said. He read the outside of the lilac envelope. "Boston, huh?" Taking the letter out of the envelope, he noticed it was scented, and he held it to his nose. It was the scent of spring, and it made him wish it was April instead of October. Opening the letter, he saw the impeccable handwriting, which read:

September 20, 1881

Dear Mr. Sawyer,

This letter is in response to your advertisement in the Boston Herald *regarding a mail-order bride. I believe*

I meet the qualifications you specified in your advertisement.

My name is McKenzie L. Worthington. I am a Boston native, twenty-four years of age, possess an outgoing demeanor, and am well educated. I am the middle child of three daughters born to Arthur and Florence Worthington, and, for generations, our family has attended Fourth Street Presbyterian Church.

I look forward to receiving your response.

Most sincerely,

McKenzie L. Worthington

1589 Wild Willow Avenue

Boston, Massachusetts

The letter was brief in comparison with the other letter, and Zach felt grateful for the difference—not only in length, but also in content. He stared at McKenzie's letter and felt his breath catch in his throat. He didn't know McKenzie L. Worthington, but something within him told him he soon would. *If this is the woman You have planned for me to marry, Lord, please make it clear to me,* he prayed silently.

CHAPTER SEVEN

$\mathcal{D}$id you hear the news?" Lucille whispered to Wilma
Waterston, the wife of the town blacksmith, Wayne.

"What news is that?" Wilma asked, turning her right ear
to Lucille. She lived for the moments when her closest friend
had new information to share with her. With little happening in the remote, Western town, news was precious.

"Zach received not one, not two, but *seven* responses so far
to his advertisement for a mail-order bride!" Lucille's excitement precluded her from speaking as quietly as she had hoped.

"Surely you jest!" Wilma gasped. "Seven responses
already? Hasn't it been only three months since he placed the
ad? I bet Mr. Victor will be kept quite busy at the post office
once Zach receives even more responses. Why, I'd wager that
Pine Haven has never seen as much mail as it's about to see."

"I agree. What's more, I asked him just the other day—"
Lucille began, but she was interrupted.

"Now, what is it that y'all are talking about?" Eliza
Renkley asked. "Here we all are, sittin' in a quiltin' circle, and
Lucille, the bearer of all news, good and bad, is whisperin' to
Wilma. Do share with the rest of us, Lucille," Eliza begged in
her Tennessee accent.

"Yes, Lucille, what news have you to share with us today?" Marie Kinion asked.

"Well, you see, I was just telling Wilma about the latest on Zach's mail-order bride situation," Lucille said. She began her news conference the same way each time at the quilting circle. She'd share the information only with Wilma, but when the rest of the women begged her, she'd then tell them, as well. Lucille loved the attention. Although she knew gossip was wrong, she consoled herself with the fact that she never told news that would scathe or slander another person. Her news was usually good news; in the case of bad news, she shared it only if it might protect or even save another person's life. Such had been the case when she'd heard rumors of a planned bank robbery in Pine Haven. She'd told Marie's husband, Sheriff Clyde, all the details, and he'd been able to foil the robbery attempt. Lucille had been a heroine for a month. The recognition had done wonders for business at the mercantile.

"Yes?" Marie asked. "Do go on." She put down her needle and sat up straight in her chair, ready to receive the information Lucille was about to give.

"Zach received seven responses already to his advertisement. Can you believe that?" Lucille asked.

"I can believe it," said Wilma. "I always wished my daughter would have married him instead of the man she chose." Several women nodded in agreement, knowing that Wilma's daughter hadn't made the best of choices in selecting a spouse.

"Anyway, I asked him the other day which ones he was going to respond to. He mentioned that he's been praying real hard, and he's chosen but one," Lucille said.

"Really?" asked Eliza. "I imagine it must have been hard for him to choose which one. Did he say anything about what was in the letters?"

Lucille shook her head. "As hard as I tried to pry it from him, I couldn't get him to utter one tidbit of information to save my life. He was very private about it and said that there were three letters that he'd ruled out completely without even having to think about it. He said that he'd be in soon to purchase some stationery to write a response to the one he'd chosen."

"Can you imagine being a mail-order bride?" Marie asked.

"I think it sounds romantic," said Lucille. "I wish I'd met my Fred that way."

"Oh, I agree. I met my Billy Lee through my brother, because they always went possum huntin' together. I think meetin' someone as a mail-order bride would be much more excitin'," said Eliza.

"I can't wait to see the woman who accepts his offer. Do you think someone from the East could even begin to fit here in Pine Haven?" Wilma asked.

"I was from the East, and I did fine," said Myrtle, Reverend Eugene's wife, speaking up for the first time that afternoon. It was known that she didn't appreciate gossip and prayed that, although Lucille thought her information was innocent, she'd learn the truth one day. For now, Myrtle did her best to set a good example and attempted to avoid the temptation of gossip herself.

"You're right, Myrtle, you fit right in," agreed Marie. "Maybe Zach's new wife will be someone like Myrtle. That would be nice. It's too bad you don't have a sister, Myrt."

"Yes, it would be nice, indeed, to have another Myrtle," said Wilma, who shared in Marie's high opinion of Myrtle, as did all of the townsfolk.

"We must do our very best to make the woman Zach chooses feel welcome," said Lucille. "As you all know, Zach is like family to me."

There were several utterances of agreement among the women. "He deserves a kind and beautiful wife," said Doc Orville's wife, Diane. "I hope that's the type the Lord blesses him with."

"That would be a benefit to all," said Wilma. "Especially Rosemary. She would practically have to live with the woman."

"That's the truth. Wouldn't that be an utter disgrace if the woman Zach chose was a disagreeable sort?" said Diane.

"I'm sure that Zach, with the Lord's help, will choose a woman who not only treats him with respect, but who also treats his help the same way," said Myrtle.

"I certainly hope so, y'all. Rosemary is one of the sweetest people I know," Eliza said, shaking her head. "It's a shame she couldn't be here today, with her not feelin' well and all."

"It's that nasty bug that's been going around since late fall arrived. My husband said he's been seeing quite a bit of it in these parts," Diane added.

"Well, I say that once we get Zach married off, let's focus on that ranch hand of his, Jonah, and find a wife for him," Marie suggested.

"I do agree with you, Marie. Jonah is such a friendly fellow. I may have to talk him into placing an advertisement in a newspaper," said Lucille.

"You might be able to start your own business, at this rate," said Wilma. "I can see it now: Lucille's Love Connections." She pretended to write the words in the air.

Lucille grinned, adoring the attention. "I might just have to do that, Wilma. If Zach's union is a success, I may be arranging marriages for the long term."

CHAPTER EIGHT

Figuring that this might be the only day this week he'd be able to make a trip to town, Zach hitched up his horses. The weather was threatening snow, and he wanted to pick up a few supplies before any storms hit.

As he drove along toward town, he pondered the turn his life was taking. He'd spent much time in prayer seeking God's guidance and knew that McKenzie's letter was the only choice. However, since he'd made his decision to pursue McKenzie, he'd put off responding to her letter for several days. Something deep within him had continued to nag at him until he'd relented and decided to proceed with the plan that Lucille had so carefully and confidently outlined. He acknowledged that he needed to respond to the one letter that had intrigued him, the letter he felt God was leading him to choose, even if his letter made McKenzie choose never to respond again.

It wasn't that McKenzie's letter said anything special compared with the others, or that it was unusual in any way. But each time he read the letter, the words jumped out at him, and he could almost hear what he imagined McKenzie's voice sounded like reading it to him. What's more, her letter had seemed so gracious, and when he'd prayed about making the right choice, McKenzie's name had come to his mind every time.

Three of the letters had been easy to weed out. Dovie's letter, of course, was absurd. There was another letter like it that he had dismissed. It had resembled Dovie's so closely that her own sister could have written it. Another letter had demanded that wealth be a part of the matrimonial equation. One letter was too short and provided no personal information, almost as though sending it had been an afterthought for the woman. Of the two remaining letters, one woman was nearing fifty years of age, and the other one was not a Christian. These details had made his choice even easier.

He may have been rather ignorant about the rules of courtship, but Zach at least knew he needed to purchase some attractive stationery on which to write back to McKenzie. Unfortunately, the only place to purchase such stationery in town was at Granger's Mercantile, and doing so would invite many questions. Still, Lucille would meet McKenzie one day if she came to Pine Haven to marry Zach. And, if the outcome was a success, Zach would have Lucille to thank for making the suggestion in the first place. Therefore, he knew it was futile to think Lucille would not be involved in just about every step of his mail-order adventure. He figured he might as well purchase the stationery from her and not give it another thought.

The snow was beginning to fall when Zach reached Granger Mercantile. Winter's arrival was not far off, and, before long, the harsh weather would make his trips to town less frequent. Zach would venture there on Sundays to attend church, as well as once during the week, if he needed to purchase absolute necessities at the mercantile. He enjoyed his trips to town—they gave him a chance to pray and spend some quiet time with the Lord—so he would welcome spring for more than just the nice weather.

When Zach reached the mercantile, he climbed down from the wagon, hitched his horses, and entered the store. As usual, Lucille was leaning over the counter, engaged in a deep, private conversation with a customer.

"Can I help you, Zach?" Fred asked, looking up from the shelf he was dusting. For a moment, Zach was tempted to ask Fred for help in locating some stationery, but he changed his mind. Fred probably knew even less than he did about fancy writing paper.

"Hi, Fred. I think I'd better ask for Lucille's help on this one," he said, reaching forward to shake Fred's hand. "How are you doing?"

"I'm doing well. How about you? I hear you've had some responses to your advertisement," Fred said with a wink.

"Word travels fast in these parts," Zach answered. "Yes, I've had a few responses. But only one that strikes my interest."

"Oh? Are you sure that Lucille has heard that yet? You know how that beautiful bride of mine loves the latest news."

"I'm afraid I know all too well about Lucille's love for sharing information. I feel like I've been helping her these past few months in her quest to make sure everyone in Pine Haven is kept current on events." Zach grinned. "I'm here to ask her opinion about some stationery."

"Glad you're asking her. I'm afraid I don't know much about things like that." Fred scratched his head. "Come to think of it, I can't say I've ever written on nice paper."

"Did I hear someone say my name?" Lucille asked. Her head was cocked as though she had a special type of sixth sense to let her know that she was being summoned. She finished with her customer, then came out from behind the counter and scuttled over to Fred and Zach.

"Zach here just needs some of your expertise," said Fred.

"Is that so? What can I help you with today, Zach?"

"I was wondering if you had any fancy stationery so that I could write to one of the women who responded to my advertisement."

"I'd heard that you had chosen one of the women! Do tell me about her. What's her name?" Lucille asked.

"Now, Lucille, you'll find out in due time. Right now, I just need some stationery. If she happens to be the one I choose as my bride, you'll be the first to know."

"Oh, all right, Zach. I usually have a nose for news and don't give up quite that easily, but I'll give you some mercy today. Now, let me see. I have four designs for you to choose from." Lucille spread the selections on the counter in the shape of a fan.

"Which one would you recommend?" Zach asked.

Lucille held her right hand to her heart. "You're asking my opinion, Zach? I am so flattered."

"I figured you'd be knowledgeable about such matters," said Zach, winking at Fred.

"As a matter of fact, I am, indeed." Lucille paused. "I believe that if I was receiving a letter from a man who was courting me via the mail system, I'd most expect to see the pale blue stationery."

"Then the pale blue stationery it is," said Zach.

"Very well, then. I'll add that to your bill." Lucille busied herself with writing the charge down in the appropriate place. "Will that be all for you today?"

"Rosemary needs five pounds of sugar, too."

Lucille fetched the sugar and wrapped both it and the stationery in brown paper, then placed the packages in a burlap sack to protect them from the elements. "Do let me know, Zach, if she writes you again, would you?"

"I'll do that. Have a good day, Fred and Lucille." Zach tipped his hat and headed out the door. He wondered to himself what Lucille would do if she didn't have the townsfolk of Pine Haven to keep tabs on every day. He figured she'd probably be bored.

Zach watched from the kitchen as his four-year-old son, Davey, carried the brown crocheted blanket from the rocking chair by the fireplace, went out the front door, and began searching the yard for his dog. "Duke!" he called. "Where are ya, boy?"

The retriever walked slowly around the edge of the house in response to his owner's voice. "There you are, boy! I've been lookin' for you!" exclaimed Davey. Dropping the blanket on the frozen ground, he ran toward the dog and wrapped his chubby arms around his neck. Then, Davey stepped back to pull a piece of jerky from the pocket of his trousers. "I've been savin' this for you all day." He giggled as Duke reached up and bit the jerky from his fingers. Duke finished it, then covered Davey with slobbery kisses in appreciation for the special treat. "I like jerky a lot, too, Duke. That's why me and you, we are the best of friends and always will be." Duke wagged his tail, as if to confirm Davey's vow.

"Now, Duke," continued Davey, deepening his voice to enhance his authority, "me and you, we got things to do today. See, today, we are in the Pony Express, and we have to deliver the mail. We have to take it all the way from Missouri to Sackermento." Davey paused and pushed his cowboy hat firmly on his head. "Don't be afraid none, Duke. I've got my gun here in case any bears come after us." Davey lifted his wooden, toy gun from his makeshift holster. "Now, there ain't no time to waste, Duke. Pa told me all 'bout the Pony Express and how quick they had to ride for their 'portant job." Davey bent down and whispered something in Duke's ear.

Next, Davey walked over to the brown crocheted blanket. Stooping down to open it to its full size, he spread the blanket on the ground and smoothed away the wrinkles. With determination, he folded it, matching the corners until it was a perfect square. "There we go, Duke. That took some doing, but I think I got it. Reckon I have to get one more thing, and then we'll be ready. Now, you wait here, Duke, and I'll be right back."

Davey scanned the area, clearly looking for something. Zach saw him run over to one of the large, flat rocks by the side of the barn and attempt to lift it. Clearly, it was too heavy, but Davey wasn't daunted. *That's my boy*, Zach thought.

Davey came back to where Duke was waiting. "That rock is too heavy, but I have a plan," he said, stooping to pick up the folded blanket. "Now, you follow me, boy, to that flat rock over yonder."

Duke followed Davey to the rock, where Davey positioned Duke just so. Speaking to the dog again, Davey stood on the rock and threw the blanket over the back of his dog.

Not a good idea. Zach decided to head outside before one of them got hurt. As he approached, he could overhear Davey saying, "Now don't move, boy; we're almost done." Standing on tiptoe on the rock, Davey attempted to climb on to the back of Duke. "Now, don't be scared none, Duke. You're gonna be my horse, and I'm gonna be a Pony Express rider!" Davey stretched his short leg up and over the dog until he was sitting on his back.

"Davey?"

Davey looked up. "Hey there, Pa," he said.

"Davey, what are you doing?"

"I'm a Pony Express rider, and Duke's my horse. This blanket here is the saddle. I have a long way to go to deliver that mail, Pa, so you'll have to 'scuse me now."

Zach began to chuckle. There was never a dull moment with Davey. Kneeling down so he was the same height as his son, Zach put his hand on Davey's shoulder. "Davey, you can't ride Duke, son."

"But why not, Pa? He's my horse, and I'm a Pony Express rider."

"Davey...."

"Are you worried for me, Pa? Iffin' you are, don't be. I got my gun right here in case a bear comes after us. I'll be just fine. Besides, we got to get the mail to Sackermento before suppertime."

"Davey, you could really hurt Duke by putting your weight on him," said Zach. "Here, I'm going to help you get off now."

"But why, Pa?" Davey stood up, and Zach knelt down once again to face him. "Dogs aren't meant to be horses, Davey," he said, his voice gentle. "Their backs just aren't strong enough. I know how much you love Duke, and that you wouldn't want to hurt him."

"But I was just pertendin'," Davey pouted.

"I know you were, Davey. But, you see, dogs aren't meant to be ridden, especially Duke. He's getting old, and his bones aren't as strong as they used to be."

"How old is he?" Davey asked.

"He's about eleven years old by now," said Zach.

"But how can I play Pony Express if I don't have a horse?"

Zach scratched his head. "Well, Davey, it's like this," he began, searching for words. "You can still play Pony Express, just change it a little."

"How's that?" asked Davey.

"Duke is a special horse in the Pony Express."

"A special horse?" asked Davey, his eyes brightening.

"Yes, a special horse. You see, he doesn't carry riders. Instead, he carries the mail."

"He does?"

"Yes, he does," Zach said. "I'll tell you what. I have a small, leather pouch in the barn. Let's use that for the mail. I know we can find a couple pieces of paper in the house. We'll put the papers in the pouch. It will be Duke's job to carry the pouch. It weighs less than two pounds. We'll fold it over his back so it stays on, and it'll be just like the real Pony Express."

"Thanks, Pa!" Davey exclaimed.

Zach smiled. Never in the world would he have wanted to miss out on the child God had so unexpectedly placed in his life and under his care.

❦

That night, after the chores had been finished, supper had been eaten, and Davey had been put to bed, Zach sat down to write to McKenzie. He'd pondered the words on his way from Pine Haven so many times that it should have been easy for him to write them on the pale blue paper. Instead, what he wanted to say had become increasingly confused and muddled in his mind, and he sat in the silent room, dark except for the illumination of the candle on his desk, tapping his pencil on the desk and staring at the package of paper. He'd even washed his hands twice to make sure he wouldn't smudge the fine stationery.

Worries and questions filled Zach's mind. What if she didn't respond? What if she found him to be unintelligent and unworthy of her time? What if she came to Pine Haven and didn't like him after she met him? What if she didn't accept Davey? What if she was an unbearable woman who was only posing as a distinguished young lady in her letters? What if she'd lied about herself in her letter? What if...? "Lord, I'm having a hard time with this," he prayed. "If it's Your will that I write this letter, would You please help me and give me the words to say? Without Your help, I don't see how I'll be able to write it."

He sat in the stillness for a while longer before bending his head toward the paper and beginning to write:

October 28, 1881

Dear Miss Worthington,

Thank you for your correspondence. Please, call me Zach.

Have you ever been to the Montana Territory? Pine Haven is a lot different from Boston. We do have several business establishments for a population of 232. There is a church, a school, a telegraph office, a café, two saloons, a lumberyard, a millinery, a Chinese laundry, a one-page newspaper, a dressmaking shop, a blacksmith, a bank, and a dry goods store.

It is beautiful here. The good Lord has certainly out-done Himself with the mountains He created, which are within view of the house and are only a few miles away. There are also two rivers and many trees.

I own a ranch two miles from town. We have cattle, horses, chickens, pigs, and a dog named Duke. Besides my home, there is also a bunkhouse and another house.

Sometimes, the work on the ranch is hard and seems never ending. Would this be a problem?

I look forward to further correspondence with you.

Sincerely,

Zach

When Zach had finished writing, he addressed the envelope before setting down the pencil. With rugged hands more used to driving cattle and planting crops that folding paper, he gently pressed on the folds of the paper once more before placing the letter into the envelope.

He would mail the letter when he went to town next week. Until then, Zach would do all he could to dismiss the anticipation in his heart at the thought of the woman who might be interested in becoming his wife.

CHAPTER NINE

*T*he horses' hooves clip-clopped on the cobblestone streets as the carriage took McKenzie and her friend, Helen, home from a tea party at the Kirkbride Estate. "That was so much fun!" exclaimed Helen.

McKenzie giggled. Helen thought every party and ball they attended was fun. Her exuberance was contagious, though never imitated, and, at times, McKenzie found herself wishing she possessed the same vivacious demeanor. Perhaps, then, she would be married by now instead of on the verge of becoming an old maid. As quickly as McKenzie allowed the thought to enter her mind, another thought competed with it. *Still,* McKenzie reminded herself, *you won't be an old maid for long if a man by the name of Zach Sawyer responds favorably to your letter.*

"I'm going to have to take the long way to your house, Miss Helen," said Lawrence, the Worthingtons' driver. "It appears there's an obstacle up ahead."

"That's fine, Lawrence. We're having fun discussing the tea party, anyhow," said Helen.

While Helen didn't mind taking the long way to her home, McKenzie's opinion was quite different. She felt a lump form in her throat at the thought of taking 18th Street instead of Clearmont Avenue to Helen's house. Taking the alternate route would resurrect old memories that were better left laid to rest. Yes, memories of a broken heart and a friend's betrayal were better left buried.

"McKenzie, are you all right?" Helen asked.

"Yes, I'm fine."

Helen looked thoughtful for a moment. "Oh, McKenzie, I'm sorry. I forgot." As fun-loving as Helen's personality was, it was equally matched by heedlessness. "This is the way that takes us past Louis and Pearl's house, isn't it?" Helen reached over, put her arm around her friend, and gave her a quick hug. "Let's just glance the other way when we pass. That way, you won't be thinking at all about what might have been."

McKenzie sighed. For all of her effort to make her feel better, Helen had failed miserably at the task. "I'm fine, Helen, really." McKenzie patted her friend's arm and squeezed her eyes shut tight. How many times had she taken pains to avoid this route? How hard had she tried to forget how Louis had broken her heart?

Lawrence turned the carriage onto Lupine Street from Clearmont Avenue, and McKenzie sucked in her breath. In a few short seconds, they would be passing the home that should have been hers.

"McKenzie, look this way," Helen said, pointing in the opposite direction.

"Helen, it's fine. It'll be nice to see the home again." McKenzie attempted to convince herself that it really didn't matter to her as they passed by the stately, redbrick house. McKenzie gazed at the edifice as if she'd never seen it before—the two-story home with six stairs, edged by a wrought-iron railing, leading up to the front entrance. The grandeur of its fashionable curtains and splendid gardens made gazing at it all the more difficult. Lupine Street was in one of the wealthiest districts of Boston, and the surrounding homes did little to hide that fact. McKenzie imagined for a moment that Lawrence was delivering her to this home rather than the one she shared with her parents. She visualized walking up the six stairs, past the clay flower pots on the front porch, and through the front door, into the front hall with its winding staircase—and coming upon her husband, Dr. Louis Clarence III.

"I'm home, darling," she announced as she handed her cloak to their butler.

"Oh, my darling McKenzie, I've missed you," Louis said. He embraced her and kissed her firmly on the mouth.

"But I've been gone such a short while," McKenzie teased. She gazed with admiration into the dark eyes of her husband of one year.

"Any moment without you is too long," Louis said, taking her hands in his. "Tell me, how was the tea party?"

"Grand, as usual. The conversation was lively, and Matilda makes the best tea. How was your day at the office?"

"Busy. I have two surgeries scheduled for tomorrow. But, never mind my day. I have something for you, my sweet."

"Louis, you didn't have to—"

"I know I didn't have to, but I wanted to. I am the luckiest man alive to be married to you, McKenzie. Now, close your eyes and hold out your hand." Louis stepped away from her and reached for a velvet box on the nearby desk. He placed it in McKenzie's open hand. "Open your eyes."

McKenzie opened her eyes and beheld the velvet box. When she lifted the lid and looked inside, she saw a pearl necklace— the most ornate pearl necklace she'd ever seen. "Oh, Louis, it's beautiful!"

"Just like you, my sweet. Now, let me help you put it on." He turned her around and fixed the clasp around her neck....

"McKenzie? McKenzie?" Helen waved her short, stubby fingers in front of her friend's face.

"Huh? Helen? Oh, sorry. I was just thinking about things."

"Thinking about Louis, no doubt," Helen said.

"You're right," she said, sighing bitterly. "Someday, I shall get over him."

"Perhaps your idea to become a mail-order bride will cure your broken heart," Helen suggested.

"Not likely, Helen, but thank you for always being so positive."

"You never know—people have fallen in love under stranger circumstances."

"But most high-society women who are merely searching for their sisters do not fall in love with ranchers in the Montana Territory," McKenzie reminded her.

"What if he's handsome and dashing, like Louis? What if he's really a doctor or a banker and has a grand home right next to a creek—the grandest home in all of Pine Haven?"

McKenzie smirked at her. Obviously, she'd told Helen too much information about her plan. Although she knew that Helen would keep the plan a secret, McKenzie still wished she hadn't divulged so much to her friend. "That's not going to happen, Helen. Besides, falling in love with him would be disastrous, since, once I've retrieved Kaydie, I'm returning to Boston—without him."

"Yes, yes, you're right. And, if all goes according to your plan, you'll then be the heartbreaker instead of the heartbrea-kee." Helen tilted her head back and waved her hands about.

McKenzie giggled. "Thank you for cheering me up."

"I just know, McKenzie, that, someday, you'll find the man of your dreams. Why, never in my most wild imaginings would I have thought I would be marrying Holden, but I am. You'll see. It will happen for you, too."

McKenzie doubted her friend's words, but it would be nice if somewhere in the city of Boston a man would make her his wife and love her forever. But she wasn't sure she could ever trust her heart to a man again. And she'd never allow herself another best friend. She'd learned that lesson the hard way.

McKenzie trudged up the stairs to her bedroom. It had been a long afternoon, and she was eager to rest her head on her feather pillow. As she removed her hat and gloves, she heard a knock on her door. "Miss McKenzie?"

McKenzie opened the door to see Biddie, one of the Worthingtons' maids. "Yes, Biddie?"

"This letter just arrived for you."

"Thank you, Biddie." McKenzie reached for the enve-lope. Upon quick examination, she saw that it was a letter from Zach Sawyer, and her heart leaped. It had seemed so long since she'd penned her letter to him that she hadn't been sure he would respond. Yet, the proof lay in the form of the pale blue envelope in her hand.

Peeking out into the hallway, McKenzie glanced from left to right before ushering Biddie into her room. "Biddie, may I speak to you for a moment in private?"

"What is it, Miss McKenzie?"

McKenzie closed the door and lowered her voice. "Biddie, I'm going to be receiving many of these letters in the near future. Can you please take special care that you continue to deliver them to me personally? It's critical that no one else knows of these letters."

Biddie nodded. "Yes, miss. So, these letters are much like the letters you receive from Miss Kaydie, which are also to be kept secret?"

"Similar," McKenzie assured her. "It's very important that I am the only one who sees these letters after they arrive."

"What shall I do if you're not home when a letter arrives?"

"Carry it around in your apron until I come home. Whatever you do, please don't leave one lying around the house for Mother or Father to see."

"I won't, miss," Biddie said.

"Very well, Biddie. Thank you. I appreciate being able to count on you."

"Thank you, Miss McKenzie," Biddie said with a smile. "If there is anything else you need, please just let me know."

McKenzie nodded. "I will. Thank you, Biddie."

McKenzie hid her excitement until Biddie left the room, then slowly opened the envelope, pulled out the letter, and began to read. She would at least give Zach credit for selecting beautiful stationery. His writing wasn't at all hideous, either, considering most men she knew had scripts that were scarcely legible. It gave her a strange feeling inside her stomach when she read the first line: "Please, call me Zach." She reread it three times. The part where he described the work as never ending failed to bother her. She merely thought that his work seemed without end. Zach had described the town in which he lived, the animals, and even the local surroundings of Pine Haven. Although none of it thrilled her the way she was thrilled by rides through the streets of Boston, with its tall buildings and elegant homes, it still made her eager to know more of the place that would soon be her destination. It also helped her to know what to expect.

McKenzie picked up her pencil to respond to Zach's letter. Although she was very tired and anticipated taking a nap before dinner, she knew she'd find sleep an impossibility due to all the thoughts in her mind. Besides, the sooner she was able to convince Zach that she should become his bride, the sooner she could rescue Kaydie. And that was all that mattered. She thought about what she would write, then began to form the words on the stationery:

November 12, 1881

Dear Zach,

Pine Haven sounds small but lovely. And, you are right, quite different from Boston.

No, I have never been west. However, I have traveled throughout Massachusetts, New York, Vermont, New Hampshire, Connecticut, and Pennsylvania. Have you lived in the Montana Territory your entire life? Do you have family nearby?

It sounds like you have many animals on your ranch. I have never ridden a horse before and would very much like to try.

No, your hard work on the ranch does not present a problem. Do you have any hotels in Pine Haven? Have

you ever heard of a town called Canfield Falls? If so, do
you know how far it is from Pine Haven?

> *Most sincerely,*
> *McKenzie*

McKenzie reread her letter before folding it and placing
it in an envelope. Tomorrow, she would ask Biddie to mail
it for her. Hopefully, Zach did live near a town known as
Canfield Falls, as Kaydie had mentioned it in her last letter.
Even if her matrimonial arrangement was only for Kaydie,
McKenzie imagined she'd at least have some fun traveling to
a place she'd never been before.

CHAPTER TEN

Zach was working in the barn when he looked up to see Jonah Dickenson, one of his hired hands, approaching. "I picked up some mail for you while I was in town," Jonah said when he came inside.

"Thanks, Jonah." Zach knew from the color of the envelope that it was a response from McKenzie, and he stifled a sigh of relief. Now that she had begun to correspond with him, he always anticipated her letters.

"I know it's none of my business, Zach, but is it from the mail-order bride?" Jonah asked with a conspiratorial look in his eyes.

"You're right, Jonah—it is none of your business," Zach said, pretending to slug his friend in the arm. "But, yes, it is from the mail-order bride."

"You know everyone is dying to know her name. You should see Lucille today. She's beside herself wondering about the details, and I could hardly escape the post office with my life after she saw that purple envelope in my hand."

"Poor Lucille. What would she do if there was no new news in Pine Haven?" Zach shook his head. "Her name is McKenzie. She's from Boston."

"McKenzie?" Jonah asked. "Isn't that a man's name?"

Zach shrugged. "She says it's her name. I'm going to trust that she's telling me the truth."

Jonah laughed. "I didn't mean that, Zach. It's just that I've never heard of a woman with that name, unless it was a surname. So, when is she coming to Pine Haven?"

"We're just corresponding for now. What is it that Lucille called it? Oh, yes, that I was courting her through the mail system."

"That sounds like something Lucille would say. I'm surprised she became a mercantile owner instead of a writer of love stories, with that imagination of hers," said Jonah.

"I agree." Zach's eyes lingered on the initials M.L.W. and the return address on the envelope. At this point, it still seemed like he might never meet her.

"You know, Zach, I can't imagine ever finding a bride this way—or any way, for that matter."

"I wasn't sure I should do it at first. I'm still not sure. I have to admit, though, that it's been an interesting way to meet a woman."

"Were any of the other letters you received any good?"

"No. This was the only one. You're welcome to respond to some of the other letters. Be warned, however, that unless you're wealthy and of high standing in society, you probably won't get a response."

"I reckon I'll pass," Jonah said. "But I am happy for you, Zach. I know how much you've been in prayer about this whole thing, and I hope it works out for you."

"Me, too. You know, when I promised Will that I would take Davey as my own son, I never imagined at the time that he would need a mother. I mean, he's got me, and Rosemary is a good mother figure in his life. After his fourth birthday, I realized that I wasn't really holding up my end of the bargain in adopting him. I want him to have two parents. I know what it's like to be an orphan, and I wish someone had adopted me. I made out all right, by the grace of God, but it still would have been nice to have people to call Ma and Pa."

"You have to want to marry her for you, too, not just for Davey," Jonah pointed out.

"I know. I talked awhile to Asa about that. I would like to get married for my own sake. I see Asa and Rosemary and the strong marriage they have, and I remember the loving marriage my parents had before they died. And even Fred and Lucille love each other, despite Lucille's sometimes difficult personality. So, yes, it's for me, too, and I hope she will want to be married to me because she loves me, not because she's able to tolerate me for the sake of a marriage of convenience."

Jonah shrugged. "Marriage isn't for me; that's one thing I'm sure of. But, I know that's not the case with most folks. Since you've prayed about it, God knows your heart, and your desire is true."

"Thanks, Jonah," Zach said.

"I best be getting back to work. Besides, I'm probably keeping you from opening that very important letter," Jonah said with a wink.

Zach chuckled. "You're right about that."

After Jonah left, Zach tore open the letter. His eyes traveled down the words that had been so precisely penned on the page. "McKenzie Worthington, I can't wait to meet you," he said out loud, surprising himself.

That night, Zach wrote yet another letter, as if responding quickly would ensure receiving a quicker response from McKenzie.

November 26, 1881

Dear McKenzie,

No, I have not lived in the Montana Territory my whole life. I was born and raised in Chicago, and I have no siblings. My parents died when I was twelve, and I was placed in an orphanage near Chicago because I had no other known living relatives.

Two years later, I left the orphanage to strike out on my own. A photograph I once saw of the Montana Territory prompted me to ask questions about the land. I had always wanted to own my own ranch, as did my Pa, so after much prayer, I traveled to Montana. I worked for several ranches in various different towns to get experience. When I was nineteen, my best friend, Will Mitchell, and I decided to purchase some land together near Pine Haven and set up a ranch. The Lord blessed us beyond what we could ever imagine. Although Will and his wife, Bess, died of the fever three years ago, I continue to run the ranch with the help of some hired hands.

There are no hotels in Pine Haven. The nearest hotel is fifty miles north, in Windsor. Yes, I have heard of Canfield Falls. I once worked for a ranch in that area. It is about twenty-five miles west of Pine Haven. The closest town, Oak Winds, is fifteen miles away.

What are some of your hobbies? Does your family live in Boston? Have you ever been married? What made you decide to answer my advertisement?

Sincerely,

Zach

Zach stared at his completed letter. He felt tempted to erase the last sentence, but he really did want to know why she had responded to his ad—why she had chosen him. Hoping the question wouldn't deter her from responding again, he folded the letter and placed it in the envelope.

❧

Zach and McKenzie continued to correspond throughout the following months, each writing a response the same day they received a letter, and almost always the moment after reading it.

December 13, 1881

Dear Zach,

I'm sorry to hear about the death of your parents and the deaths of your best friend and his wife. Both of my parents are still living, as are my sisters, so although I cannot truly understand your loss, I can and do sympathize.

Some of my hobbies are social activities, knitting, taking care of Mother's flower garden, and dancing. I attend many balls and tea parties in the city during the year. What are your hobbies?

Yes, my family lives in Boston; I've lived here my entire life. I reside with my parents, Arthur and Florence. My older sister lives in Boston with her husband, Maxwell, and their son, Maxwell Jr., whom we call Nate. (His middle name is Nathaniel.) My other sister moved away from Boston about three years ago.

No, I have never been married. I decided to answer your advertisement because I have long found the West to be intriguing. I am also matrimony-minded, and your advertisement was among the ones I found to be of interest. What made you decide to advertise for a mail-order

bride? I'm sure you received many responses. I am curi-
ous about your decision to choose mine.

What are some of the social activities in Pine Haven?
Do you travel to Canfield Falls often?

Most sincerely,
McKenzie

McKenzie sat in the chair in her room and thumbed
through the letters she had received from Zach. She had
lost count of the times she had read each letter. Thoughts of
the man she would someday meet filled her mind, and she
found herself thinking about him more often than she cared
to admit. Did he think of her often? Was he eager to meet
her? Would he help her find Kaydie? *Yes, Kaydie,* thought
McKenzie, *the very reason I find myself preparing to make*
such a carefully planned trip to a place thousands of miles away.
Not to get married, but to rescue Kaydie. McKenzie sighed. It
would still be some time before the weather was conducive to
travel, and she was growing more and more concerned about
Kaydie's safety and well-being.

McKenzie reached for the decorated, wooden box on
her desk. She opened the lid and carefully placed Zach's letters inside. She then knelt down on the floor and slid the box
under her bed until it was pressed flush against the wall. No
one would ever think to look there.

So far, it had been somewhat easy to keep her correspondence with Zach Sawyer a secret. Biddie had kept her promise of hand-delivering any letters to McKenzie as soon as
they arrived, and McKenzie made sure that her parents never
knew about the envelopes she received from the Montana
Territory.

The next day, McKenzie spent the afternoon Christmas shopping with Helen. "I will carry in your parcels, Miss McKenzie," Lawrence announced as he helped McKenzie down from the carriage when they returned to the Worthington residence after driving Helen home.

"Thank you, Lawrence. You may bring them up to my room, please." McKenzie reached for Lawrence's hand and stepped carefully out of the carriage. Holding up the corner of her dress, she made her way up the porch steps and opened the front door.

Her mother came out of the sitting room. "Finally, you're home," she said, her voice flat with apparent frustration.

"Hello, Mother. I was just shopping with Helen. Is something wrong?"

"What is the meaning of this letter?" her mother asked, rushing toward McKenzie and waving an envelope in her hand.

"What—what do you mean, Mother?" McKenzie held her breath. She recognized the blue envelope and wondered how her mother could have acquired possession of it.

"I mean this letter here," her mother said, her voice rising in pitch.

"Oh, how nice! I received some mail?" McKenzie smiled with feigned surprise. She reached out and attempted to retrieve the letter with all the ladylike assertiveness she could muster.

"Oh, no, you don't," her mother warned her. "You're not getting this letter until you tell me what this is all about. Why would you be receiving a letter from someone in the Montana Territory, of all places?"

"The Montana Territory?" McKenzie asked. She racked her brain to come up with a reasonable explanation for the letter. If she told the truth, her mother would forbid her to continue corresponding with Zach, which would ruin McKenzie's plans to meet him—and to rescue Kaydie. The only thing left to do was lie. *Quick, McKenzie, think of something.* McKenzie willed her mind to think of a convincing excuse that would quell her mother's concerns. She reached up to twirl a tendril of hair between her thumb and forefinger. Thankfully, Zach hadn't written his name in the return address but had written only, "Pine Haven, Montana Territory." That left McKenzie with more room for creativity.

"You sound as though you're surprised to be receiving a letter from a place that's far enough away to be on the other side of the earth," her mother fumed.

"Mother, may I look at the envelope?" McKenzie asked, making her voice sound syrupy sweet.

Her mother paused for a moment, then relented and handed McKenzie the letter. McKenzie stared down at the envelope, eager to remove herself from this uncomfortable confrontation with her mother and even more eager to read Zach's latest letter. "Was this letter just delivered?" McKenzie asked, confused as to why Biddie hadn't kept it for her to read in secret.

"About twenty minutes ago," said her mother. "I nearly opened it myself because it seemed as though you would never return."

McKenzie nearly let a gasp escape her lips. What if her mother had opened the envelope? McKenzie didn't allow herself to imagine the consequences that would have come, had her mother been any more impatient.

"Where's Biddie?" McKenzie asked. She should have known better than to have trusted Biddie with something so important. While she liked the maid, McKenzie also knew that Biddie could be scatterbrained at times.

"Biddie?" her mother asked. "What does Biddie have to do with the letter?"

"I just remembered that I hadn't seen her today," said McKenzie.

"You haven't seen her because she's not here."

"She's not here?"

"No, she is ill today. At least, that's what she says. You know hired help. Completely unreliable in times of need," her mother said, rolling her eyes.

"She's ill?" asked McKenzie. *Of all days for Biddie to be ill, this had to be the day.*

"Yes, McKenzie, she's ill. She stayed home today. Now, let's stop speaking of something so insignificant and return to the matter at hand. Who is the letter from?"

"Oh, yes, the letter," said McKenzie. "I'd almost forgotten." She turned the envelope over in her hand. *Quick, McKenzie, think of something, anything!* "Poor, poor woman," McKenzie said after a moment, shaking her head and closing her eyes.

"What poor woman?" her mother asked, sounding curious.

"The one who wrote me this letter."

"A poor woman wrote you that letter?" her mother asked. "I will say one thing for the *poor woman*—she has nice penmanship. But, never mind that. Tell me the details."

"May we sit in the parlor, Mother?" McKenzie asked. "My feet are tired from shopping all day."

"Of course," she said, following her daughter to the parlor.

McKenzie sighed. *Please, Mother, don't ask me to read you the letter,* she thought to herself. She clutched Zach's letter and sat down on the sofa next to her mother.

"Now, do tell," her mother demanded.

"The story is so very sad, Mother. You may need your handkerchief," said McKenzie, covering her mouth with her hand.

"Go on," said her mother.

"You see, there is a young woman in the Montana Territory whom I learned of through some of my charity work. Her name is...Isadora Jones."

"Isadora? What a dreadful name," said Florence. "You're right, I will need a handkerchief."

"Anyway, Mother, as I was saying, I learned of Isadora through my charity work. She is a young woman with eight children—"

"Eight children? Goodness gracious! How old is she?"

"My age."

"And she has eight children? You're right—she *is* a poor woman!"

"Mother, times have been difficult for Isadora," sniffled McKenzie. "So difficult, indeed. You see, two of her children are twins."

"Twins?" her mother exclaimed. "That would make life difficult. I was always thankful I didn't have twins."

McKenzie nodded, reaching into the depths of her imagination to add to the story, being sure to make it tragic yet credible. "The twins are very ill. They have had difficulties since birth. As a matter of fact, one of them cannot even walk."

"How old are they?"

"I believe Isadora told me in her letters that they are four years old. Not only that, but Isadora's husband was injured when he fell off a horse last year. He hasn't been able to work."

"He shouldn't have been riding a horse," her mother declared.

"Because he hasn't been able to work, the family has no food and no clothing. Their only shelter is a meager cabin with but two rooms. It's dreadful, Mother…." McKenzie pretended to cry then, burying her face in a handkerchief.

"I had no idea," said her mother. She dabbed at the corners of her eyes with her own handkerchief. "What can we do to help?"

McKenzie lifted her head and faced her mother. "The church has been supporting her, and I have been acting as a liaison between the two parties. I knew you wouldn't mind my corresponding with her, because of your kind and generous nature. Please don't be angry with me. I was only doing what we privileged are called to do, and that is to provide charity and encouragement to those in need."

"Now, don't cry, McKenzie; it's not becoming of a proper lady. I'm not angry."

"Oh, thank you, Mother. It is my guess that this is an update on the status of her and her family's condition." McKenzie fanned herself with Zach's letter. "I would let you read it, Mother, but I promised her—oh, how I promised—that I would keep her matters secret. I have already told you more than I should. It's quite humbling, you know, when one cannot afford to buy a bag of flour."

"No, no, that's fine. I don't need to read the letter. I'm just relieved. At first, I thought it might be from Kaydie. We haven't heard from her in so long."

"No, Mother, it's not from Kaydie," McKenzie said, gazing wistfully at the missive in her hands. "I surely wish it was."

"I suppose you're right."

"Now, if you'll excuse me, Mother, I must go upstairs and read this letter in the privacy of my room. It's the only way I will be able to see what else I can do for the Jones family."

"Yes, by all means, please do so," her mother agreed.

"Thank you, Mother." McKenzie stood to her feet, dragging them slowly, as if still overcome with anguish over Isadora's plight. "I'll be down for dinner," she said.

"Very well."

McKenzie found it difficult not to take the stairs quickly, or even two at a time, in her excitement to open Zach's letter. *That was a close one, McKenzie,* she told herself. She felt her heart racing and knew that it had only been a miracle that her mother believed her far-fetched story. Rushing into her room and closing the door, McKenzie sat down on her bed. Carefully opening the envelope, she retrieved Zach's letter....

December 28, 1881

Dear McKenzie,

Thank you for your sympathy. Although it has been difficult at times, God has carried me through and will continue to do so. I always thank Him for that and feel very blessed.

When I'm not working, I enjoy spending time with my ranch family, riding horses in the nearby mountains, fishing, and reading the Bible. Do you read the Bible often?

I received seven responses to my advertisement from several places in the East. I chose yours because it was the most genuine, and, after much prayer, I decided you were the one with whom I would choose to correspond. I, too, am matrimony-minded and look forward to meeting you in person someday.

Because Pine Haven is small, there aren't many social events, but it is a very close-knit community. Church potlucks, barn dances, and picnics are among some of the activities. There is also a quilting circle, in which many of the women in town participate.

No, I don't travel to Canfield Falls very often. It is smaller than Pine Haven and has a reputation for being rough and wild, due to the success of mining in the area. However, if you would like to visit, I would be happy to take you there.

I hope that you and your family had a blessed Christmas.

Sincerely,
Zach

More letters traveled over hundreds of miles and continued with frequency throughout the winter months. Both McKenzie and Zach shared details about their lives and showed interest in each other's lives. It was at the beginning of April that Zach worked up the courage to ask McKenzie to come to Pine Haven and be his bride. He received this response:

April 14, 1882

Dear Zach,

Spring has finally decided to come to Boston. I am always thankful when the new leaves and the flowers begin to poke their heads from their winter hiding places and look to the forthcoming summer sunshine. I admit that spring is my favorite time of year. Are the winters long in Pine Haven?

Yes, I accept your proposal for marriage. June seems like an acceptable time to travel to Montana. I will make arrangements to arrive there on June 16.

I've never been on a train for such a long journey, so I will be sure to bring plenty of reading and sewing. I admit I also like to daydream a bit and am sure my mind's fanciful wanderings will keep me company throughout

*the journey. I have also never been on a stagecoach, so
that will be a new experience for me. Of course, the whole
idea of traveling west will be new—an experience I never
in my wildest dreams imagined I would consider.*

I look forward with anticipation to meeting you, Zach.

Most sincerely,

McKenzie

As McKenzie affixed a stamp to her letter to Zach, she
felt somewhat guilty for having expressed excitement to meet
him, for she knew that he would take her words differently
than she intended him to. Although she did think of this
as an adventure and looked forward to meeting him, what
she was really awaiting was seeing her sister again after so
many years. That, and the thought of bringing Kaydie back to
Boston, where she'd be greeted with open arms by her family.
No more would she have to be married to Darius and suffer
the mistreatment she'd experienced at his hands.

McKenzie dismissed the tinge in her conscience that
she was being devious or misleading—after all, the despera-
tion of the situation demanded she take desperate action.
McKenzie knew that if it were she instead of Kaydie in this
predicament, she'd want someone to rescue her, and that
someone would likely be Kaydie. Besides, if she was on good
terms with Zach, then he would be more willing to assist her
in finding Kaydie—and, hopefully, less angry with her when
she revealed her plan.

Just then, a disturbing thought entered her mind: How
would she tell Zach the truth when it came time to do so?
How would she tell him that she could no longer remain
married to him and must return with Kaydie to Boston? Not
that McKenzie was going to tell him the second she stepped
off the stagecoach about why she was really in Pine Haven.

No, that would wait until she'd at least had the opportunity to locate her sister. If she was unsuccessful, then and only then would she ask for Zach's assistance. With any luck, she'd be married for less than a year to the man with whom she enjoyed corresponding clandestinely.

CHAPTER ELEVEN

JUNE 5, 1882

With the blow of a whistle, the train began to move. Clutching her carpetbag tightly, McKenzie slid down lower in her seat and closed her eyes, as if to hide herself from anyone who might be watching the train from the platform in search of a passenger who was running away to the Montana Territory without her parents' knowledge or blessing. *If I am even half successful with this scheme, it will be a miracle,* she thought to herself. *All that matters is finding Kaydie and bringing her back to Boston.* She felt the thump-thump of her heart and wondered if the rest of the passengers could hear it, as well.

A few moments later, McKenzie opened her eyes. She scanned the train car, checking every seat for any familiar faces. Seeing no one she knew, she pushed aside the red curtain and stared out the window at the passing scenery, watching as Boston slowly disappeared. She then looked about the train car again, just to be sure of her safety. If her father somehow were to have found out about her plan, McKenzie wouldn't have put it past him to have hired someone to go after her. He surely had the means and even more likely had the concern and tenacity to do so. Seeing no one suspicious, McKenzie heaved a sigh of relief and settled in for the long ride, knowing it would be at least a week and a half before she reached her destination.

Several minutes later, McKenzie opened her carpetbag and located a piece of yellowed paper—her most recent letter from Kaydie. Unfolding it, she smoothed the creases and read the letter for what was probably the hundredth time.

When she had finished, McKenzie refolded the letter and placed it safely back in her purse. "Hold on, my dear sister, I will be there as quickly as I can," McKenzie whispered. *I just hope I'm not too late,* she thought to herself. Fears filled her mind. Darius was a dangerous man—one whom McKenzie had never liked, even when he had begun courting Kaydie. Yet, there was something in Darius Kraemer that had drawn Kaydie to him. For the life of her, McKenzie couldn't figure out what that had been. He was a con artist and a bank robber, always on the run from the law. He had dragged Kaydie across the United States to the primitive and unsettled West, where she'd discovered too late who he really was. He'd taken her dowry, lied to her, mistreated her, and now was holding her as his hostage. McKenzie covered her mouth with a gloved hand. It was up to her to rescue her sister. If only she could know for sure that she would be successful in that feat. All she knew was that the desperate situation in which Kaydie found herself called for McKenzie to take desperate measures.

By now, McKenzie's parents would likely have received the letter she'd left for them on the kitchen table. She drew a deep breath and hoped that they wouldn't take any rash actions based on what she had decided to do. The last thing she needed was for her parents to follow her. Still, McKenzie reassured herself that the possibility of that happening was unlikely. Her mother would never want to travel west, and her father had a heart condition. Yes, they could hire someone to follow McKenzie, but, hopefully, before they decided to act on that plan, she would have completed the task she had set out to do.

McKenzie thought again about the letter she had left for her parents. She'd spent a good deal of time composing it last night. She'd wanted to make her intentions known without giving away too much information. The words she'd written now flowed through her mind:

Dearest Father and Mother,

By the time you read this letter, I will be well on my way to the Montana Territory to rescue Kaydie and bring her back to Boston. Please, I beg of you, do not come after me or send anyone else to retrieve me. It is necessary that I go, and that I do this on my own. After all, Father, it is you who constantly tells me that if I had been your son rather than your daughter, I could have become a partner in your law firm due to my tenacity, strong will, and forthrightness. Clearly, I have what it takes to tackle this problem on my own. Please, do this for me—and for Kaydie.

I will write to you once I reach my destination, and you may also stay in contact with me by writing me in care of the Sawyer Ranch, Pine Haven, Montana Territory. Such an address is that of a friend of Isadora Jones, the poor woman with all the children and the injured husband, whose plight I related to you recently, Mother.

*Please do not fear for my safety, as I am more than
capable of taking care of myself. Instead, take joy in the
knowledge that, before winter arrives in Boston, your two
daughters will have returned to spend Christmas with
the family.*

Yours truly,
McKenzie

McKenzie tried to imagine how her parents would react
when they read the letter. Her mother would likely weep quietly about the betrayal she felt regarding her daughter's plan
to do something without her knowledge. She would then
send for McKenzie's older sister, Peyton, with whom she
would share all of the grievous details.

McKenzie's father, with his thinning, wavy, red-gray hair,
and his mustache, which curled on the ends that he twirled
when he was nervous, would likely pace the floor, pondering
his plan of action. Or, perhaps, he would be at his law office
until ten o'clock that night, as he was on many nights. After
all, he devoted most of his time to the law practice started
by his father, Peyton Worthington, after whom McKenzie's
older sister had been named.

McKenzie thought of how her father seemed to prefer
spending his time at the Worthington law offices rather than
at home with his family. An introvert, he found preparing for
upcoming cases in the confines of a book-filled den prefer-
able to actually trying the cases in court. He spent large sums
of money to be sure his home was staffed with competent
people who could handle any difficulties that arose so that
he could devote more time to his work. He'd hired a butler,
two maids, a gardener, and a business manager. He dressed in
only the finest of linens from the most reputable of shops in
Boston and made sure that his family was clothed in the same

quality clothing as he wore. When his three daughters were young, he'd hired a nanny to care for them to relieve his wife of the demanding work of childcare and free her to do volunteer work with the Ladies' Society of Boston. He'd suffered beside his socialite wife through many gatherings and events in order to bolster his reputation and solidify his presence within the community.

Yes, while her father always gave self-assured presentations, inside he was a nervous, anxious man. McKenzie had seen stress get the best of her father during momentous legal cases. It was in those times that his eyes, which always appeared to be staring, became tired and weary. He was thin and tall, standing over six feet on long legs, which McKenzie had inherited. One thing she hadn't inherited, however, was his serious, stoic demeanor, which found humor in few things.

McKenzie was proud of her father for many reasons. He was well respected and highly regarded for his knowledge, prestige, and influence, and he quickly and generously gave donations to those organizations that he found worthy. Yet, although he was efficient in helping the less fortunate, he rarely found time to spend with his own daughters or helped them with the difficulties that arose in their privileged lives. For that reason, McKenzie had always felt an emptiness inside her heart. Even so, her father had made it clear that he thought highly of his spunky, feisty, determined middle daughter. McKenzie smiled. She would have liked to be an attorney. Instead, her father had been obliged to settle for Peyton's husband, Maxwell Adams, a timid and unskilled attorney.

Realizing that her leg had fallen asleep, McKenzie shifted herself into a more comfortable position within the confines of the train seat. Watching the passing scenery, she smiled to herself. The time had finally arrived for McKenzie Worthington to begin her adventure to Pine Haven, Montana Territory.

CHAPTER TWELVE

Zach sat down in his rocking chair on the front porch to spend the calm, crisp evening with the Lord. He looked forward to the summer evenings, when he could have his quiet time outside. Not that he didn't enjoy such times by the fireplace during the winter months, but summer evenings in Pine Haven were as close to perfection as he'd ever experienced. On winter nights, he would read first to Davey before tucking him in and saying good night. He would then sit quietly, read from the Bible, and reflect on those verses. The light of the fire always reminded him of the warmth the Lord had placed in his heart—a warmth of knowing he was never alone, and that his future was secure in the arms of Christ. It didn't matter where he spent his time with the Lord, whether outside on the porch or inside on cold, winter nights. The important part was that Zach yearned to know more about the God he loved.

Zach continued his reading in the book of 1 Samuel. He found the entire Bible fascinating, but in the Old Testament, his favorite Scriptures were found in 1 and 2 Samuel and Psalms. He read about Samuel anointing David to be the next king of Israel. His eyes traveled through the text as he read of Samuel's fear for his life at the hands of King Saul when the news was told of God's decision for the next leader of His chosen nation. Zach stopped when he came to verse 7. Something about the words resonated within him. He paused to stare up at the moon and stars overhead. Then, he returned his gaze to the page and read the second half of the verse: *"For the LORD seeth not as man seeth; for man looketh on the outward appearance, but the LORD looketh on the heart."*

Zach fingered the stack of letters he'd received so far from McKenzie Worthington, which he had tucked safely in his Bible. It amazed him that she hadn't sent a photograph, considering she seemed to be of higher class in Boston. Surely, photographs were commonly taken, not as they were in Pine Haven, where, every few years, a traveling photographer would take photos of eager residents for a modest fee.

Zach opened one of the letters and glanced briefly at McKenzie's perfect handwriting. What did she look like? In one letter, she'd mentioned she had a fair complexion and green eyes, but that had been the extent of her descriptions of her appearance. He wondered if she was tall and slender or short and plump. He wondered if her eyes brightened when she spoke about things that brought joy to her heart. He pondered whether she had dark or golden hair, if she smiled often or was of a more sullen nature.

He thought again about 1 Samuel 16. It was clear that God had chosen David not because he was the tallest or oldest in his family, but because of his heart. God had chosen David because he was *"a man after mine own heart,"* as God had called him in Acts 13:22.

What if McKenzie was stunted in growth, plump, and exceedingly homely? What if her plain features left nothing to stand out against the other women in her city and left nothing to be desired by the men of Boston—or anywhere else, for that matter? What if she was missing teeth and had a nose large enough to fill the faces of two women?

Zach felt convicted for his focus on outer appearances. "Yes, Lord," he whispered. "Even if McKenzie Worthington is all of those uncomely and unattractive things I just thought of, I will still love her. I will love her for her heart and for what is on the inside, just as You do. I strive to be more like You, Father, so that is what I will do. If my mail-order bride is ugly and hard on the eyes, I will still love her as Christ loves the church. This I promise to do."

Zach again thought of McKenzie's letters. He'd been unsure she'd accept his proposal after learning about Davey, but it hadn't mattered to her. For that, he was grateful. It had also improved his esteem of her character. For a woman to take on a child who wasn't her own and love him as though he were spoke volumes about her integrity. "Thank You, Lord, for letting her be willing to be my wife," Zach prayed aloud. "She easily could have refused."

Four-year-old Davey William Mitchell Sawyer was sweet yet mischievous, boisterous yet shy. Zach thought of his young son, and how he rarely even recalled that he was adopted. Davey had become so much a part of his life, much like an appendage, and Zach couldn't imagine life without him. Zach's mother had been right when she'd told him he would never truly know how much she loved him until he himself had a child of his own.

Rosemary had even remarked once that Davey resembled Zach. While Zach knew that there was no way Davey could have directly inherited any of his traits, he knew that Davey had a similar personality, and that was one of the things that made Davey a Sawyer. Folks had often remarked that Davey's biological father, Will, and Zach looked enough alike to be brothers. As close as they had become, Zach had considered them brothers. Now, Zach prayed daily that he would be able to raise Davey in a way that would please the Lord. He prayed that he would raise Davey in a way that would have made Will and Bess proud of the choice they'd made to leave their son in Zach's care.

Zach closed his Bible and sat for a moment longer, his fingers intertwined in prayer. His own mother had been a beautiful woman, both on the inside and on the outside. Anytime she'd giggled, which had been often, everyone around her would laugh, too, for her happiness had been contagious. Hers had been a laugh that began low and throaty and then rose to a higher pitch as her jollity mounted. She'd been barely five feet tall, and, based on her roundness, no one ever could have said that she lacked for decent meals. Yet, her stature had been unimportant. Her face had been lovely and smooth, despite the harsh life she'd endured as the child of unloving, neglectful parents. Her eyes had been a deep brown, like rich chocolate, and her hands had always been warm, ever quick to give a touch of love to anyone who needed it. She'd prayed continually for Zach's future bride, and Zach remembered hearing those prayers as a young child. He only wished she could have lived long enough to see whom God had chosen for him. She would have giggled, for sure, at the unconventional way in which Zach was pursuing his bride.

The most difficult part of this pursuit was waiting— waiting to meet McKenzie.

As Zach sat, reflecting, McKenzie was traveling at that very moment by train across the United States. Was she as excited at the prospect of meeting him as he was at meeting

her? Did she look forward in anticipation at the thought of a
new life as Mrs. Zachary Sawyer? After meeting him, would
she be pleased she'd accepted his proposal? Or, would she
take one look at him and climb back aboard the stagecoach
bound for Boston? Would she find his appearance and personality agreeable, or would she find them offensive in some
way? Zach's own modest disposition had never allowed him
to accept himself as the fine, handsome man others often said
he'd become.

Zach's thoughts again turned to his future bride. Yes, if
it was God's will for him to marry McKenzie Worthington,
it wouldn't matter what her stature was or if she would never
turn the heads of those in Pine Haven. What did matter was
the heart that beat within her, and, based on the letters he'd
received, Zach was sure that she was a sweet, kind woman.
That was enough for him.

CHAPTER THIRTEEN

McKenzie gazed absently out the train window, thinking about Boston, the place she had called home for all twenty-four years of her life. She stifled the tears that threatened to fall and instead kept her focus on the future.

After a time, she settled back in her seat. The commotion around her helped to take her mind off missing her family, and she began to daydream about the day when she'd bring Kaydie back to Boston. She felt confident that her hopeful daydreams and fond memories would carry her through the long miles and months ahead.

"We're almost there, Kaydie," McKenzie said, reaching over to hug her sister. They were in their seats on the train, eagerly anticipating their arrival at Boston & Lowell Station.

"Thank you again for coming all the way out to Montana to rescue me, McKenzie. I don't know how I would have made it home, had it not been for your bravery." Kaydie sniffled, and McKenzie offered her a handkerchief.

"You would have done the same for me, Kaydie. Now, we'll be together and never have to be separated again. We can put the entire Darius Kraemer episode behind us, and it will be just as if you never left Boston."

"What a treat that will be," Kaydie said with a wistful sigh. "I was so foolish to fall in love with him."

"Never mind that—you're almost home now. Wait until Mother and Father see you."

"If it had not been for your sacrifice, McKenzie, this moment would not be happening. How I have missed our parents!"

"Wait until you see our nephew! Nate has grown so much since the last time you saw him. I'm sure he's grown even more since I left Boston. He's such a sweet child."

"I can't wait to see him," said Kaydie. "Tell me, McKenzie, how did you become brave enough to venture so many miles all by yourself?"

McKenzie giggled. "It wasn't easy, I'll grant you that. Of course, the most difficult part was keeping my plans from Mother and Father. To my knowledge, at first, they were none the wiser about my decision to rescue you. Had they discovered what I'd decided to do, there is no way they would have allowed me to follow through with my intentions." McKenzie glanced out the window. "Look, Kaydie, there it is! The train station!" She pointed and found it difficult to remain seated.

Kaydie's eyes followed where McKenzie was pointing. "Oh, please, McKenzie, say this is real and not just a dream."

The train slowed to a stop, and the passengers began to shuffle down the aisles to the exits. "I see Mother and Father on the platform!" Kaydie exclaimed.

McKenzie looked and saw her parents, along with Peyton, Maxwell, Nate, her dear friend, Helen, and Lawrence, waiting patiently as other passengers disembarked.

"Kaydie!" their mother exclaimed when the two sisters finally stepped off the train, flinging herself with open arms at her long-lost daughter. "I never thought I'd see you again!"

Kaydie returned her mother's embrace. "Nor did I, Mother."

"Save some hugging for me," their father said as he wrapped Kaydie in his arms, then turned to face McKenzie. "If it hadn't been for you, McKenzie, this happy reunion would not be happening. Thank you for bringing our youngest daughter home."

"Yes, you were the missing piece of our family puzzle, finally complete again," their mother said, wiping her tears.

Peyton stepped forward. "McKenzie, I must admit, I was so very wrong about you. Please accept my profound apologies for my behavior. You are to be commended for the courage you exhibited in rescuing Kaydie and returning her to us. I could never be as brave as you."

"Of course, I accept your apology," McKenzie said, attempting to hide her surprise. Never had Peyton apologized for anything, especially not to McKenzie. Maybe this would be the start of a new relationship between them. No more would they argue and harbor blatant dislike for each other. No, now they would be the best of friends, just as McKenzie and Kaydie were….

❧

The train slowed with a screeching of brakes, bringing McKenzie back to the present. Yes, the day when she returned to Boston with Kaydie would be marvelous, and, while she did hope for the happy ending that she'd just played out in her mind, she knew that two things would never be: the barrage of warm embraces from her parents, and Peyton's humble apology and newfound kindness toward McKenzie.

McKenzie had been so caught up in her daydream that she'd forgotten all regret about how her plan to return to

Boston would affect the man she was going to marry. And he wasn't the only one who would be affected—McKenzie now knew that he had a son.

She opened her carpetbag and pulled out the second to the last letter she'd received from Zach. Her eyes were drawn to two paragraphs in the middle of the page:

> *McKenzie, forgive me for not telling you sooner, but I have a four-year-old son named Davey. He is a sweet boy with a pleasant demeanor, ruffled blond hair, and the bluest eyes you ever saw. I love him more than life itself and can't wait for you to meet him. I hope the fact that I didn't inform you of this fact sooner doesn't change your mind about accepting my proposal.*
>
> *Also, I wanted to say that I am more than willing to pay for your travel to Pine Haven. Please let me know the cost of your train and stagecoach tickets, and I will mail the amount to you right away.*

McKenzie folded the letter and returned it to her carpetbag with the rest of the letters from Zach. She hadn't minded finding out that Zach had a son, although she had wished that he'd been honest with her from the beginning. But, the fact that there was a young Sawyer was of no consequence to her. Her main and only goal for this trip was not to become a wife or a mother, but to find her sister. McKenzie would make every attempt, no matter how difficult, to not become attached to the sweet boy with the creative imagination. However, she knew that might be difficult.

Already, she'd found a great deal of pleasure in picking out some items for Davey and had packed them in one of her trunks. Perhaps, when she arrived in Pine Haven, she would give him the swirled lollipop she'd purchased from Holmes'

Candy Shop on Eighth Avenue. Later, if she were still in Pine Haven when the proper time arose, she would present him with the ball and the harmonica. Surely, such things weren't easy to come by in remote, Western towns. McKenzie had chided herself for purchasing the items, but she hadn't been able to resist doing so. She only hoped the gifts would not endear her to Davey too much.

McKenzie scarcely noticed the changes in scenery as the train traveled west. She'd save the sightseeing for her return trip, when she and Kaydie could observe the landscape and marvel together at its variations.

Days later, McKenzie found herself aboard a stagecoach for the first time. The bumpy ride and uncomfortable quarters did nothing to impress her, and, as she had often done on the train, she lapsed into daydreams or reminiscences. Her heart broke once again as she relived the moment when she'd learned of Louis Clarence's decision to marry Pearl.

"Miss McKenzie?" Biddie called, tapping on McKenzie's bedroom door. "Miss Pearl is here to see you."

"Thank you, Biddie. Tell Pearl I'll meet her in the parlor. Would you please have Nellie prepare us some tea?"

"Yes, miss," Biddie said.

McKenzie set down the novel she'd been reading, left her room, and walked down the winding staircase to the parlor. Pearl was seated on the blue sofa, wringing her hands. "Pearl? What a pleasant surprise!"

Pearl practically jumped to her feet at the sight of McKenzie. "McKenzie! I need to talk to you."

"Surely, we can have some tea first. Nellie will be right in."

"Oh, I really haven't the time for tea. I need to talk to you now—it's important."

McKenzie looked intently at Pearl. Why was she acting so peculiarly? They always had tea when she came for a visit. And why did she seem so nervous and agitated? They'd been friends for eighteen years. Surely, nothing had arisen to cause dissension between them. McKenzie searched her memory. Had she said something to offend her best friend? Had she done something to hurt Pearl's feelings? She was very sensitive.

Pearl reached out and took McKenzie's hands in her own. That was when McKenzie saw the large, diamond ring on her left ring finger. Don't let yourself jump to conclusions, McKenzie chided herself silently. She had a habit of thinking the worst in situations.

"McKenzie, it's about Louis," Pearl told her.

"Yes?" McKenzie asked. "Is he all right?"

"Yes, yes, he's quite all right. You see, McKenzie…." Pearl gulped.

"What is it, Pearl?"

"Louis—Louis asked me to marry him last night."

McKenzie felt as though someone had hit her hard in the stomach and knocked the air out of her lungs. "What did you say?" she asked. Perhaps, she'd misunderstood her friend.

"I know that you have always fancied Louis, McKenzie, but, the fact is, he's been in love with me for years. Last night, he took me to dinner—and proposed to me." Pearl pulled her left hand away from McKenzie's and meekly splayed her fingers, displaying her glittery ring right under McKenzie's nose.

McKenzie let go of Pearl's other hand and narrowed her eyes. "How could you, Pearl?" she asked.

"McKenzie, please, keep your voice down."

"I will not keep my voice down. Do you realize how badly you have hurt me?"

"I'm so sorry, McKenzie. I never meant for this to happen. You have to realize, though, that you and Louis weren't courting. You hadn't been courting since we were in finishing school, and that was for only a short while. Louis and I have been courting for a month now, and he told me he's always loved me."

"Pearl, you knew I loved him—I told you all my secrets. I told you all my hopes and dreams for our future. How could you steal him away from me like this?"

"I didn't steal him from you, McKenzie. He was never yours to begin with. Oh, how I wish you would be happy for me, so we could celebrate together!"

"Happy for you? You are—sorry, were—my best friend. We did everything together. We told each other our deepest, darkest secrets. You know me better than anyone, except Kaydie. Did you decide that our friendship mean nothing to you when you accepted Louis's proposal?"

"No, of course not—your friendship means so much to me, McKenzie. I was hoping that we could remain best friends. I would be esteemed if you would be my maid of honor at the wedding."

Was she crazy? "Most certainly not. I could not be your maid of honor now, not after what you did. I love him, Pearl."

"As do I." Pearl narrowed her beady, gray eyes. "I have loved him just as long as you have, if not longer. We have so many dreams for the future—dreams that you and he never could have had."

"How do you know?"

"Please, McKenzie, take no offense, as I mean this in the kindest of ways. Louis and I are better suited for each other. I am calm, abiding, and pleasant; you are rather loud, and you always want to have your own way. Louis needs a wife who will listen to him when he comes home after a long day at the clinic. You would only offer unwanted advice and argue with him at every turn."

"I can't believe I am hearing this," said McKenzie. Her anger had reached its height, and she found it difficult to resist giving Pearl a shove. As it was, she determined to push Pearl out of her life forever.

"You need to believe it. Besides, I thought it would be better coming from me than if you were to hear it at some tea party or from your sister, Peyton. News travels fast in our social circles, McKenzie. I think I should at least be thanked for having had the decency to tell you, myself. It wasn't easy for me to do this."

"I'll have you know, it isn't easy being on the receiving end of such a cruel betrayal. I trusted you, Pearl. I trusted Louis. I'll not trust either of you ever again."

"It wasn't a betrayal, McKenzie. Louis wasn't courting you. He was free to marry whomever he wanted. He wasn't yours."

"Please leave, Pearl. I've heard more than enough."

"Here's your tea, miss," Nellie said, bustling into the parlor.

"Thank you, Nellie, but we no longer need it. Pearl was just leaving." McKenzie narrowed her eyes at Pearl, as if to dare her to do otherwise.

"Please, come to the wedding, even if you're still angry with both of us," Pearl implored her. "I'll send an announcement in the coming weeks."

"I will not attend your wedding, and that is a promise," said McKenzie, aware that her voice was loud enough to carry into the kitchen and beyond. "Good-bye, Pearl."

"Good-bye, McKenzie," Pearl said, then turned and left the parlor.

McKenzie had kept her word. She hadn't attended the wedding, and she hadn't seen Louis or Pearl, except from a distance, *since the day Pearl had brought her the news of their engagement. Louis and Pearl had exchanged wedding vows; meanwhile, McKenzie had made a vow never to trust another man with her heart, and never to have another best friend—with the exception of Kaydie, of course. The stakes were too high.*

"Miss? Miss, are you all right?"

The voice of another passenger in the stagecoach shook McKenzie out of her reverie.

"I beg your pardon?" McKenzie said.

"You were crying, and I wanted to make sure you were all right."

McKenzie studied the woman speaking to her. She was a motherly sort, and her face held concern for McKenzie's welfare. McKenzie reached inside her carpetbag for a handkerchief and blew her nose. "I'm fine. Thank you so much for asking," she told the woman.

"Are you returning home for a mournful occasion?" the woman asked.

"No, I'm actually going to a small town in the Montana Territory to get married."

The woman looked shocked. "Is that why you were crying?" she asked.

McKenzie attempted a laugh in the midst of her tears. "Oh, my, no," she said. "I was simply saddened by a memory of the past."

"Thank the good Lord for that," said the woman. "Nothing could be worse than crying at an upcoming marriage—unless, of course, you're crying tears of joy."

McKenzie nodded. "Thank you again for your concern. I'm sorry if my sobs were a bother."

"They were nothing of the sort," the woman assured her. She smiled and leaned forward to pat McKenzie's arm. "Congratulations, dear, and may your marriage be one grounded in faith in the Lord and filled with happiness for many, many years to come."

"Thank you," McKenzie said, suddenly disbelieving that, by this time tomorrow, she would be a married woman—but not for the reasons most women chose to become wives. She would be celebrating the successful avoidance of spinster-hood, and yet her marriage would be peculiar in its being temporary, with an end that would come before it truly began.

Still, the thought of meeting Zach filled McKenzie with nervous anticipation. What would he think of her? Would he find her worthy of marrying him? She hadn't sent him a photograph. Surely, he would find her attractive. Most men she knew did. Why, then, should he be any different? Still, she felt a wave of insecurity rise within her at the thought. A more worrisome question remained: Would she find him attractive? Although the marriage would be annulled once she returned to Boston, she wouldn't want anyone to find out she'd married a homely man, even if it had been for a practical reason and for a short time.

McKenzie sighed. She would be living with a man she didn't know and relying on him to assist her in locating her sister. Of course, she would wait until the time was right to ask him for his aid. Pretending to be in love with him and marrying him would be an interesting task, but McKenzie knew she could use her creative imagination to her benefit.

Yes, McKenzie had had moments of success with manip-ulation, but this particular task would stretch her beyond anything she had ever accomplished. If Zach hadn't changed his mind and still wanted to marry her tomorrow, she would not only have a place to stay while searching for Kaydie, but she'd also have Zach's help in rescuing Kaydie from a man who would never let her go without a fight.

Kaydie's plight continued to haunt McKenzie's mind. Unfortunately for Zach and Davey Sawyer, it was imperative that McKenzie succeed in carrying out her plan. She couldn't afford to worry about whom she had to mislead and manipulate in order to execute that plan. Kaydie's life depended on its success, and that was all that mattered.

CHAPTER FOURTEEN

Zach watched as the passengers stepped off of the stagecoach one by one, and his eyes alit on a woman who looked to be by herself—McKenzie? She looked nowhere near how he had expected her to, not that he'd really known what to expect. A part of him was grateful that she wasn't as hard on the eyes as he had once dreaded—not that outer appearances mattered, he reminded himself. He moved away from the building he'd been leaning against, his nerves on edge.

What if she didn't like him? Forever was a long time to be married to someone who didn't care much for you. What if she didn't like Pine Haven, with its dusty, dirty streets and primitive, wooden buildings?

Another thought disturbed Zach: What if McKenzie changed her mind and boarded the stagecoach tomorrow to leave as quickly as she had arrived?

Zach wanted to approach her, but something kept his feet still. His knees shook, and he hoped that no one else would notice his nervousness at meeting the woman to whom he was ready to commit the rest of his life.

Zach noticed that a crowd had gathered, as it always did whenever the stagecoach arrived, and McKenzie herself had attracted the attention of quite a few onlookers. Not that he was surprised. From where he was standing, he could see that McKenzie was beautiful, even if she did look completely out of place. She stood out as a member of high society in a town where every other woman wore plain calico and shirked fancy frills.

McKenzie's face was partially hidden by a large, embellished hat, and on her hands—such slender fingers—were white, lacy gloves. Her blondish hair cascaded down her back in ringlets, and her tall, lean figure was accentuated by her flowered velvet dress, complete with an exaggerated bustle. A string of tiny pearls encompassed her slim neck, and a lace collar fringed the top of her dress.

"Would you please gather my belongings?" he heard McKenzie ask one of the stagecoach drivers.

"Yes, ma'am," the driver replied. He retrieved two trunks from the top of the stagecoach and then reached inside, grunted, and carried out two more. Never had Zach seen someone travel with so much luggage! *She must be fixing to stay awhile*, he thought to himself. *Either that, or she's fixing to open up her own shop—she must have room for fifty dresses in those trunks!*

Zach finally urged his feet to move from their stalled position and made his way toward McKenzie. The last thing he wanted was for her to feel unwelcome in her new home. This was no time to be his habitually shy self. He'd prayed for bravery and for the words to speak from a mouth that usually said little, especially to people he didn't know. He hoped God would answer those prayers, and that the impression he made on his future bride would be positive. Zach straightened his shirt and stretched his shoulders in an upward, circular motion to loosen up the tension in his neck. "McKenzie?" he said. When she turned around, he extended his hand. "I'm Zach Sawyer."

McKenzie fixed her eyes on Zach—first his face, then his clothing, then his outstretched hand. He hoped she wasn't afraid that he'd soil her gloves with his rough, work-worn hands. She smiled and slowly reached her right hand toward his, her fingers slightly curled under, and curtsied. "McKenzie Worthington," she said.

Zach gently took her hand in his. He hoped she knew that he was offering not merely a handshake, but also support, should she need it. Last week, he'd pored over *The Gentleman's Guide to Manners*, which he'd found at Granger's Mercantile. The book explained in detail how a gentleman should conduct himself in the presence of a woman. Zach remembered how Lucille had taken such joy in helping him locate the book, and it was a good thing he'd read it. He didn't want McKenzie to find him completely uncivilized. He had, after all, spent the first twelve years of his life in a city, and so he knew something of the ways of city life, even if he was fourteen years removed from that experience.

～⌘～

Well, this isn't awkward or anything, McKenzie thought, standing there staring at the man she would marry tomorrow. Surely, Zach felt just as bewildered, looking at her.

Finally, Zach cleared his throat. "I'll load your things into the wagon," he offered.

"Thank you," McKenzie said. *At least he's an attractive man,* she remarked to herself as she watched him load her trunks, one by one, into the back of his wagon. She'd been concerned that he might look older than his twenty-six years—balding, perhaps, or having a thick, shaggy beard. No—as far as his appearance went, McKenzie couldn't have been more pleased. His nearly black hair appeared clean, and his blue eyes held a kindness in them she'd not seen in any man before. Zach had broad shoulders and a lean, strong-looking body; he was probably about six feet tall, which was good for McKenzie, nearly five feet eight inches, herself. A brief realization that Louis Clarence's handsome looks paled in comparison with those of Zachary Sawyer entered her mind, but she quickly pushed it aside.

She needn't have feared that he'd possess a harsh manner, either, for he was polite and seemed eager to please her. Too eager, perhaps. He was also too rugged for her taste. McKenzie would have to work on both of those attributes, and the sooner, the better. She planned to find Kaydie in less than six months and then proceed with making plans to return to Boston in late spring, if not earlier. If she wanted to survive those six months, she would have to mold Zach into a man she could live with.

"Can I help you into the wagon?" Zach asked, interrupting McKenzie's thoughts.

"Please," McKenzie replied, holding out her hand.

With extreme gentleness, Zach assisted her as she climbed into the wagon, and then he jumped up beside her. "Welcome to Pine Haven," he said, smiling.

He seemed so kind, and McKenzie thought how it would be such a shame to hurt him in the way she would need to once she'd found Kaydie, returned to Boston, and had their marriage annulled. *But, what must be done, must be done,* she thought with a sigh. There were far more important things in life than the feelings of some stranger she'd just met, even if she had grown fond of him through his letters. Still, something odd and unrecognizable tugged at her heart at the very thought of hurting Zach.

"You're probably exhausted, so I'll give you the full tour later," Zach said. "But do you need to stop anywhere before we head out to the ranch?"

McKenzie was taken aback at his question—where in town would she stop? She glanced around but wasn't enticed by any of the storefronts, especially since none of them looked like dress shops or high-class cafés. "No, thank you," she said, "although I would like to send a telegram to my family and let them know I've arrived safely."

Zach nodded. Her response had seemed a bit short to him, but he figured it must have been due to nervousness. After all, she had traveled a great distance all by herself to an unknown place to marry a stranger. It must have been a shock for her to see a place so very different from what she knew. The thought of living out the rest of her days in Pine Haven instead of Boston was surely disheartening at the moment. But, he hoped she would one day become accustomed to the quaint and friendly town and would cherish it as her home. Until then, he would do all he could to make her feel welcome. And he would have the patience of Job with her as she adjusted to her new life in Pine Haven.

CHAPTER FIFTEEN

*M*ost of the two-mile ride from town to the ranch was spent in silence. McKenzie gazed at the open world around her, amazed at the contrasts between Boston and the surroundings in the life she'd been thrown into as a sacrifice to find her sister.

An occasional wagon passed them on the road—far fewer than the carriages that clattered along the streets of Boston—and McKenzie watched as Zach waved at each driver. The homes that dotted the road on the way to the ranch were modest and small, some no larger than a single room. The homes in the neighborhood where McKenzie grew up were magnificent and grand, large enough to house not only the residents, but also their staff. In all likelihood, four or five of those houses in Boston could accommodate most of the population of Pine Haven.

McKenzie marveled at the strangeness of finding herself so many miles from home. Had she ever been so brave in all her twenty-four years? No. She'd never once set foot outside the confines of city life. She'd never once felt the discomfort that comes when a situation does not go according to plan, with two exceptions: Pearl and Louis' betrayal, and Kaydie's elopement with a man who'd made her a hundred promises and kept only one—the promise to move Kaydie to a life so many miles from home that only a miracle would bring her back. McKenzie cringed to think of the letters Kaydie had written to her in secret. Where Kaydie had found the money to mail those letters was beyond her. Perhaps, some kind stranger had offered to pay the postage fees so that Kaydie could stay connected to her closest family member.

Now, McKenzie found herself in a similar situation, using the kindness of strangers to find Kaydie. It would be worth it, however, the day she and Kaydie boarded the stagecoach, and then the train, on their way back east. It would be worth it the day she followed Kaydie through the front door of their Boston home. Yes, it would be worth any discomfort, any sacrifice, and any manipulation of others to have her best friend and dearest sister safe home again and far from the clutches of the evil liar, Darius Kraemer.

McKenzie remained deep in thought until the sudden jolting of the wagon nearly threw her to the ground. She grasped the back of the seat and felt nausea creeping in. "Are you all right, McKenzie?" Zach asked, slowing the wagon to a stop.

"Yes, I think so," McKenzie answered. She was almost afraid to breathe, and she closed her eyes for a moment, as if to will the world to stop spinning around her.

"I'm so used to that big hole that I don't even notice it anymore. Please forgive me for not slowing down and taking into consideration that you've never been on this road," Zach said, sounding genuinely remorseful.

McKenzie slowly opened her eyes and pursed her lips together. The nausea was still there, although it seemed to be waning. "I'm all right," she said. "But that hole ought to be filled in before someone gets seriously hurt!"

"Yes, you're right," Zach said. He touched her arm, and she flinched. "I'm sorry, McKenzie. Why don't I come out here tomorrow and fill in the hole so we don't have that happen again?"

McKenzie held her breath. His touch had shocked her. "Are you sure you're all right?" Zach asked. "I guess I was so intent on getting us to the ranch that I was deep in thought about some unfinished tasks."

McKenzie nodded. "I'm fine." She noticed that his hand was still gently placed on her arm, and she saw the worried look in his eyes. Was he always so concerned about others? Yes, he should have been sorry for not having avoided the large hole in the road, but did he have to be so worried about her welfare? She swallowed. Such compassion would be easy to take advantage of, and she wished his personality wasn't such that manipulating him would be so simple.

༺✌༻

"All right, then," Zach said, flicking the reins to get the horses moving again. Already, he'd made a bad impression on McKenzie—he should have expected as much. She seemed so delicate and so fragile, and his protective nature rose to the surface. He only hoped she would be able to handle the hardships that came with living in Pine Haven.

A few minutes later, when they reached the ranch, Zach was humbled, just as he always was, when they rounded the corner and drove under the large arch he'd constructed with the words "Sawyer Ranch" carved into it. God had blessed him so richly in his life. It wasn't just the ranch, but also the friendships he'd formed and the town where the Lord had led him. How the Lord had taken an orphan and given him such a full life would always be beyond Zach's comprehension. He cleared his throat. "McKenzie, this is Rosemary and Asa's home," he said, nodding to the right at a small, well-kept cabin. "Rosemary helps out in the kitchen and prepares all the meals, and her husband, Asa, is one of my ranch hands. They're good friends—almost like family."

As they rode a little further, Zach's house came into full view. "And this is my—our house." He nodded to a cabin with a pointed roof and a large porch that encompassed most of the front of the home. It had dormers on the partial second level, which, he thought, lent character to the house, as did the two chimneys from the fireplaces, which kept the place warm in the wintertime. While not fancy in the least, Zach's home was one of the nicer ones in the Pine Haven area, and his own hands had done most of the work.

McKenzie's eyes veered from the road toward the house. Next to the house was a barn, and, further down the road, she saw what appeared to be more living quarters. She'd never lived in a place with so few neighbors.

McKenzie had noticed when Zach had corrected himself and called the house theirs instead of just his, and the thought disturbed her slightly. She thought of the more appropriate chances for matrimony that abounded in Boston and wondered if Zach believed that a woman whose parents had the means of hiring servants, a butler, and gardeners would really leave all that behind for a life that would include only hardship, backbreaking work, and little rest. Yet, Zach seemed proud of his home, even though it looked to be in desperate need of fresh paint, and the land that surrounded it.

For today, at least, she would be proud of his accomplishments, too, even though, in Boston, only members of the lower class would find themselves in such a setting.

"And look at that!" Zach pointed in the opposite direction where the sun had begun to set.

McKenzie directed her gaze in the direction he was indicating and gasped to see the vivid, orange sunset. Its staggering beauty more than made up for the lack of glamour and finery of the home, the surrounding land, and Pine Haven, itself. The bright hues transfixed McKenzie, as did the towering mountains silhouetted against the glowing sky, which she'd made no particular notice of until this moment. She turned and saw that the upstairs dormers of the house faced the mountains, and she wondered which residents got to enjoy the breathtaking view from their bedroom windows. Never before had she beheld such a majestic scene, or, if she had, she'd failed to notice it. She sucked in her breath. To say that she had found herself surprisingly enchanted would have been an understatement, and, for a moment, she entertained the thought that she might never tire of staring at the scenery under the vast, Montana sky.

"Wait until you see those mountains in the winter," said Zach. "They're even more amazing when they're covered with snow. Sometimes, they even have a bluish tint to them. It's the most beautiful thing you ever saw. When I first moved here, I saw this land and knew that if it was the Lord's will, someday, it would be mine. I still can't believe that I live close to something as amazing as those mountains."

McKenzie turned to stare at Zach as he spoke. *In the winter?* If things went according to plan, she would be making preparations to return to Boston long before then.

CHAPTER SIXTEEN

hen Zach stopped the wagon in front of his house, Asa, Rosemary, Jonah, and Davey were waiting outside to greet them.

"Pa!" Davey ran from his place beside Rosemary and leaped into Zach's arms when he stepped down from the wagon. "Is this my new ma?" He pointed a finger at McKenzie.

Zach swung Davey around. "Yes, son, this is McKenzie." He set Davey down and helped McKenzie out of the wagon.

With his nose scrunched in curiosity, Davey held out his hand. "Nice to meet you," he said.

McKenzie shook his hand. "You must be Davey."

Davey blushed. "Yes, but my full name is Davey William Mitchell Sawyer." He puffed out his chest at the sound of his own voice announcing his name. "And this is my fav'rite dog in the whole world. His name is Duke Sawyer."

"What a sweet dog!" McKenzie exclaimed. "And, my, what a big name for such a small fellow as yourself," she added with a smile.

Davey made a silly face at McKenzie. "I'm not so little," he said, standing on tiptoe. "I'm four years old. Soon, I'll be five, and then six, and then seven! Why, someday, I'll even be a hundred years old. Then I'll be as old as Grandpa Asa."

"Now, now, Davey," Asa interjected. "Don't forget that after a hundred comes a hundred and one, and then you'll be as old as Grandma Rosemary."

Rosemary playfully punched her husband in the arm. "Now, Asa, you know you're older. Don't be putting ideas into his head."

McKenzie watched the interaction between Asa and Rosemary and tried to figure out where they fit into Zach's family. She recalled that Zach had mentioned in one of his letters that his parents had died. That meant that Asa and Rosemary must be Davey's maternal grandparents. The thoughts of Zach's having been married before, and Davey's losing his mother, brought on a mix of emotions, which McKenzie decided to deal with later. Hadn't Zach mentioned something about Asa and Rosemary on the way to the house? She wished now she had paid closer attention to his explanation.

"McKenzie, let me introduce you to everybody," Zach said. "Remember the small cabin we passed when we first got to the ranch? It belongs to Asa and Rosemary. Asa is one of my hired hands, and Rosemary helps in the kitchen. They've been like parents to me, so Davey calls them Grandpa Asa and Grandma Rosemary."

McKenzie nodded and greeted them. So, the two were not the parents of Zach's late wife? She wondered where her parents were, and why they weren't helping rear their grandson. As the daughter of a lawyer, McKenzie had been instilled with an inquisitive mind, and she was constantly working to assemble any details she learned, like the pieces of a puzzle. This seemed to her like just another puzzle to solve.

"This is Jonah Dickenson, my other hired hand," Zach said, nodding toward a man who looked about Zach's age, with copper-colored hair and gray eyes. "And you've already met Davey."

"It's nice to meet everyone," said McKenzie, trying to sound genuinely enthusiastic.

"Supper should be just about ready," Rosemary announced. She looked at McKenzie to say, "I bet you're very tired and hungry from such a long day of traveling."

"I am, actually," said McKenzie. She shifted her weight. It had been a long day, and all she wanted right now was to crawl into a nice, warm bed and go to sleep. She would even forfeit dinner if it would mean getting a peaceful night's sleep as soon as possible.

"Why don't you go on into the house?" Zach suggested. "Jonah, Asa, and I will unload your trunks."

"Thank you," McKenzie said, then followed Rosemary into the house. She wasn't sure what to expect, since everything in Pine Haven was opposite of that in Boston, but she couldn't have anticipated how plain-looking the interior would be. Not one curtain hung in the windows; instead, mismatched blankets had been hung, many of them askew. To the right was a stone fireplace, near to which a large pile of logs were stacked, and two chairs. A crude coat hanger was nailed to the wall just left of the door, and past it was the kitchen area, with a stove, a rustic, wooden counter stacked with dishes, and a large table, surrounded by six chairs. A few shelves lined the kitchen walls, as well, which were plain, unlike the wallpapered walls of McKenzie's house. Past the kitchen was a set of stairs leading up to the bedrooms, McKenzie surmised.

The atmosphere was dark and gloomy, except for in the kitchen, where two candles were lit, and, although the house was larger than she had expected it to be, it was nowhere near the spacious size to which she was accustomed. Still, while the cabin may have failed to meet her expectations, the aromas of whatever Rosemary had prepared for dinner offered hope. When the men came in from outside, everyone took a seat, leaving a chair for McKenzie between Zach and Rosemary.

Zach pulled McKenzie's chair out for her, which she hadn't exactly expected. "Thank you," she said, her voice barely above a whisper. She sat down and listened as Zach blessed the meal, and she was struck by how personal it sounded. Her father's prayers were always short and simple: "Dear Lord, bless this food. Amen." In contrast, Zach's prayer was longer and more conversational, as if he knew God intimately. "Dear Lord, we thank You for this day and for all the blessings You have given us. Thank You for this food. Please bless the hands that prepared it. We also thank You for McKenzie's safe travel to Pine Haven. We pray that You will help each of us to make her feel welcome in her new home. Please bless our wedding tomorrow and guide us in our marriage so that it may be pleasing to You. In Jesus' name we pray, amen."

As the other voices chimed in with an amen, McKenzie thought about how Zach had thanked God for her safe travel to Pine Haven and asked Him to bless their marriage. McKenzie had never heard such an intricate prayer. She wondered if her parents had ever prayed for her specific needs or offered praise for acknowledged blessings. Somehow, she doubted it.

"Would you please pass the potatoes?" Jonah asked. McKenzie watched as the potatoes went from Asa to Jonah. In her own home, Nellie would arrange each table setting with the food Cook had prepared. No one passed any food on the table. If something was needed, Nellie or Cook would fetch it. McKenzie was unsure of how to go about preparing her own plate.

"Would you care for some potatoes?" Rosemary asked her.

"Potatoes?" McKenzie asked.

"Yes. They're mashed with butter—quite tasty. I guess you'd say that they're an important staple in this family." Rosemary smiled.

This family? McKenzie thought. This wasn't a family—not when only two of the six were related.

"There're also biscuits and turkey. Almost like Thanksgiving with all these trimmings." Rosemary was now staring at McKenzie, awaiting her response.

"Pardon me, yes. I'll take a biscuit, a spoonful of potatoes, and a few slices of turkey. I'd also like some tea to drink, please," McKenzie answered.

Rosemary raised her eyebrows. "I beg your pardon?"

"I said, I would like one biscuit, a spoonful of potatoes, and a few slices of turkey on my plate. I'd also like tea to drink." McKenzie's voice rose to a higher pitch at her annoyance of having to repeat herself. She never had to do such a thing at home.

Rosemary looked dumbfounded, and McKenzie noticed that the room had gone completely silent. Finally, Rosemary stood to her feet and began arranging food on McKenzie's plate to McKenzie's specifications. When she was finished, she placed it in front of her guest.

"I don't have any tea to offer you," she said, sitting down again. "Perhaps, Zach could pick some up for you the next time he's in town. We have fresh milk or water."

"Thank you," said McKenzie. She could feel the stares of the others on her face and wondered why they seemed displeased. She took a bite and was thankful when the conversation around the table resumed.

After McKenzie had cleaned her plate, she said, "Rosemary, I'd like another biscuit, please. I'm finding that my appetite is quite large after that long trip." With that, she placed her hands in her lap and waited for Rosemary to serve her.

Rosemary reached for a biscuit and placed it on McKenzie's plate.

"You don't, by chance, have any honey, do you?" McKenzie asked. "We have the most delicious honey in Boston."

"I'm sorry," said Rosemary. "We don't have any honey, but we do have some strawberry preserves."

"That would be lovely," McKenzie said with a smile. "Cook used to make homemade preserves, and strawberry is among my favorites." She handed Rosemary her biscuit, then watched as the woman stood up and walked over to one of the shelves in the kitchen. She retrieved a jar of preserves, opened it, and smoothed the jelly onto the biscuit.

"That was delicious," McKenzie said when she was finished eating. "My, how that lengthy train ride and dirty trip on the stagecoach have taken a toll on me. Would you mind drawing a warm bath for me, Rosemary?"

❧

"Zach?" Rosemary said, looking down the table, her eyebrows arched in disbelief.

Zach had debated how to handle McKenzie's treating Rosemary like a lowly servant, and his first inclination had been to take a stand for Rosemary against McKenzie. But, then, he'd thought better of it—he didn't want to upset

McKenzie on her first night here. He'd seesawed back and forth in his mind and prayed for wisdom throughout the meal. Now, he knew what he must do.

"McKenzie, may I speak to you in private for a minute?" he asked. She looked surprised but nodded, and so he pulled out her chair for her, then led her out to the front porch.

"McKenzie..." Zach started. He wasn't sure how to say what he needed to say. He knew that every marriage had its conflicts, but he hadn't expected them to encounter one so early.

"Yes?" McKenzie said, seeming oblivious to anything amiss.

"McKenzie, did your family have servants?" he asked her.

"Yes, of course. We have Biddie, who does all the cleaning and washing; Nellie, who helps serve the food and does many odd jobs; Cook, who prepares the food; Lawrence, our butler and chauffeur; and Manuel, our gardener. Why do you ask?"

The stream of hired help McKenzie listed made Zach dizzy. No wonder she was unaccustomed to serving herself! The way things were done on the ranch would be quite a shock to her. "McKenzie, Rosemary is not a servant, and neither is Asa or Jonah," he patiently explained. "Granted, they are hired help—they're paid for what they do—but they're more like family than employees. Rosemary doesn't serve people, unless it's assisting Davey with his food. She makes all the meals and cleans the kitchen afterward and takes care of the house, but she's not a maid. It's a lot of work to feed this many people, and she does a fine job, but, soon, you'll be helping her with those duties. Everyone has to pull his own weight around the ranch in order for it to be successful. Does that make sense?" Zach tried to keep his voice low and gentle. He wanted to avoid embarrassing her at all costs. But it didn't look like he'd succeeded, judging by the tears in McKenzie's eyes and her quivering lower lip.

⁓

McKenzie felt the tears start. She'd been here for less than two hours, and, already, she was making an utter fool of herself. What must Zach and the others have thought when she kept asking Rosemary to serve her? They must think her to be such a spoiled brat. And why hadn't Zach spoken up prior to this, instead of allowing her to carry on like a nincompoop? She sniffled. What she wouldn't give to be back home again! The reminder that she must endure many hardships for Kaydie's sake was the only thing that kept her from running from the house, going into town, and ordering a ticket for the earliest stagecoach heading east.

"McKenzie, please don't cry," Zach pleaded. But she couldn't stop the sobs. She was so miserable, so alone, so far from home.

Zach took a step toward McKenzie. "Shh, McKenzie," Zach said, his voice a whisper. "It's all right. No one will think anything of what happened." He reached his arms out and wrapped them loosely around her. "Everyone here knows things were different in Boston. Don't worry about it."

McKenzie looked up at Zach. Shouldn't he be saving his kindness for a woman who would really love him? Shouldn't he be concerned about the feelings of a woman who would make good on her vows to remain married to him forever? Instead, he held in his arms a woman who would leave in a few short months, after she'd finished the task she'd set out to accomplish. The thought made McKenzie feel even worse. "I'm sorry, Zach," she said, apologizing for more than just the meal episode.

"No harm done," Zach said. "It'll take a little bit to get used to the way things are around here. I remember when I moved here from Chicago, and life was so different. In time, you'll fit right in, and no one will be able to tell that you haven't lived here your whole life."

"I need to apologize to Rosemary," McKenzie said. She doubted she'd ever come to like the woman who'd embarrassed her in this way, but she knew that the right and proper thing to do was to ask for forgiveness.

"I think Rosemary would appreciate that," said Zach. "She's a godly woman—one of the most loving, caring people I've ever met. She's like a second mother to me, and I think you'll come to see her that way, too, in time. If she knew you were upset, she'd feel badly, herself." Zach paused for a moment, then said, "McKenzie, if you want, I'll draw you a bath."

All she wanted to do was escape to her room and sleep. "Thank you, Zach, but I think I'll have a bath tomorrow, instead. I'm quite tired."

"I imagine you are. I'd be happy to draw a bath for you tomorrow, then."

As she stood in Zach's arms, she wondered whether she should lift her arms to hug him back. Her stomach felt strange, and she figured it was due to the eventful day and the tumult of emotions it had brought. In the end, she decided to keep her arms where they were. Something about feeling secure in Zach's arms made her decide against making even the slightest movement.

"Are you as nervous as I am about our wedding tomorrow?" Zach asked.

"Yes," McKenzie admitted. If only he knew just how nervous she was! Of course, she was more concerned about what she needed to do when she found Kaydie than the ceremony itself.

Zach grinned. "I imagine everyone gets nervous before getting hitched."

McKenzie nodded. He was right. But not everyone had as many things to be nervous about as McKenzie Worthington did.

CHAPTER SEVENTEEN

That night, McKenzie sat on the bed in her new room, trying to block out her bleak surroundings and fight the tears that threatened to fall. Her shoulders sagged hopelessly as she longed for the life she left in Boston.

McKenzie thought of her bedroom at home—the same room she'd had ever since she'd been a little girl, and the same room she would keep until the day she entered into marriage with a suitable Bostonian bachelor. Her room was three times the size of this one, but it was cozier, too. She missed the fireplace, complete with a grandfather clock on the mantel, and the burgundy wing chair with its brass studs. How many times had she sat in that chair to lace up her boots in the morning or to brush her hair before turning in at night? The walls were papered with a rich, paisley print of burgundy and yellow hues, and the polished, wood floor was covered with a plush Oriental rug. She had a wide, comfortable bed with a wrought-iron headboard, a private bath area, and a spacious closet to house all of her frocks and gowns. Every week, Nellie or Biddie would fill the vase on her bureau with fresh flowers from the garden outside. In the wintertime, dried flowers replaced the fresh ones, and they were kept in perfect condition. Nellie and Biddie also took great pains to be sure McKenzie's room was dusted and the furniture was polished regularly. They made her bed, drew her baths, and did everything they could to make her comfortable.

McKenzie sighed at the memory. This room had just enough space for a bed, a small, wooden table, which, McKenzie supposed, was meant to be a desk, and a bureau with two drawers. At least a washbowl and pitcher had been placed on the bureau—they would be helpful when she felt the need to freshen up. But the walls were neither painted nor papered, and the window was covered with a threadbare-looking, brown blanket. A tattered, faded quilt had been spread across the bed, and McKenzie had already noticed that the straw mattress would be anything but comfortable. There was nothing beyond the bare essentials—no decor, nothing homey.

McKenzie stood up and walked over to the window. How she wished either Nellie or Biddie was here right now to draw her a warm bath. She especially loved how Nellie always brought her a steaming cup of tea to sip while she bathed. Now, so many miles from home, there was no Nellie, no Biddie, and no tea.

While McKenzie knew that this room was probably used only by the occasional guest, she wished some time had been set aside to make it warmer and more welcoming. The closet-sized space had scarcely more character than a prison cell, in her opinion, even though she'd never been inside a prison, much less a cell. Yet, this would be her room for the duration of her stay in Pine Haven, for she doubted very much that she would ever move into Zach's room, as he likely expected her to do starting tomorrow, when they were married.

What had she been thinking when she'd decided to answer Zach's advertisement? Her life had been close to perfect, or so it seemed in hindsight, and, now, it was topsy-turvy, thanks to her plan to rescue her sister. Maybe Kaydie didn't even want to return to Boston. Maybe after McKenzie located her, she'd want to stay in Montana. Then what? It would all have been for naught. Even if she did follow McKenzie back to Boston, would this sacrifice be worth it? Would Kaydie, so timid and lacking in common sense, again follow her heart and have to be rescued once more?

McKenzie returned to the bed, crying softly as she let down her hair and brushed it with the pearl tortoiseshell comb her mother had given her for her tenth birthday. She determined that she would adhere to her time frame to find her sister and return to Boston. Any longer than that, and she wouldn't survive the harsh surroundings of a dismal life she neither desired nor would ever find acceptable.

McKenzie put on her nightgown, climbed into bed, and laid her head on the pillow, then reviewed the day's events in her mind. First, there was the bumpy ride on the uncomfortable stagecoach. Second, her first glimpse of Pine Haven and the depressing realization that the town had no dress shop, nor any other marks of civilized society. Third, meeting Zach face-to-face, followed by another bumpy ride, this one in his wagon. Fourth, the incident with Rosemary, the embarrassment from which McKenzie knew she would never recover. She decided right then to dislike Rosemary with all the effort she could muster. Finally, her discussion with Zach on the porch, where she heard him deliver an explanation of the error in her ways with more sensitivity than she'd ever seen in a man. She recalled the way he'd put his arms around her to console her, and how, though she would never admit it to anyone, she had enjoyed the comfort he'd provided.

McKenzie closed her eyes and imagined traveling back to her home in Boston. She pictured her elegant, two-story home with the pointed roof, which she loved. The rounded porch in the front, and the additional porch on the right side, which made summer evenings so pleasurable, especially when seated on the porch swing built by Manuel, with the calico cushions sewn by Biddie. The five thick, white pillars on the front porch, and the four pillars on the side porch, which lent to the extravagance and superior craftsmanship of the enviable home. McKenzie sniffled at the thought of her parents' bedroom, with the private balcony that extended over the front door. She and Kaydie had spent many afternoons there, playing Rapunzel. In her mind, she strolled around the manicured gardens and shrubs, which Manuel took such pride in maintaining. She imagined entering through the front door and walking into the parlor, with its four fireplaces and walls lined with portraits and paintings. Her eyes alit with fondness on the Oriental rugs, the gold-framed mirror, the exquisite, winding staircase that led upstairs, and her mother's beloved piano, stately situated in the corner. She saw the long, rectangular table in the dining room, where the family dined and entertained guests.

McKenzie would never want to invite guests to Zach's house. There was no back kitchen entrance for the hired help, nor any area where the staff could sit during a meal and wait to be summoned to refill the water goblets or clear the table. This area was a place to which McKenzie had escaped many a time to sit and visit with Nellie or Biddie while they tended to their chores. Although they were paid to do so, McKenzie wanted to believe that they listened to her and helped her sort out her life's problems because they cared. Had they been here at this moment, she would have shared with them the depressing thoughts that obsessed her regarding her new life.

Closing her eyes tighter and willing herself to fall asleep, McKenzie thought of how, tomorrow, she would become a married woman. She only hoped all this would be worth it. *Wherever you are, Kaydie, this is for you,* she thought before drifting into a fitful sleep.

CHAPTER EIGHTEEN

*E*arly the next morning, Zach hitched up the horses and headed into town. He still couldn't believe that in a few short hours, he'd be a married man. *Lord, please let this be Your will,* he prayed silently. He'd known McKenzie such a short time, and yet, after several months of correspondence, and now, with her here, he felt like he knew her as well as he could, given the circumstances. Besides, God willing, he had a lifetime to continue getting to know her.

Along the way, Zach pulled over, got out of the wagon, and used a shovel to fill in the hole in the road that had rattled McKenzie on her first trip to the ranch. Then, he loaded the shovel back into the wagon and continued to the church, laughing to himself all the while. Who would have guessed that Zach Sawyer would be wearing his Sunday best on a day other than Sunday? He was willing to put up with the itchy, uncomfortable clothes two times this week, though, for it wasn't every day that a man got married.

At the thought of marriage, his mind traveled back to a conversation he'd had as an eleven-year-old with his father while they were fishing.

Zach swung his legs over the dock and held his fishing pole tight. Maybe today would be the day he'd finally catch a fish. How many times had Pa taken him fishing, and he'd caught nothing? Yes, he knew today would be different.

"What are you so deep in thought about, son?" his father asked.

"Oh, I was just hoping that today will be the day I catch a fish," Zach answered, smiling up at his father.

"I think you just might be right. But, if you're not, don't be discouraged. There'll be plenty of other times for you to catch that fish." Joseph Sawyer patted his son on the back.

"Pa, was Ma kind of like a fish?" Zach asked. He wasn't sure where the odd question had come from, only that he wanted to ask it.

"Your ma? Like a fish?" His father chuckled. "If she were an animal, I guess I'd think of her as more of a doe than a fish."

"No, Pa, I don't mean that!" Zach was suddenly embarrassed.

"What did you mean, son?" His father turned to look at Zach, giving him his full attention.

"I mean, before you and Ma were married, how did you try catching her as your wife?"

His father chuckled again. "I see what you mean, now. Well, your ma didn't grow up in the best of homes, so she lived on her own from an early age. She began caring for my aunt's children as their live-in nanny when she was fourteen because my aunt had become quite ill. That's when I first met her. She was the most beautiful woman I had ever seen—and the sweetest I'd ever met, too. She loved my cousins as if they were her own children. She read to them, bathed them, fed them, and taught them all about our Lord."

"So, did you ask her to marry you right then?" Zach asked. In all the stories his parents had shared with him, he'd never heard one about how they'd met.

"No, not right then," his father said with a laugh. "I was two years older and so busy working for my pa. We were very poor, and, as my pa's only child, I had a lot of duties fall to me, especially since Ma had passed on only a year before. When your ma turned sixteen, I decided it was time for me to start courting her. I knew I was the most blessed man alive. Everywhere we went, folks loved your ma. I've never heard one ill word come from her mouth in all these years we've been married. She's not perfect, but she's always had that gift of holding her tongue and not letting words destroy delicate relationships."

"Well, she did get mad at me that time I brought my pet snake into the house," Zach said.

"That's different. She's your ma, and you're to obey her. You knew better than to bring Mr. Green into the house. Your ma is terrified of snakes. Still, the look on her face…." His father trailed off into laughter, then cleared his throat. "You're right—your ma wasn't too happy that day. So, getting back to the story, I asked your ma to marry me five months after I began courting her. I had prayed and prayed that if I wasn't supposed to marry her, God would make it clear. I'd also prayed that I wouldn't be too much of a coward to propose to her. God confirmed that she was to be my wife, and He did give me the courage I needed to ask for her hand in marriage. I had nothing but the clothes on my back, but I had all the care any man would ever need for the love of his life."

Zach felt his face flush. He hadn't thought about his parents being in love before. "And then you had me," he said.

"Yes, we had you after many years of praying for a baby. You are our blessing, Zach. I want you to know, too, that *someday, you'll be fishing for a wife, so to speak. When you do find her, remember what the Bible says about loving your wife. In Ephesians, the apostle Paul wrote,* 'Husbands, love your wives, even as Christ also loved the church, and gave himself for it.' *Remember that, son. God wants you to love the woman He gives you as much as Christ loved the church. That's a lot of love. Remember, too, the book of First Peter, which says,* 'And above all things have fervent charity among yourselves: for charity shall cover the multitude of sins.' *Love your wife with all you have, and don't make a big deal about the small things."*

"All right, Pa," Zach promised, although, as far as he was concerned, girls were a nuisance and he'd likely not be marrying one in the near future.

"That's a long way off, son. You're only eleven," his father said, as if reading Zach's mind. "But your ma and I have been praying that, someday, God will bless you with a godly wife. And He will. When He does, you remember what I've told you."

⤞⤟

McKenzie put on the wedding dress she had purchased before leaving home. It wasn't an expensive one, but it was beautiful, nonetheless. She pressed on the delicate, lace pleats of the gown. It would certainly be the fanciest wedding dress ever seen in Pine Haven, of that she was sure. McKenzie closed her eyes and thought for a moment. If this were a real wedding....

⤞⤟

McKenzie's mother finished pinning up her daughter's hair. "You look beautiful, McKenzie," she said. "Your father and I are so proud of your choice."

McKenzie smiled at her mother and gave her a quick hug. "Thank you, Mother. I'm pleased, as well." She thought of the man who would be her husband within the hour, Louis Clarence III—wealthy, charming, tall, handsome, and intelligent. He was one of the most respected physicians in the Boston area, and he loved her more than any man had ever loved a woman in all of history. He'd surprised her with the most superb engagement ring and had promised her a life of luxury.

"I think you're ready," Mother said, taking her daughter's gloved hand in hers. "You'll never forget today—your wedding day. You look lovely, so let's not keep Louis waiting." McKenzie turned, and the long train of her gown trailed behind her. It was the most exquisite dress in the entire State of Massachusetts. Father had spared no expense in making sure his middle daughter was dressed in only the best.

McKenzie and her mother walked down the staircase to the first floor of the church. There, Mother continued through the doors into the sanctuary, where music played softly as her husband escorted her to the front pew on the left-hand side. He then returned to the back of the church, where he took McKenzie's arm and waited to walk her down the aisle to meet her groom. McKenzie smiled at him as she looped her arm through his, and he smiled back at her and kissed her gently on the cheek. "Your mother and I love you so much, McKenzie," he said.

"I love you, too, Father," McKenzie replied, trying not to cry.

When Wagner's "Bridal Chorus" began to play, McKenzie's father accompanied her down the red-carpeted aisle to the altar, where Louis was waiting. McKenzie glanced up to see her groom and knew such a day could be only in her dreams....

A knock at the door interrupted McKenzie's daydream, and she sighed, annoyed by the interruption. "Yes?" she asked, hoping she didn't sound as irritated as she felt.

"McKenzie, it's Rosemary. Are you almost ready, dear?"

"Yes, Rosemary. I'll be right out," McKenzie replied.

"Is there anything I can help you with?"

"In a moment, if you don't mind, I'd appreciate your help with my hair."

"I'll be back in a few minutes, then," Rosemary said. McKenzie could hear her footsteps descending the stairs.

For the moment, McKenzie wanted to dive back into her daydream. She attempted to reenter the dream, but it didn't work. Reality had set in. She wasn't marrying Dr. Louis Clarence III, and she never would. He had chosen her best friend, Pearl, to marry, instead. No, the man McKenzie was marrying was Zach Sawyer, a poor rancher with rough, dirty hands and a plain home in the middle of nowhere. He wasn't a prestigious doctor, and he wasn't charming. He was handsome and kind, she would give him that, but she doubted he was very smart, given that he'd chosen to leave Chicago and move to an untamed area out West.

Unlike in McKenzie's dream, her father wasn't here to walk her down the aisle, and not once had he told her that he loved her. Oh, she knew that he did—he'd always provided for her and had often shown interest in what she had to say. But he'd never said those words that would have meant so much to her.

Neither was her mother here to help her prepare for the biggest day of her life. Instead, McKenzie had only Rosemary, a plump, dowdy ranch wife, who seemed more inclined to hinder than help. The dress McKenzie was wearing was nowhere near as exquisite as the gown she would have worn to wed Louis, either. Moreover, it was likely that she and Zach would ride away from the church in his rickety wagon rather than the classy carriage that would have whisked her away on a honeymoon with Louis. Her life was turning out all wrong. Yet, she still had hope that, someday, after she'd found Kaydie and returned to Boston, she'd find a wealthy gentleman to marry and still have the wedding ceremony of her dreams. Her "real" husband would never know her secret past—her father could legally make sure of that. Until then, she would pretend to be enchanted with the idea of marrying a man she'd met through a newspaper advertisement.

"McKenzie?" Rosemary knocked again on the door, and McKenzie rolled her eyes. That woman's constant presence would have to change once McKenzie became Mrs. Sawyer. As a matter of fact, a lot of things would be changing in this house.

"Come in, Rosemary," McKenzie said, her voice low.

When Rosemary entered the room, McKenzie had to keep herself from gasping. Rosemary's appearance had much improved from yesterday. Her dingy, faded calico had been traded in for a clean, crisp, blue dress. She'd pulled her light brown hair into a bun, from which several silvery strands had escaped, to a surprisingly elegant effect. McKenzie thought she looked almost beautiful.

"You mentioned needing some help with your hair—how may I help you, dear?" Rosemary asked.

"Would you mind putting in a few pins?" McKenzie asked. Without a mirror, it was especially difficult to fix her hair the way she desired.

Rosemary quickly went to work pinning McKenzie's hair. "You look gorgeous, dear," she said. "I'm thrilled for you and Zach."

McKenzie turned to look at Rosemary. "Thank you, Rosemary. Does there happen to be a mirror in the house?"

"Yes, in Zach's—er, your and Zach's room," Rosemary said, adjusting her glasses on her nose.

"Thank you. I would like to see how I look." McKenzie stood up and followed Rosemary into Zach's room. It was the first time she'd entered the space, and she felt as though she were invading his privacy by doing so. Although the bedroom would be hers to share with Zach in a few short hours, she had already determined never to spend a night there.

This room was much more spacious than hers, but it was just as plain, furnished with a large bed, a bureau, and a rocking chair. McKenzie studied her reflection in the mirror above the bureau and saw that Rosemary had done a fine job on her hair. The dress accentuated her slim figure, and she was pleased enough with the overall effect. Thankfully, Zach had drawn her a warm bath early this morning, and the dirt from yesterday's travel had been washed away.

Yes, she was ready to act the part of blushing bride.

⁓

Several minutes later, McKenzie climbed into Rosemary's wagon, and the two women left for the church. McKenzie's stomach was full of knots, and she hoped Rosemary wouldn't talk the entire way into town.

"There's a big hole in the road just up ahead," Rosemary said. "Hang on; I don't want you bouncing out of the wagon."

McKenzie nodded. Yes, she remembered the hole in the road, and she cringed, bracing herself for the impact.

Rosemary maneuvered the wagon down the road, then slowed to a stop. "Well, I'll be!" she exclaimed. "The hole used to be right here." McKenzie joined her in craning her neck to look down at the ground. "That's odd," Rosemary said with a shrug. "It's been completely filled in. I guess we needn't have worried about it, after all."

"You said the hole was filled in?" McKenzie said.

"I guess so; can't imagine how else it could have disappeared. It's been here just about forever."

McKenzie sat in silence at Rosemary's observation. Had Zach filled in the hole? He'd promised he would, but so soon? McKenzie shook her head in disbelief. Perhaps it was someone else who'd become impatient with the hole in the road.

"You know, Zach is a kind and wonderful man," Rosemary said after a while.

"I beg your pardon?" McKenzie asked.

"Zach is a good man, McKenzie. You're fortunate to be marrying him." Rosemary's voice had quieted so much that McKenzie could barely hear it above the horses' hoofbeats and the wagon's rumble.

"Yes, he seems like a nice man," she agreed.

"Oh, he is. He's honest, kind, and thoughtful. I always wondered when he was going to marry. Of course, there aren't many eligible women in Pine Haven. Asa and I have prayed for him for many years now that the Lord would send him the wife he was meant to have—someone who would cherish and love him."

McKenzie couldn't think of what to say, so she merely nodded. She knew she wasn't the kind of woman Zach deserved, any more than he was the type of man she desired. However, there was nothing she could do. The circumstances were the way they were, and, as far as she could tell, there wasn't anything she could do to change them.

CHAPTER NINETEEN

$\mathcal{M}$cKenzie stared at the small chapel as Rosemary parked the wagon. The wooden structure was painted white and had a steeple topped with a rough-hewn cross. Three wooden stairs led up to the double-door entrance. It was a far cry from the church her family attended in Boston—a massive, redbrick building with a large bell tower and a steeple with a cross fashioned from high-quality oak by a skilled artisan. The interior was impressive, as well, with red-carpeted aisles and maple pews, and colorful light flooded the sanctuary through the stained-glass windows.

A wedding at that church would have been so glamorous, McKenzie thought with a sigh as she followed Rosemary up the front steps. The woman opened one of the double doors and peeked her head in, then turned to McKenzie and patted her arm. "It's time to go in, dear. They're ready for you."

Seeing the inside of the church for the first time, McKenzie held her breath. The chapel was plain, with no carpet on the floors, and it held perhaps one-tenth as many pews as her church at home.

She felt Asa's arm loop through hers and fought the resentment that welled within her at being given away by a man she didn't even know. She guessed it was fitting, though, considering the man she was about to marry was also a stranger. And so, McKenzie matched her steps with Asa's down the short aisle, keeping her eyes focused straight ahead. She knew none of the people in the pews, anyway, with the exception of those from the ranch. Best not to become too acquainted with them, anyhow. It wouldn't be long before she was on a stagecoach heading to the train depot, where she'd board the locomotive that would deliver her home again.

When they reached the front of the church, Asa gently released McKenzie's arm and sat down in the front pew next to Rosemary. McKenzie stood in silence and faced Zach, her eyes slowly meeting his. She was conscious of Reverend Eugene, standing to her left, and of Davey, huddled near Zach and holding a ring. She desperately desired to turn and run from the church, from Pine Haven, and from Zach. Had she not loved her sister more than life itself, she would have picked up the train of her dress and run as fast as her long legs would allow her, somewhere, anywhere but here.

Her thoughts of escape stopped when Reverend Eugene began speaking. "We are gathered here today to witness the matrimonial union of McKenzie Lonelle Worthington and Zachary Joseph Sawyer. It is my honor to perform this marriage, which, I pray, will endure through the test of time." Reverend Eugene smiled at Zach and McKenzie before continuing. "Will you please turn in your Bibles to Genesis chapter two, verse twenty-four? In this passage, we are told, 'Therefore shall a man leave his father and his mother, and shall cleave unto his wife: and they shall be one flesh.' Zach and McKenzie have stated their desire to unite as husband and wife and live as God intended in holy matrimony. You, Zach, and you, McKenzie, have made the decision to place each other as the second most important in each other's lives after a love and devotion to Jesus Christ.

"Now, would you all please turn with me to the book of Ephesians? In Ephesians four, verse thirty-two, it states, *'And be ye kind one to another, tenderhearted, forgiving one another, even as God for Christ's sake hath forgiven you.'* We pray that Zach and McKenzie will heed these important words of the Lord and treat each other with kindness and love, and that their hearts would be full of merciful forgiveness, just as Christ forgives us in His infinite mercy each and every day."

McKenzie hadn't realized the Bible spoke about marriage and provided guidance on how to treat the one to whom you were married. The list of vows for her to uphold as a wife were overwhelming, and she feared she would faint at the mere thought of all the promises she was expected to fulfill for Zach. She had attended many weddings yet had never paid attention to the words of the clergy until this moment. She regretted that now. Thank goodness this situation would be temporary! She already knew that there would be days in her short time as Mrs. Sawyer when she would feel little or no desire to be any of those things toward Zach. She had seen her own parents engage in an occasional disagreement, and she knew that, in the midst of a heated argument, it was too much to ask of someone to be kind and loving, let alone forgiving. And to admit wrongdoing and ask forgiveness was something else, altogether.

McKenzie's idea of marriage was saying "I do," moving into a big, beautiful house, and fluttering here and there to participate in volunteer activities while her husband was working outside the home in a notable profession. To her, being a wife meant living a life of ease, complete with a nanny to raise the children, maids to attend to the household duties, and a cook to prepare the meals. She glanced down at Davey, thinking it ironic that she would have to play the role of nanny, maid, and cook for a child she didn't know.

McKenzie jolted herself back to the reality of the situation and pretended to listen intently to what Reverend Eugene was saying. She wouldn't listen closely, for concentrating on his words would probably bring about a fainting spell, and she would rather feign interest than risk making a scene. Even so, McKenzie began to feel dizzy with the beginnings of a headache.

"If there are any objections to this union, which the Lord has brought together, may they be stated at this time. If not, may you forever hold your peace." Reverend Eugene waited for a moment, and then, when no objections were voiced, he continued. "Will you, McKenzie Lonelle Worthington, hereby have this man, Zachary Joseph Sawyer, to be your lawfully wedded husband, to live together after God's ordinance in the holy estate of matrimony? Will you love him, comfort him, honor and keep him, for better, for worse; for richer, for poorer; in sickness and in health; and, forsaking all others, cherish him from this day forward, until death do you part?" Reverend Eugene completed the wedding vow and waited for McKenzie's response.

McKenzie opened her mouth to speak, but the words would not come. Instead, much to her horror, strange gasping noises escaped from her mouth. The wedding vows were all so much to agree to—so much that she *didn't* want to agree to, nor even contemplate. After all, wouldn't her father, as an attorney, advise her that a wedding vow was a legally binding contract? Could she agree to the aforementioned items and pledge to uphold them? For worse? For poorer? In sickness? To love him forever, or, at least, until one of them died? To love him and comfort him? The inconceivable thoughts made her pulse quicken all the more, and she was overcome with light-headedness. She felt herself sway as her weakened legs wobbled beneath her. A marriage vow to Zach? But he was so opposite from the man she was meant to marry. He was so.... Fearing she would lose consciousness, she reached forward and attempted to steady herself by grabbing Zach's arm. That was the last thing McKenzie remembered.

Zach's quick reflexes allowed him to catch McKenzie before she thudded to the church floor in a heap. Commotion filled the building, with many people offering to help. Zach lifted McKenzie and carried her over to the front pew, where Rosemary and Asa moved aside to make room for her to be laid down.

Doc Orville was soon at McKenzie's side, checking her pulse. "She'll be fine," he assured Zach after a minute or so. "I believe you just have a very nervous bride."

Zach nodded and looked at McKenzie. She appeared peaceful in her unconscious state, and he felt guilty for not having arranged a private ceremony at the ranch. He'd simply taken it for granted that McKenzie was accustomed to large crowds, and a large crowd by Pine Haven's standards would probably count as only a small gathering in Boston. He'd assumed that she'd want a large wedding, but he'd never asked. Now, he regretted not asking her opinion. He'd figured that she would have had enough on her mind, making travel plans and preparing to part with her family, without having to think about the wedding ceremony details, as well.

Moments later, McKenzie regained consciousness. "Where am I?" she asked, reaching up to rub her temples with her fingers.

Zach leaned down beside her. "You're in Pine Haven, in the chapel. It's, uh…it's our wedding day."

"What?" McKenzie sat up quickly—too quickly, it turned out, and she felt the shooting pain of a headache.

"Just take it easy, McKenzie. I'm Doc Orville," said a man standing over her. "You're going to be fine, but you must lie here awhile."

McKenzie gulped. Where had Zach said she was? For a minute, everything was hazy, and she begged her mind to awaken from this nightmarish dream that had overtaken her. Had he said they were at a wedding? *Their* wedding?

"Would you like a glass of water, dear?" Rosemary held a cup of water in front of McKenzie and reached out an arm to steady her as she slowly lifted her head.

"Let's give her some space, folks," Doc Orville suggested, and the crowd around McKenzie began to disperse.

"I'll be outside when you need me," Reverend Eugene told Zach, patting him on the shoulder. "Don't be too concerned. You're not the first groom in history to have a fainting bride, and, I daresay, you won't be the last."

"Thanks, Reverend," Zach said. He'd envisioned every possible scenario of how this day could go, or so he'd thought, but none had included this. He took McKenzie's hand in his and stroked it with his thumb.

McKenzie looked up at Zach, then down at her dress. She seemed to be remembering the reason she was here, lying on a church pew.

"Are you all right, McKenzie? You gave us all quite a scare," Zach said quietly. He wished he could lean down and kiss her on the cheek to reassure her that everything would be all right, but he thought the gesture might be a bit forward, especially since they weren't married yet.

"I—I think so."

"Good. I'm sorry this day has been so stressful for you. I hadn't thought to ask if you would have preferred a small, private wedding on the ranch. I guess I took it for granted that you would want to have a church wedding. And, of course, whenever there's a wedding in this town, the entire population attends. I hope you'll forgive me, McKenzie."

⸎

McKenzie saw the look of remorse in Zach's eyes, and, for a moment, her heart sank. He truly believed she had fainted because of the pressure of getting married in front of a crowd of people. If only he knew that she encountered twice as many people on a trip to the mercantile on any given day in Boston. "It's fine, Zach," she assured him. She couldn't tell him the real reasons she'd passed out: because she was marrying a poor stranger with no family instead of a wealthy, reputable man with a prestigious pedigree; because she was trapped in a town with no modern conveniences instead of enjoying the high-class culture of Boston; because she had no family nearby with whom to celebrate this occasion; and because she would be making a vow and breaking it almost as quickly. But it was better that he believed she'd had a case of nerves.

Half an hour later, McKenzie and Zach were standing at the front of the chapel with Reverend Eugene, ready to declare their vows of matrimony. This time, however, their audience was limited to Davey, Jonah, Asa, and Rosemary. McKenzie hoped she wouldn't faint again, and she attempted with every fiber of her being to act as happy as everyone else seemed to be about the occasion.

Reverend Eugene cleared his throat and repeated the words that had sent McKenzie into a state of unconsciousness a short while before: "Will you, McKenzie Lonelle Worthington, hereby have this man, Zachary Joseph Sawyer, to be your lawfully wedded husband, to live together after God's ordinance in the holy estate of matrimony? Will you love him, comfort him, honor and keep him, for better, for worse; for richer, for poorer; in sickness and in health; and, forsaking all others, cherish him from this day forward, until death do you part?"

McKenzie pretended not to hear the words and instead focused on Zach. She was still surprised by his uncommonly handsome looks, and an odd feeling sprouted in her stomach, but she dismissed it as nerves. "I will," she squeaked on cue.

"And will you, Zachary Joseph Sawyer, hereby have this woman, McKenzie Lonelle Worthington, to be your lawfully wedded wife, to live together after God's ordinance in the holy estate of matrimony? Will you love her, comfort her, honor and keep her, for better for worse, for richer for poorer, in sickness and in health; and, forsaking all others, cherish her from this day forward, until death do you part?

"I will," said Zach.

"Do you have the ring, Davey?" Reverend Eugene asked, turning to the boy.

Davey stepped forward and handed Zach the ring. "Thank you, son," Zach said, then turned and slid the ring onto the appropriate finger of McKenzie's left hand.

"Forasmuch as Zachary and McKenzie have consented together in holy wedlock, and have witnessed the same before God and this company, and thereto have given and pledged their troth, each to the other, and have declared the same by giving and receiving a ring, and by joining hands, each to the other, I pronounce that they are man and wife, in the name of the Father, and of the Son, and of the Holy Spirit. Amen." Reverend Eugene smiled at the couple and added, "Zach, you may kiss your bride."

Taken aback at those words, McKenzie was unprepared for what happened next. Zach took a step toward her and leaned forward, placing a tender kiss on her lips. She was surprised by the sensation and pressed a hand to her stomach, as if to steady the flutters. His lips were gentle and unassuming, yet filled with affection and subtle fervor. Had McKenzie ever been kissed the way Zach had kissed her? The answer came quickly: no. But, then, she'd been kissed only a handful of times by hopeful beaus, none of whom had ever captured her heart—not even Louis, she realized.

Would every kiss be as overwhelming as Zach's or had the situation made her overly excitable? The questions popped into her mind faster than she could answer them, and she decided, for the moment, to cherish the feeling of her husband's first kiss.

CHAPTER TWENTY

"I present to you Mr. and Mrs. Zach Sawyer! Congratulations!" Reverend Eugene exclaimed after Zach and McKenzie ended their kiss. He patted them both on the back and sent them on their way down the aisle to see the townsfolk waiting outside the chapel.

A group of women, including Rosemary, quickly approached the newlyweds. "Congratulations, dear! I know you and Zach will be very happy," Rosemary said, stepping forward to hand McKenzie a handmade quilt. "On behalf of our quilting circle, I would like to present you with this gift."

McKenzie looked down at the quilt as she took it from Rosemary and felt humbled. It was not as thick and luxurious as her bedding at home in Boston, which she had ordered from a specialty imports store, but it had probably taken the women hours of effort, and she appreciated it. "Thank you," she said.

"You're quite welcome! Let me introduce you to the ladies in our circle," Rosemary said, then gestured to each woman in turn: "This is Myrtle, Reverend Eugene's wife. Here is Lucille Granger; she owns Granger Mercantile with her husband, Fred. This is Diane Orville; she's married to Doc Orville.

Then, we have Eliza Renkley; she and her husband, Billy Lee, have a ranch not too far from yours. Marie Kinion, here, is married to the sheriff, Clyde Kinion, and Wilma Waterson's husband, Wayne, is a blacksmith."

"Nice to meet you all," McKenzie said. Zach had left her side and was speaking to several men in the shade of a tree, and she felt odd standing in the middle of a group of women who were so opposite from herself in every way. She doubted any of them had ever been to a city like Boston or lived in a fine home.

"We would love for you to join us in the quiltin' circle," said Eliza. "Do you sew?"

"I do," McKenzie replied.

"Well, that settles it, then," said Lucille. "You're our newest member!"

"All in favor of inviting McKenzie Sawyer to join the quilting circle, say aye," said Marie.

Each woman voted in McKenzie's favor, and several of them gave her a hug. "We're happy to have you in Pine Haven, and we'll do whatever we can to make you feel welcome here," said Myrtle.

"We've baked some goodies for the potluck," Diane put in, "so, after you're finished meeting and greeting, please help yourself to a meal. Wilma also baked a grand wedding cake for you and Zach—it's over on the far table."

"Thank you," McKenzie said again, surprised at the charity of these strangers. While she delighted in spending time at teas and parties with her friends back home, she doubted they'd ever prepare a meal or bake a cake for her. Why should they? Only cooks and maids did such menial tasks.

The townspeople continued to greet McKenzie, and she floated from stranger to stranger, amazed at their genuine kindness.

When she felt a tug on her arm, she looked down to see Davey smiling up at her. "Can I call you Ma now?" he asked.

McKenzie couldn't believe how quickly Davey's clean appearance during the wedding had taken a turn for the worse. His trousers were caked with mud, and his once white shirt was spattered with dots of different colors, probably from his lunch. McKenzie could almost hear her own mother scolding him for being so ungentlemanly and telling him to pass his clothes immediately to Nellie to launder.

"Well, can I?" Davey persisted.

"Yes, Davey. That would be fine," McKenzie answered with a smile. *How quickly Davey is earning a place in my heart,* she thought. The realization both touched her and troubled her at the same time.

After the potluck reception, Zach and McKenzie rode most of the way to the ranch in silence. McKenzie turned her gaze to the band on her finger. Had she married Louis, she would be wearing only the finest of diamonds mounted on a pure gold band. But she had married Zach, and the plain ring in no way could be considered exceptional. She doubted the band was real gold, and it certainly wasn't studded with any diamonds. She wondered why one would even bother to purchase such a dismal piece of jewelry.

She opened her hand and then folded it into a fist, watching the ring maintain its secure place on her left ring finger. *It doesn't matter,* she reminded herself. In a few short months, the ring would be removed and tossed away, never to be seen again.

⤬

As Zach drove the wagon, he watched McKenzie out of the corner of his eye. He wished he knew what was going through her mind. She had shared so little with him since her arrival, and his own shyness prevented him from asking her the questions that traveled through his mind like a runaway horse. Was she happy? Was she still thinking about losing consciousness during the wedding? Did she regret her decision to become his wife? *Lord, enable me to be the kind of husband You designed me to be,* he prayed silently. *And, thank You, Lord, for letting McKenzie be so easy on the eyes.* He stifled a chuckle. After all, he'd convinced himself not to be concerned at all about his new wife's appearance, and now, here he sat, next to the most beautiful woman he'd ever seen. Watching her walk up the aisle with Asa during the wedding ceremony had taken the breath from him. Not that he would have hesitated to marry her, had she been plain, but he felt a sense of honor and privilege to think that God had chosen someone so beautifully made for him. *Please, let her love me the way I promise to love her,* he prayed.

CHAPTER TWENTY-ONE

On Wednesday morning, a tiny voice and a knock at the door interrupted McKenzie's sleep. "Ma? Ma?" McKenzie rolled over and sat up in her bed. What was that?

"Ma? Ma? Come quick!"

McKenzie bolted from her bed and rushed to the door. When she opened it, she saw Davey standing there. "What is it, Davey? Is something wrong?" She realized that responding to the name "Ma" would take some getting used to.

"No, Ma; nothing's wrong. It's just that your wedding present is here."

"Davey, it's not even morning yet. Go back to bed, please." McKenzie winced. She'd only been Davey's 'ma' for less than a day, and already she was telling him what to do.

"No, I can't go back to bed. Besides, it's mornin' time. The rooster already crowed." He reached for McKenzie's hand. "Come on. I can't wait for you to see your wedding present!"

McKenzie sighed. What could be so important that she would be awakened at least two hours before her normal rising time? "Just a minute, Davey. Let me put on my cloak." She slipped her arms through the garment and buttoned it over her nightgown.

"We don't got too much time," Davey said.

"You mean, we don't *have* too much time," McKenzie corrected him.

"That, too. You'll see why when you come out to the barn." Holding McKenzie's hand, he led her through the house and outside.

"Did you say my wedding present is here?" McKenzie asked when the words finally clicked in her mind.

"Yep! I can't believe it. Pa says it's perfect timing. Wait till you see it!"

McKenzie was hoping to receive a jeweled broach or a pearl necklace. However, if her gift was in the barn, as Davey had said, it probably wasn't a piece of jewelry. Perhaps, Zach had purchased for her a new armoire with a gold-framed mirror. She smiled at the notion.

"Wait a minute," Davey said, interrupting her thoughts.

"What is it?" McKenzie asked, her hand still firmly gripped in Davey's.

"Look at that sunrise, Ma. Isn't it bootiful? Pa says only the Lord could create somethin' so bootiful."

McKenzie turned her head in the direction Davey pointed. Sure enough, pinkish hues fanned the sky as the vibrant sunrise made its appearance. Feeling somewhat ashamed, she realized that she'd never before marveled at a sunrise. Had it been because the buildings were so tall in Boston that they blocked the magnificence? Because she had never awakened early enough to see it? Or, because she simply never had taken the time to view such a piece of artistry? "Yes, it is beautiful, Davey."

"I think I like God's sunrises even better than His rainbows," Davey admitted.

McKenzie stared down at Davey. His blond hair stuck up in odd places from last night's sleep and made a ruffled design at the back of his head. His blue eyes were bright, and a dimple creased his right cheek. "Do you like rainbows, Ma?" he asked her.

"I do," McKenzie said, even as she realized she'd never seen a real rainbow. She'd seen paintings of them, of course, but never the real thing. "Do you have a lot of rainbows here?" she asked.

"Only sometimes, after it rains. It's 'cause God told Noah He'd never flood the world again. It's a promise."

"Really? That's why we have rainbows?" McKenzie asked him.

"Yep."

McKenzie stared at Davey in awe. She had never learned about the origin of rainbows. *Davey will be a smart man some-day*, she mused.

"We better get to the barn. Pa's waitin'," Davey said, pulling again on McKenzie's hand.

They entered the barn, and McKenzie scrunched her nose at the unfamiliar smell of hay. She saw Zach rise from his crouched position beside a white horse.

⸎

"Good morning, McKenzie," Zach said, standing up when he saw her and Davey. He attempted to hide a smirk at the sight of McKenzie's white nightgown peeking out from beneath her cloak and the look of her hair in disarray.

"Good morning," McKenzie replied. "Davey said my wedding present was in the barn?"

"Yes—she's right here." Zach leaned down again and scooped up a small, brown and white foal. "Isn't she beautiful?"

"I beg your pardon?" McKenzie said, sounding incredulous.

"I named her Starlight," Davey spoke up. "I hope that's okay. It's 'cause she has a star on her forehead. See?" He pointed to the foal's head. "She can't stand very good, either. It's 'cause she's just born."

Zach laughed. "You're right, Davey. But, each day, she'll become stronger and stronger, and, before long, she'll be able to walk and run, just like her mother, Sugar."

"The horse is my gift?" McKenzie asked, staring blankly at him.

"The foal, yes," Zach said. "I know she's tiny now, but I thought you'd enjoy having your own horse. It's really something to watch a foal grow up, and, if she's anything like her mother, she'll be easy to train. She'll make a good horse."

"You are giving me a horse for my wedding present?"

What was making it so hard for McKenzie to understand? "Yes, I am giving you a horse for your wedding present," Zach confirmed, creasing his eyebrows in concern. Did McKenzie not like her gift? He'd been so sure she would embrace his idea, since she'd said in a letter that she'd never ridden a horse but was eager to try. He remembered the first time he'd had a horse of his own, and how ecstatic he'd been.

"I guess I don't believe it," McKenzie said, her voice quiet. "Thank you, Zach, for the horse," she said after a moment. "I guess I was just expecting something different. But, thank you all the same."

Zach stared at McKenzie. Unsure of how to respond, he prayed for guidance, and then said, "I'm sorry if I disappointed you. I truly thought you'd like a horse." The last thing he'd wanted to do was disappoint her, but he'd done it. As he watched McKenzie walk out of the barn, he recalled what his father had told him about not making a big deal of the small things. Although her response to his gift had crushed more than his ego, he decided to classify this incident as a small thing and think nothing more of it.

CHAPTER TWENTY-TWO

*M*cKenzie walked into the house and up to her room. Of all the odd things she'd encountered so far on this mercy trip, the gift of a foal had been the most unexpected. She had wished so much for a more fitting present. When she'd been a child, she'd always received everything she had asked for and more. While she didn't fault Zach for not knowing what she would want for a wedding gift, she did wish he had asked her.

McKenzie plopped onto her bed with a sigh. It was still early in the morning, and she wondered whether she would be able to fall back to sleep. Lying back down on the bed, she closed her eyes. Perhaps she should get dressed and help Rosemary with breakfast. After all, that's what Zach probably expected of her. It seemed as though the work on the ranch never ended. No sooner had one meal been served than another one had to be prepared. To add to her troubles, McKenzie felt herself growing increasingly lonely. Suddenly, she felt a wave of self-pity at her plight. She had expected her plan to find Kaydie to turn out differently than it had thus far.

When McKenzie had come to Pine Haven, she had sent a brief telegram to inform her parents of her safe arrival. She hadn't yet taken the time to write them. She figured now was as good a time as any, especially since she was missing them and felt the need to vent her feelings. So, she opened one of her trunks and pulled out some stationery and a pencil. Then, sitting at the little wooden table, she began to write.

Dearest Mother and Father,

I hope this letter finds you well. As for me, I am noth-ing short of miserable. I don't even know where to begin.

First of all, there is something I need to tell you. I'll not go into detail now, but I am now a married woman. Please do not be alarmed, as this is only a marriage of convenience with a man who wanted a mail-order bride; it will last only until I find Kaydie. I know Father will find it fitting to annul it once I return to Boston.

Zach, the man I married, seems to find it fitting to make ridiculous demands of me. He fails to treat me kindly and expects me to live in a home that is worse than those inhabited by poverty-stricken folks in Boston. I have no friends here, and there are no modern conve-niences. In short, I don't know how much longer I can remain on this temporary adventure I have decided to undertake.

I have not yet located Kaydie, but I hope to place a posting in town and inquire of as many people as pos-sible about whether they know of her whereabouts. I keep hoping that I will find her soon, for her sake as much as for mine.

Yet, as bad as things are, I again ask that you not come for me.

Please tell Biddie, Nellie, and Helen hello for me.
Your daughter,
McKenzie

PS: I might as well tell you now that there is no woman
named Isadora Jones. The person I was writing to wasn't
a destitute mother, but the man I married, Zach Sawyer.

Later that day, McKenzie accompanied Rosemary to town on some errands. Her first stop was the post office, where she handed her letter to Mr. Victor to mail. The sooner someone else knew of her plight, the better.

⤜⤛

The following weekend, everyone on the ranch went to church together on Sunday. Zach assisted McKenzie onto the wagon seat beside him, and Davey, Rosemary, Asa, and Jonah climbed into the back of the wagon.

The congregants meandered up the stairs of the church, each shaking Reverend Eugene's hand on their way inside. McKenzie followed Zach and sat down in a pew between him and Davey. Earlier that morning, her family would have attended the service at their own church in Boston. Suddenly, she missed those Sunday mornings at church, which were usually followed by an afternoon meal at the home of close friends. She knew no such thing would be occurring in Pine Haven today.

"Welcome to Pine Haven Chapel," Reverend Eugene said when the service began. "Would you all rise and join me in signing hymn number fifty-eight, 'The Solid Rock'?"

McKenzie watched as those around her reached for the hymnals scattered about in the pews and opened them. Zach leaned closer to McKenzie to share his hymnal with her.

As Myrtle began to play the tune on the piano, the people lifted up their voices to the Lord, singing, "On Christ, the solid Rock, I stand, all other ground is sinking sand; all other ground is sinking sand."

McKenzie had always sung along with the hymns at church, yet, the music had never moved her much. Like the tradition of going to church, it was just another ritual that had to be observed every Sunday before she could go about her other activities.

When the hymn ended with an amen, Reverend Eugene asked that everyone sit down and join him in prayer. "Dear heavenly Father, we thank You for allowing us to meet here today to worship You. What a blessing it is that we have the freedom to do so. Please prepare each heart for the sermon I am about to deliver and enable me to deliver that message in a way that is pleasing to You. It is in Your precious name that we pray, amen." Reverend Eugene looked out at the congregation and smiled. "It is nice to see all of you here today. I would like to take a minute to welcome a new person to our fellowship. Mrs. Zachary Sawyer, would you please stand?"

Feeling nausea rise within her, McKenzie slowly stood to her feet. "Welcome, Mrs. Sawyer. We are so blessed to have you here. As many of you know, this dear lady married our own Zach Sawyer last week. Please make her feel welcome."

"Thank you," McKenzie said, her voice barely audible. She sat back down and attempted to conceal the quick, shallow breathing that had overtaken her. Had she ever been welcomed in such a way before as she was continually being welcomed in Pine Haven? No. Not even at the tea parties and balls did anyone give a second thought that she was in attendance. Yet, here, people seemed to genuinely care that she was now a part of their town. She stifled the tears that threatened to come. If they only knew her real reason for being here, and what she intended to do once her goal was accomplished, she doubted they'd be so glad to have her in their midst. If she had come to Pine Haven without an ulterior motive, she would have been humbled by the outpouring of kindness. She might even have come to like the people of the town and cultivate friendships with them. After all, they had given her a warmer welcome and more ready acceptance than anyone else ever had.

Zach patted McKenzie on the arm. He spoke no words, but she could see in his eyes a mixture of compassion and hope. She realized that she hadn't thought about or appreciated anyone other than herself for a long time, and, now, she thought of the man beside her. A man who had been nothing but kind to her. If only she could be what he wanted her to be. If only she could stay with him and love him in the way he deserved. If only....

"Please turn in your Bibles with me to Proverbs ten, verse twelve," Reverend Eugene said, interrupting McKenzie's thoughts. The sounds of pages turning prompted her to begin leafing through the pages of her own Bible. She had no idea where the book of Proverbs was, or that it even existed. The pages in her Bible were crisp from lack of use and difficult to turn one at a time. Her fingers didn't want to work, and she felt embarrassed being the only one still struggling to find the passage Reverend Eugene had mentioned.

Zach had found the Old Testament book with apparent ease. He looked over at her, flipping futilely through the pages. Out of the corner of her eye, she saw him smile sympathetically. Leaning over, he whispered in her ear, "McKenzie, may I help you find it?"

She nodded, embarrassed and grateful at the same time, and Zach lifted her Bible, placed it in his lap, and turned to the correct page before handing the book back to her.

"Thank you, Zach," McKenzie whispered.

Zach nodded and turned back toward Reverend Eugene.

McKenzie looked down at Zach's Bible, open on his lap. She'd seen the cover earlier—although it likely had once been stiff, it was now bent in places and worn all over. Inside his Bible, the pages were wrinkled and yellowed. Pencil marks underlined certain verses, as if to make them stand out. Perhaps, the next time she was in town, McKenzie would purchase a new Bible for Zach. Maybe that could be her wedding gift to him.

"Proverbs ten, verse twelve, states, *'Hatred stirreth up strifes: but love covereth all sins.'* I want us to consider this verse for a moment. Solomon, who is credited with writing most of Proverbs, gives us insightful clues on how to live in a manner pleasing to our Lord. We all know someone who, at one time or another, has stirred up trouble...."

As the reverend went on, McKenzie was convicted like never before about the times when she had stirred up strife. She wished that she could disappear, so that no one would see her shame, which surely was obvious. As she listened to Reverend Eugene speak about the importance of love, she realized that she was unaccustomed to reading and really thinking about God's Word. She was unfamiliar with 95 percent of what the Bible taught, for rarely had she turned the pages of her book.

McKenzie swallowed hard. How many times had she started arguments with Peyton? Could the letter she'd sent to her parents become a means of causing strife with her and Zach if he found out about it? Her heart felt heavy, yet she did not know how to ease her discomfort.

CHAPTER TWENTY-THREE

In the week since the wedding, Zach had asked McKenzie each night if she'd care to join him on the porch to spend time with the Lord. And, each night, she'd refused. However, after hearing Reverend Eugene's sermon that morning, McKenzie wanted to learn more about the Bible and the God she claimed to worship. So, this time, when Zach extended the invitation, she accepted.

The first thing she wanted to know was why he "spent time with the Lord" every night.

"I spend time every night with the Lord, reading His Word and praying, because the Lord has been so good to me," Zach began. "He sent His Son to die for me in my place, and He didn't have to do that." He paused for a moment. "He has blessed me beyond measure. He gave me a son, good friends, a roof over my head, food, and He gave me you." Zach reached over and squeezed McKenzie's hand.

McKenzie held her hand still, worried that, if she moved it, she would spoil the moment Zach had created. As it was, she felt safe and secure next to him on the porch. She decided to ask another question.

"How can you say that God has blessed you when He took your parents from you?"

"I do miss my parents; I think about them often and wish I could have had just one more day with them. I'd give anything for that. But, God is sovereign, and He has a plan. He alone knows why they had to die at such a young age. As a child, it was difficult for me to understand why they died, especially since they both loved the Lord with all their hearts. They served Him, devoted their lives to Him, and raised me to love Him, as well." Zach paused again. "I was only twelve when they passed away, and I remember not being able to stop crying for days. Later, I was taken to the orphanage. I had my pa's Bible—the one I use to this day," Zach said, patting the worn volume in his lap. "I began reading it from beginning to end. I didn't want to miss anything. I wanted to find out why God had let them die. I remember the first time I read the verse in Romans that says, *'And we know that all things work together for good to them that love God, to them who are the called according to his purpose.'* Finally, I stopped asking God why and focused on the fact that He had a reason. Even though I didn't know what it was, He had a reason, and that was good enough for me. Besides, who was I to argue with the One who spoke the world into existence?"

Even in the dim light of the candle flickering on the table beside them, McKenzie could see the emotion in Zach's eyes. She imagined him only eight years older than Davey and losing his parents. He'd been carted off to an orphanage. His parents were gone. "But then God took Davey's mother from you, too," she said quietly.

Zach looked up at her with a surprised expression. "Yes, I do miss Davey's ma *and* pa," he said. "I forgot to tell you this, since I tend to forget, myself, but I adopted Davey. His pa,

Will Mitchell, was my best friend. We met at the orphanage in Chicago and later decided to come out West together. My pa had always dreamed of owning his own ranch but never had the chance. It had become a dream of mine, as well, and Will thought it was a great idea, too. He later married Bess, and they had Davey. When Davey was one year old, they both died of the fever—first Bess, then Will. On his deathbed, Will made me promise that I would adopt Davey and raise him as my own. I never had any siblings, and Will and I were like brothers. There was no way I would not make that promise to him. I had already grown to love Davey like my own son, anyway."

McKenzie attempted to hide her shock. Davey was adopted? She never would have guessed it. "So, then, you weren't married before?" she asked. Somehow, knowing that she didn't have to compete with the memory of another woman would make her life easier.

"You are my first and only wife, McKenzie," Zach said, squeezing her hand again.

McKenzie gulped. She may be his first wife, but she knew she wouldn't be his only one. "I had no idea Davey was adopted," she said.

"I forget that he is adopted most of the time, too. Because of my love for him, and because of the large part he plays in my life, he is truly mine," said Zach. "He looks a lot like his parents—an equal mix, I would say—but he acts like me in a lot of ways. Maybe that's because I've raised him." Zach turned to look at McKenzie. "He sure has taken to you."

"Yes," McKenzie said, chuckling softly. "He asked me right after we were married if he could call me Ma."

"That sounds like Davey," Zach agreed.

"So, did you want to marry so that Davey would have a mother?" McKenzie asked. It hadn't mattered before what his motives had been, but now, oddly, it did.

"I did want Davey to have a mother," Zach conceded, "but that wasn't the only reason I wanted to get married. I wanted to have someone special with whom to spend the rest of my life. I saw how much my pa loved my ma, and I prayed God would give me a wife to love like that."

"So, you took seriously all the things Reverend Eugene said at our wedding ceremony about loving and serving each other and all of that?" McKenzie asked. She was thankful that she no longer felt nervous around Zach. In fact, sitting with him on the porch and having this discussion with him made her feel as though she'd known him all her life.

"Yes, I took it very seriously, McKenzie. You see, a marriage that is founded on God's principles is a marriage that lasts."

McKenzie doubted that was true in all cases, and she knew that, whether or not their marriage was founded on God's principles, it would soon come to an end.

"Everything we ever need to know about anything is in the Bible. Everything we face, God understands. He created marriage, so He knows firsthand the good and the bad that comes with that commitment."

"Really?" McKenzie didn't know that such a wealth of knowledge could be found in the Bible.

"Yes, really."

"How do you know all this?" she asked.

"I've spent a lot of time getting to know God by reading His Word," Zach said. "I won't know Him completely until I go to spend eternity with Him, but I want to learn all I can while I'm here on earth. So, I spend a lot of time reading His Word, praying, and worshipping Him. He's my life."

"Does the Bible speak of loneliness?" McKenzie asked. She didn't want to bare too much of her soul to Zach, yet the words tumbled out before she could stop them. She had felt so lonely in Pine Haven without her family and close friends.

"It does, McKenzie. In Hebrews, it says, '*For he hath said, I will never leave thee, nor forsake thee.*' I know that it's been difficult for you to move here and adjust to a new lifestyle, but God promises us that, no matter where we go, He will always be with us."

"I never realized all of this, Zach. I guess I should spend every evening on the porch with you."

"I'd like that. I also hope that, someday, you'll feel completely comfortable here, and that we can have a marriage that is truly founded on God's principles. I'd like nothing more than to spend the rest of my life with you, McKenzie."

"Oh, you don't mean that, Zach," McKenzie said, hoping she was right.

"I do mean it. I made a vow before God, and I intend to keep it."

An awkward silence followed, and McKenzie was grateful when Zach spoke again, changing the subject. "Why don't we begin our Bible reading?"

McKenzie nodded and listened while Zach read aloud and then prayed. Maybe, just maybe, she'd be able to endure Pine Haven a little more easily.

CHAPTER TWENTY-FOUR

"Hello, Mr. Victor. Any mail?" Zach asked as he entered the post office the following day during an afternoon of errands.

"Let's see, Zach. No mail for you, but I do have a piece of mail here for Rosemary." Mr. Victor handed Zach an envelope.

"Thanks, Mr. Victor. Have a good day, now." Zach turned and was about to walk out of the post office when a large piece of paper hanging on the wall caught his attention. The scribbled words seemed to leap off the page at him.

Looking for one beloved Kayde Kraemer, last seen in western Montana Territory. If seen, please contact McKenzie Sawyer at once. Your assistance is appreciated.

"Oh, yes, please tell McKenzie I haven't heard anything regarding her inquiry," Mr. Victor said.

"Uh, all right. Thanks, Mr. Victor." Zach opened the door and walked out into the street. Questions filled his mind—questions that troubled him. Who was Kayde Kraemer? The possibility that the person McKenzie was seeking was a man with whom she'd been romantically involved bothered him, but he quickly dismissed the thought and entertained other questions. Why hadn't McKenzie mentioned Kayde to him? And when had McKenzie hung the notice in the post office? Had it been recently? Zach fought the temptation to conjure up negative conclusions based only on the limited information he had.

When Zach arrived back at the ranch, Rosemary was in the kitchen, trying to teach McKenzie how to cook. Zach watched from afar as Rosemary talked about measurements, ingredient combinations, and cooking times. McKenzie seemed eager to learn, and she appeared to be listening intently. *Thank You, Lord, that McKenzie is a willing student. I know things are so different for her here. Please let her learn with ease;* Zach prayed silently. Not wanting to interrupt the lesson, he decided to wait until their Bible time that evening on the porch to approach the subject of Kayde Kraemer, provided he could wait that long. Questions continued to swarm in his mind, and he knew that the only way he could temporarily dismiss the disturbing thoughts would be to busy himself with chores.

As McKenzie tucked Davey in bed that night, she kissed him tenderly on the forehead. She delighted in the task of securing him in his bed for the night. "Good night, Davey," she said.

"G'night, Ma," he echoed.

McKenzie turned to leave the room and join Zach on the porch when Davey said, "Ma?"

"Yes, Davey?" She turned around.

"I love you," he said.

McKenzie stood in silence, her feet fixed in one spot. How could Davey love her after knowing her for so short a time? Further, how was she to respond to him?

"Ma? I love you," Davey repeated.

McKenzie's breath caught in her throat, and she found it difficult to breathe. She'd never said those words to anyone, nor had they really been spoken to her. With the exception of Kaydie, she'd never truly loved anyone—even Louis, she admitted to herself again.

She knew Davey was waiting for her to say something. Should she tell him she loved him, too, even though she didn't know if it was true? Or should she tell him good night again and go on her way? The decision was a weighty one, and she tried to reason out a course of action as quickly as possible. Finally, before Davey could repeat himself yet again, she answered him, "I love you, too, Davey."

Before he could say more, she left the room and fled down the stairs, her emotions a jumble.

Downstairs, McKenzie slowly regained her composure, preparing to meet with Zach. She picked up her Bible from the table, opened the door, and walked out onto the porch.

"Good evening, McKenzie," Zach said, patting the chair next to him. He always looked forward to the evening, when he could spend time getting to know the woman he'd married. He hoped their times together meant as much to McKenzie as they did to him.

"Hello, Zach," McKenzie replied, sitting down beside him. When she looked up at the sky, she gasped. "That is the most amazing sunset I've seen yet!" she exclaimed.

"I agree," Zach said, still looking at McKenzie. "The Lord's artistry never ceases to amaze me."

McKenzie nodded. "I thought you'd be happy to know that I learned how to make biscuits today. Rosemary has been teaching me all of her kitchen tricks."

"I thought I saw you taking lessons today," Zach said.

"I never much cared for cooking. I never had to do it in Boston. Cook always prepared the most scrumptious meals, and I never gave much thought to where the food came from or how it was made. When I was a little girl, I would sit on a stool in the kitchen and watch Cook as she prepared meal after meal. She'd never let me help her, though, because she said I was too young. Once, when I was about Davey's age, I remember begging her for a scoop of cookie dough. She finally acquiesced, and I recall thinking that nothing tasted finer than that unbaked ball of dough."

Zach listened as McKenzie took them both back in time to a life that was so different from the one she was living now. He hoped she never stopped sharing her memories with him. He reveled in those glimpses of her past. "My ma loved to bake, and she made a lot of cookies—we almost always had a batch on hand. After supper, Pa, Ma, and I would sit around the table and dunk cookies in milk. It was one of my fondest memories."

"I wish my mother had baked us cookies. I doubt she ever baked anything, much less a dessert."

They sat in silence for a while, and Zach considered asking her the question that had plagued his mind, not to mention his heart, throughout the entire day. Finally, he couldn't contain his curiosity any longer. "McKenzie?"

"Yes?"

"Who is Kayde Kraemer? Is he a relative?" Zach prayed that Kayde was merely a cousin. He wanted McKenzie to refute the worst of his fears—that Kayde Kraemer was someone with whom she was in love.

McKenzie stared at him. She actually looked frightened. But then, after a moment, she relaxed and actually laughed. Finally, she said, "*Kaydie* is not a he but a she."

Zach could do nothing to stop the sigh of relief that escaped his lungs. "Kayde is really Kaydie, and he's not a man?" he asked, just to be sure he'd heard her correctly.

"No. Kaydie is my sister."

"Your sister?" Zach hadn't thought to ask many questions about McKenzie's sisters. He knew from her letters during their courtship that she had two sisters, and that one of them was named Peyton. That was all he'd known, and he hadn't thought to ask more.

"I know it seems odd. You see, all the girls in my family are named after important male relatives. I'm named after my maternal grandfather, McKenzie Dudley. My older sister, Peyton, is named after our paternal grandfather, Peyton Worthington. And Kaydie is named after my mother's favorite brother, Kayde Dudley. Kaydie's real name is Kaydence, but I've always called her Kaydie."

"I see," said Zach. His heart felt lighter, and he praised God that his suspicion was not founded on fact. "Why didn't you tell me you were looking for Kaydie?" he asked, trying not to sound accusatory. Although this matter had concerned him, he reminded himself that it was a small thing, and he wasn't going to make a big deal of it.

"I put up the ad in the post office about a week ago. I'm sorry I never mentioned it to you." McKenzie looked pensive. "I must have written it so hastily that I looped the letters together, making the name appear to be Kayde rather than Kaydie. I'll have to go back and fix that."

Zach dismissed the hurt he felt at not knowing about something that was apparently important to McKenzie. "Mr. Victor told me to tell you that he hadn't heard any news. So, you believe your sister's in these parts?"

"I do. She ran off and married a man by the name of Darius Kraemer, who swindles and robs banks; he's been on the run from the law for quite a while now. Darius is a wicked man with an even more wicked temper, and he treats my sister abusively. He has refused to let her return to Boston and has stolen all of her inheritance. The last I heard, she was in Canfield Falls—at least, that's where her last letter had been postmarked."

"So, you want to help Kaydie escape from Darius?" Zach asked. Why hadn't McKenzie asked for his help from the start? Had she not trusted he would do everything he could to remove Kaydie from such a desperate situation?

"Yes, I do," said McKenzie.

"I would be happy to help you, McKenzie, but I wish you had told me sooner."

❧

McKenzie nodded. She didn't know what to say, but she was relieved Zach was neither mad at nor disappointed with her. For some reason she couldn't explain, his opinion of her mattered more and more to her with every passing day. With increasing frequency, she felt the same, peculiar feeling that came when she sat with him in the evenings and spent time with the Lord.

It frightened McKenzie to think that she was becoming friends with Zach. And his assistance in finding Kaydie would no doubt bring them closer together—not what she wanted, even if it would improve the odds of finding her sister faster. That meant her return to Boston would be much sooner, and the sooner she and Kaydie could get back home, the better. Still, McKenzie was wary of Zach's helping her—she was beginning to feel things for him, and it would make leaving him harder to do. *Finding Kaydie is your one and only goal*, she reminded herself. *You would be silly not to welcome Zach's help.*

"That ring belonged to my ma," Zach said, interrupting McKenzie's thoughts.

"I beg your pardon?"

"Your wedding ring. I noticed you staring at it. I thought you might want to know it has a history."

McKenzie hadn't realized she'd been staring at the gold band and was caught by surprise that he'd noticed. "It was your mother's?"

"Yes. You should have seen the look on the jeweler's face in Wilmerville when I asked if he could make it a little smaller." Zach smiled and shook his head.

"You—you had to have it made smaller?"

"Yes. There was a little more of Ma than there is of you, except for height," Zach said. "She was barely five feet tall."

The thought of having a hand-me-down wedding ring both disturbed and intrigued McKenzie. Had she married Louis, her ring would have been brand-new, with at least a two-carat diamond of the highest of quality. It would have been designed by one of Boston's top jewelers—custom-made just for her—and presented to her in a velvet box.

"It was important to me that the woman I marry have Ma's ring. She was a precious woman and meant so much to me." Zach leaned toward McKenzie and brushed a stray hair away from her face. "I would have done everything in my power to buy you one of those fancy rings that you probably saw in the jewelry stores in Boston. But this ring that you are wearing is worth much more. It has value that can't be measured by money. Your ring tells of a love between my parents that was God-honoring, God-serving, and real. They loved each other more than life itself. Their lives were difficult, and they shared together in many struggles, but they never gave up."

Zach paused. "They used to pray for me that I would someday find the wife God had planned for me. That woman is you, McKenzie. You're the one God planned for me to marry. The way it all fell into place could only be the work of His hand. Of all the responses I received, only yours was genuine. God led me to respond to yours alone, and I thank Him for you each day. I hope that this ring will symbolize yet another generation of true love—a love that can survive anything."

McKenzie felt a stab of guilt for leading Zach to believe that their love was true. Being this close to him—physically and emotionally—scared her. "But, what if—what if ours isn't true love, like your parents shared?" she stammered, hoping to plant a seed of doubt in Zach's heart that would help him better bear her departure later. "We are different people, Zach. You can't base our marriage on your parents'."

"You're right, McKenzie. I just want to love you like Christ loves the church. I don't want to duplicate every area of my parents' lives. I don't want to be my parents. I want us to be us. But I want us to have the unconditional love that my parents seemed to share."

"It sounds like your parents had a perfect marriage," McKenzie said. She thought of her own parents, who seemed more like friends or business partners than lovers.

"Not even close to being perfect," Zach said with a laugh. "They had their disagreements, just like any married couple."

He paused. "As close as Asa and Rosemary are, they have their struggles, too."

"What if our marriage never becomes like your parents', or like Asa and Rosemary's?"

Zach stared at McKenzie. He looked alarmed.

"Zach?" McKenzie could see the troubled look in his eyes.

"All we can do, McKenzie, is put our marriage in God's hands. He knows what has been and what is to come."

McKenzie thought of what Zach had said about God knowing what was and what is to come. From what she knew of the Lord, He knew of her motive for marrying Zach. He knew why she'd accepted his proposal. And He knew what would happen in the coming months. The thought that the Lord would be disappointed in her for the choices she'd made distressed her. She'd never given much thought to her Creator's opinion of her in the past. In recent days, although she hadn't realized the full extent of it, God had begun to tug on her heart.

However, whether it was in God's hands or not, McKenzie knew that their marriage would be short-lived. No matter what feelings she harbored in her heart now or later, the answer would remain the same. Her marriage to Zach would be over once she found Kaydie. There was nothing she or he could do to change that fact.

Just then, Zach drew closer to McKenzie and kissed her gently on the lips. McKenzie found herself wishing the kiss would last longer than it did. Feelings within her—feelings she'd never felt before—rose to the surface, and she struggled to define them. She needed to figure out some way to protect her heart and Zach's heart, and his kisses weren't helping the matter one bit.

McKenzie attempted to dismiss the kiss from her mind and decided to change the subject. "Perhaps—perhaps I should pick up a new Bible for you the next time I'm in town. I know this Bible was your father's, but it is looking a little worse for the wear."

"Thanks, McKenzie, but this Bible is my most prized possession," Zach said. "It shows years of wear from being read by both Pa and me. Pa flipped through the pages of this book looking for just the right verse and underlined the Scriptures that held deep meaning to him, personally. Now, I do the same thing. My parents were only thirty-one and thirty-two when they died—so young to be taken. I didn't have them for long, and I have only a few things that were theirs. I know that this Bible and your wedding ring are just things, but they somehow bring me closer to my parents and help me remember that I'll join them in glory someday. I can't wait for them to meet you."

McKenzie nodded, pretending to understand. Her parents were still alive, so she couldn't truly empathize with his loss. She wasn't as close to her parents as he had been to his, so she couldn't understand his devotion. She hadn't experienced the love of parents and child like he had, so she couldn't comprehend his dedication. She was learning so much during these evenings on the porch—so much about Zach, in addition to God and His Word. Neither subject was something she would have cared about a month ago. Likewise, going to church had become exciting to her, even without lunches and social gatherings to look forward to afterward.

"Growing up and into adulthood, God and His Word never meant much to me," McKenzie said. "My family attended church for the social aspect of it, not to grow closer to God or to learn more about Him. Church here seems so foreign to me, but in a good way."

"Keep letting God pull you closer to Him, McKenzie. He loves you so much. Together, we will learn all about Him."

McKenzie nodded. Why was it that in these moments with Zach, she felt a closeness she'd never felt before? As quickly as she'd let the question enter her mind, she dismissed it. It would be better to distance herself than to make things more difficult when the time came to leave. Besides, while she didn't want to hurt Zach, she knew it was necessary to sacrifice everything for Kaydie. Surely, when McKenzie explained to him why she had made the choices she had, Zach would understand and forgive her.

CHAPTER TWENTY-FIVE

A week later, McKenzie and Zach set out on their trip to Canfield Falls to look for Kaydie. Having Zach with her made McKenzie feel more at ease about the task that lay before her.

McKenzie had packed only what was necessary for their short trip in the back of the covered wagon. Learning to pack light was an ongoing process that McKenzie had never needed to master before. Whenever she'd traveled with her parents and even during her trip to Pine Haven, she had packed an excessive amount. Because they would be gone for only two days, McKenzie knew that to pack more than necessary would be useless and even burdensome.

Canfield Falls was twenty-five miles west of Pine Haven, and, with each passing mile, McKenzie grew more and more anxious. Her mind swam with worries and questions. What if Kaydie wasn't there? What if Kaydie was there, but Darius wouldn't let her leave? What if Kaydie was no longer alive? What if they found Kaydie, but she chose to remain with Darius, instead?

"Are you all right, my sweet McKenzie?" Zach asked.

McKenzie thought of how Zach had just begun to call her his "sweet McKenzie." She had no idea why. She had never considered herself sweet. "I'm just thinking about what will happen when we arrive in Canfield Falls," she said.

"Tell me, why did Kaydie marry someone like Darius?"

"She didn't realize who he truly was. He made her all of these glowing promises. He purchased gifts for her, he made her feel special…." McKenzie struggled to keep from becoming emotional. She recalled the day so clearly when Darius had walked into Kaydie's life and things had changed forever. "He has mistreated her egregiously."

"I'm sorry," Zach said. "I can't imagine a man treating a woman that way. We'll find her, McKenzie, and we'll get her away from Darius. I promise."

"But, how can you promise that? She may not even be alive."

McKenzie swallowed a sob, and she heard Zach gulp.

Finally, his voice filled with renewed conviction, he said, "If it is God's will, then there will be nothing stopping us."

"I hope it's His will," McKenzie said, her voice weak. "If it's not, that means Kaydie must stay trapped with Darius forever."

"If it is God's will, and I pray that it is, God will help us. In Luke, we have the assurance that 'with God nothing shall be impossible.' I believe that this will be possible with God's help."

McKenzie nodded. She wished she had Zach's faith. She glanced at his profile and thought of how he had given up two days of work to take her to Canfield Falls. Had anyone ever made such a sacrifice for her before? Would she even have noticed? Probably not. She knew she was changing, and the realization scared her. She wasn't the same woman she'd been when she'd arrived. She cringed at the thought that being different would only make the inevitable more difficult.

"Are you as close to your other sister as you are to Kaydie?" Zach asked, bringing her thoughts back to the conversation at hand.

McKenzie giggled, and her mood brightened immediately. "No, Zach. Peyton and I are not close at all. Ever since we were little girls, we've never gotten along. Mother used to sigh in exasperation at our constant quibbling. Peyton is very opinionated and has always been Mother's favorite. She's just like Mother, always attending social gatherings and raising her son the same way Mother and Father raised us. I, on the other hand, have a slightly strong will, and I'm closer to Father. Such differences have done more to make us disagreeable to each other than anything."

Zach laughed, too. "For the first time in my life, I feel fortunate I was an only child."

"You would feel that way for sure if you had Peyton for a sister. She's four years older than I am, and she married this horribly boring, spineless man named Maxwell Adams. She never wasted any time letting me know that she was superior to me, if only for the reason that she was married and I was not."

"Fortunately for me, you weren't married," Zach said. "I have to admit to you that I thought Kaydie was a long-lost love of yours when I first saw the name Kayde."

"Oh, Zach, really?"

Zach nodded. "I'd just found you, and I didn't want to lose you."

McKenzie sobered at his remark and hoped he wouldn't feel that way when Kaydie had been freed from Darius and was boarding the stagecoach with McKenzie to go back to Boston.

"You and Kaydie are pretty close, I take it," Zach said.

"We're very close. I would call her my baby when we were little, even though we are so close in age. We didn't play much—at least, not in the way children like Davey do—unless, of course, my parents were gone for the day. No, we were always taught to sit properly, not touch anything, speak only when spoken to, and be seen, but not heard. We were much like pretty doilies on a parlor table."

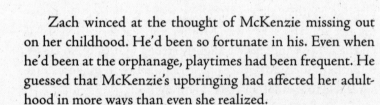

Zach winced at the thought of McKenzie missing out on her childhood. He'd been so fortunate in his. Even when he'd been at the orphanage, playtimes had been frequent. He guessed that McKenzie's upbringing had affected her adulthood in more ways than even she realized.

"I do remember one time, though," McKenzie said, placing a hand over her mouth. "I was about six, and we had this fabulous nanny named Esther. She took us to a park, not knowing that it was against Mother's wishes. Kaydie and I played games with her, had a picnic, and watched the ducks on the lake. That's my best memory from when I was a child, I think. Unfortunately, when we returned home with stained dresses and a few bumps and bruises from all our fun, Mother found it fitting to dismiss Esther at that very moment. So, that was not only my best memory but also one of my saddest ones."

"You were raised by nannies?" Zach asked.

"We were. Later in our lives, Nellie and Biddie took the place of nannies and did everything a mother would normally do. We knew for certain that our parents loved us—they provided everything for us—but it was a different kind of love from the kind you have for Davey."

Zach thought for a minute. He hesitated to ask the question that nagged at his mind but ultimately decided to do so. "McKenzie, have you given any thought to what type of ma you'd like to be for Davey, and for the children you and I have together someday?" He'd thought often about the type of pa he was and would be when he had additional children.

McKenzie drew in her breath and looked as if she might faint.

"McKenzie, are you all right?" Zach asked. McKenzie's face had gone from a rosy color to a pallor as white as snow. She had begun to sway from side to side, and Zach feared she might fall from the wagon. He reached out to steady her, and she collapsed into his waiting arms. Thankful that she hadn't lost consciousness, as she had during their wedding, Zach held her with one arm and used the other to slow the horses to a stop. "McKenzie?"

"I—I'm all right, Zach." McKenzie's breathing was quick and shallow. "I—I don't want to talk about being a mother, if it's all the same to you."

Zach was taken aback. Had his mention of motherhood really prompted her pallor and uneven breathing? "I'm sorry, McKenzie. I had no idea this discussion would disturb you so."

❧

McKenzie gazed up into Zach's eyes. She'd noticed that whenever he was particularly concerned, his eyes became bluer. Had she ever seen eyes that more closely matched the sky on a hot, summer day in Pine Haven? She doubted it. His eyes were one of the things she had grown to like most about his appearance. "I—I'm sorry, Zach. I just don't want to talk about it right now."

"That's fine. I'll not bring it up again. I know that having a child is a big change, and I am in no rush to become a father again. I'm completely content with Davey. I'll not rush you into anything, McKenzie."

McKenzie again felt as though she would faint. She hadn't even thought about having children—not when she and Zach had separate bedrooms, and when she was planning to be gone in a few months' time. The thought that Zach wanted to have children with her racked her heart with guilt. He really loved her and had already made plans for their future together. McKenzie had made plans, too, but they didn't allow for a future together, with or without children. The world around her began to spin, and light-headedness replaced her body's stability. *No, don't faint again!* she told herself. *I will not faint again!*

Zach set McKenzie's head down gently on the seat and reached into the wagon for his canteen. He dampened his handkerchief and used it to dab at McKenzie's forehead. "You'll be fine, McKenzie. Just take deep breaths," he said gently.

McKenzie obeyed Zach's suggestion. She disliked the fact that whenever she became intensely overburdened, she would faint. Perhaps, someday, that would pass, and she'd be strong, like Rosemary. "Thank you, Zach," she squeaked.

"I'm always here for you, McKenzie. Always. Even if you had a difficult upbringing, even if you're prone to fainting, even if you decide you never want to bear children, and even if you never love me the way I'm beginning to love you, I'll be there for you. After all, I made a vow."

CHAPTER TWENTY-SIX

*M*cKenzie and Zach arrived in Canfield Falls in the early evening. True to Zach's description in his letters to McKenzie, the mining town had become reckless with nominal law enforcement. The possibility of finding gold brought hungry prospectors of good and bad character alike from all over the continent in their quest to become wealthy. Some would stop at nothing to achieve that goal, and they'd brought with them a rough, wild atmosphere, with gunfights in the saloons and drunken carousing in the streets. Among the inhabitants, there were few women and even fewer families. To say that Canfield Falls and Pine Haven were opposites in terms of ambience would be an understatement. Zach had been hesitant to travel to Canfield Falls, but he knew that until they sought out information regarding Kaydie's whereabouts, McKenzie's heart would not be settled.

"I think our best bet is to find somewhere to park the wagon and settle in for the night," Zach said. "Tomorrow morning, we can begin asking questions. I doubt we'll get any answers this late in the day."

"I guess you're right," McKenzie said with a disappointed sigh.

Ever vigilant, Zach gazed down the main street of the town. On the left were three buildings: a saloon, a mercantile, and a blacksmith's shop. On the right was one building: a livery stable. Men were staggering through the street in a drunken fashion, firing random shots into the air. Zach saw McKenzie shudder, and he was aghast to think that she might have made this trip alone had he not found out about her quest to find Kaydie.

They left the town behind, and Zach found a quiet, seemingly safe spot by the river, where they would stay for the night. He built a fire, and, before going to bed, he and McKenzie ate the meal Rosemary had packed for them.

⸻

McKenzie lay alone in the covered wagon, staring up at the canvas that encased it. Worries about Kaydie—and about Zach, sleeping outside under the stars—filled her mind and made it difficult to fall sleep. She tried to make herself comfortable, but the hard wood beneath her back, combined with her racing thoughts, made it futile. At some point in the night, however, she did manage to sleep. She awoke after sunrise, and, after breakfast, she and Zach prepared to begin their mission.

Zach assisted McKenzie from the wagon at their first stop—the mercantile. An unfriendly-looking man stood behind the counter. "I'm Zach, and this is my wife, McKenzie," Zach began. "We're looking for a woman by the name of Kaydie Kraemer. We've heard that she's living in this area with her husband, Darius Kraemer."

"Don't know nobody by that name," the man said. His shifty demeanor made McKenzie suspect that he did know something but was hesitant to tell them anything.

"Are you sure?" Zach asked. He must have sensed the same thing.

"Like I said, I don't know nobody by that name. You callin' me a liar?"

"No, sir, I'm not. Thank you for your time." Zach led McKenzie out the door and into the street.

"Shall we try the blacksmith?" Zach asked.

McKenzie nodded. It was difficult not to be in tears about the lack of information they'd received so far.

"Remember, that was only one person. We'll find out where she is; don't worry." Zach gave her hand a squeeze, and they walked toward the blacksmith's shop.

"We're looking for a Darius Kraemer," Zach said when they entered the run-down building and saw the blacksmith at work.

"Ain't everybody?" the man asked. "What is you, the law?" He continued with his work without even glancing up to see who might be inquiring about Darius.

"No," answered Zach, "we aren't the law. But, tell us, have you seen him?"

"No, I haven't." With that, the blacksmith turned his back to Zach and McKenzie and walked through a door and into the attached building, as if to dismiss them from his presence.

❧

Not a person could be found in the livery, leaving only one more choice. "Let's try the saloon," Zach said. He didn't want to say anything to McKenzie, but his hopes for finding Kaydie were diminishing by the second. "I'll take this one alone, McKenzie. It's not the kind of place for a woman."

"I want to come with you, Zach. Please."

Zach stopped and turned to McKenzie. "It's a rough place, McKenzie. This whole town is rough. I used to work on a ranch a mile from town. It became so bad that the owner of the ranch packed up and left. The saloon, especially, is no place you'll want to see."

"I know that, Zach, and I know you're trying to protect me, but please. She's my sister."

Zach sighed. "All right, McKenzie, but stay right by me."

"I will," McKenzie promised.

Even before they reached the saloon, the noise of rowdy drunkards could be heard from the street. Zach pushed through the swinging double doors and into the gloomy tavern, McKenzie at his side. The smell of cigar smoke and spittoons filled his nostrils, and he thought for a moment he would lose the breakfast he'd eaten only an hour earlier.

"We're looking for a Darius Kraemer," Zach said to the bartender.

"What do you want with Darius?" the bartender asked. He was a short, balding man with a black mustache that curled on the ends and rose up and down when he spoke.

"My wife is the sister of Darius's wife, Kaydie. We're been looking for her."

The bartender sneered. "Ain't no one saw much of her. Don't know Darius' whereabouts. You might ask Bulldog over there if he knows anything." The bartender pointed to a large man in the corner.

"Much obliged," Zach said.

McKenzie covered her mouth. "Zach," she whispered, "did that man just say something about a man named Bulldog?"

Zach nodded. "I think it's that man over there," he said quietly, not wanting to draw more attention to McKenzie and himself.

"Zach, I need to talk to you for a minute," said McKenzie.

"Right now?"

"Yes. It's about Bulldog. Something I remember Kaydie telling me in her letters." She glanced over at the corner and shivered, then looked back at Zach.

Zach led McKenzie to the opposite corner in the saloon. "What is it?" he asked, making sure he stayed aware of their surroundings, in case anyone posed a threat.

"Kaydie said that Bulldog was this scary friend of Darius's, and that he would watch her every move. Surely, he must know where Kaydie is!"

Zach held his finger up to his mouth to quiet McKenzie. "Shh. He should know where she is, but whether he will tell us is another thing." He shook his head. "This Bulldog sounds like a dangerous man. Would you reconsider waiting outside, McKenzie?"

"I'm sorry, Zach, but I need to stay here with you. Please?"

Against his better judgment, Zach again agreed. "All right," he said. "Let's go talk to Bulldog."

As Zach and McKenzie were making their way to the other side of the saloon, Zach nearly ran into another man, who stumbled into his path. "Excuse me," Zach muttered, attempting to veer around the man, who was almost two heads taller than he. But his efforts were in vain.

"You tryin' to start somethin'?" the man snarled. He reached his hand forward and grasped the front of Zach's shirt, pulling Zach toward him.

"I'm sorry. I didn't mean to run into you," Zach said.

"I don't buy that for a minute. You're tryin' to start a fight, is what you's doin'!"

"I'm not trying to start anything. I need to speak with Bulldog, and I was just trying to get around you." Zach's pulse quickened. He knew he was tough—tough from years of hard ranch work, and equally tough from natural strength. His own father, although wiry and thinner than Zach, had been naturally strong, as well, and easily had been able to take on men twice his size. Still, Zach had no desire to fight this man—or anyone else, for that matter. It wasn't in his character.

The man pulled a gun from his holster. "I should just shoot ya!"

"I'm not looking for trouble," Zach said, his heart racing at the thought that he could be putting McKenzie in danger. "If you'll excuse me, I have some work to do."

"You may not be lookin' for trouble, but you found it, and I ain't excusin' nobody!" The man took the butt of his gun and attempted to whack Zach in the side of the head. But, because of his drunken state, he was slow, and Zach was able to block the attack easily.

"Yah, Sly don't excuse nobody!" someone in the saloon shouted. Zach took his focus off of Sly and turned to see who had made the remark.

"Zach, look out!" McKenzie shouted. But it was too late. Sly punched Zach in the nose.

Zach teetered, but he slowly regained his footing. "I'm not looking for a fight," he said again, holding his nose to stop the bleeding.

"You ain't, but I am. I could kill you right now and make your woman *my* woman," Sly said, eyeing McKenzie. "I could use me a wife, you know."

"Zach, let's go," McKenzie whispered, shivering visibly.

"Zach, let's go," one of the men in the saloon mimicked in a high-pitched, mocking fashion.

"Mebbe you need another punch, just for good measure." Sly hit Zach again in the ribs. "I really need a wife, and your little lady is right pretty." He leaned toward McKenzie and stroked her cheek with a filthy thumb. McKenzie flinched and tried to move away from his unwelcome touch.

Zach didn't mind what happened to him, but Sly had no business touching his wife and making insinuations. He could see McKenzie's fear, and he was enraged by the man's uncouth, lewd behavior. He regained his composure and, with all the strength he could muster, punched Sly square in the jaw. To mess with him was one thing, but to mess with McKenzie was quite another. He would always fight for her honor, no matter what the cost.

McKenzie gasped. She'd never been in a saloon before. She'd never seen a real fight before. She'd never been a spectator to violence. She felt helpless as Zach and Sly wrestled on the floor and traded jabs. *Lord,* she prayed for the first time, *please, keep Zach safe. Please, don't let him get hurt. Please, help him!* Zach was at an advantage because he was sober, even though Sly had the advantage of size. She continued to watch as Zach gained the upper hand over and over again.

From nowhere, a large man stepped toward Zach and Sly. He broke up the fight and shoved each man into a separate corner of the room. "It's too early for fightin'!" he shouted. He walked toward Zach and shoved him out the door. McKenzie hurried to follow. She watched as blood dripped from Zach's nose, and she panicked.

"What's your business with Darius Kraemer?" the man asked once they were outside the saloon.

"Kaydie, Darius's wife, is my wife's sister, and we really need to find her," Zach answered, wincing and holding his nose.

As difficult as it was to do, McKenzie held her tongue and avoided adding her input. Although she felt anything but calm inside, she knew that the investigation would take a certain degree of professionalism—even among the unprofessional.

"I know a Darius Kraemer. Can't say as I know his wife's name—might be Kaydie, might not be. Don't know." The man shifted his weight. "Name's Bulldog." He extended an enormous hand toward Zach.

"Zach Sawyer," Zach said, shaking his hand.

"Why do you want to know about Darius?" Bulldog asked. His face was covered with scars, adding to his unattractiveness, and his height was close to seven feet, McKenzie estimated. His girth was large, as well, made of muscle rather than fat. His long, stringy, dark hair hung in clumps around his ears, and his chin housed what looked like two days' worth of stubble. One of Bulldog's hazel eyes faced permanently to the left, while the other darted about, as if to compensate for his stationary eye.

McKenzie's heart raced with a surge of hope, and she grabbed Zach's arm. "Can you tell us where he is?" Zach asked.

"Not now, I can't. If you would have come by last week or earlier, I could have—for a price. You see, it was my job to keep an eye on that wisp of a wife he had." Bulldog laughed, his voice low and mean, as his shifty eye darted from Zach to McKenzie. "As a matter of fact, if you got some money on ya now, I might have some information. Then again, I might not."

Zach reached into his pocket and pulled out some coins, then handed them to Bulldog. "Please, tell us what you know," he said.

"Darius owes a lot of people money. He's heavy into gamblin' and has lost one too many times. He ain't a popular man in these parts. What's more, he's on the run from the law for some bank robberies he done committed years ago." Bulldog spit on the ground, causing McKenzie to jump.

"Did he leave town?" Zach asked.

"Yep. Last week. He and that woman of his."

"Do you know where they went?" Zach asked.

"If I knew where they went, I'd be a rich man, for sure. Everyone wants to know where he is. There's even a reward for him—he's wanted dead or alive. He owes pret' near everyone in town, and he for sure owes the law some prison time. No, I don't know where he went. He talked of going farther west, is all I know."

"His wife—what did she look like?" McKenzie asked. Before they went after Darius, she wanted to make sure he hadn't traded in her sister for another poor, gullible girl.

Bulldog squinted at McKenzie. "Didn't look none like you. 'Course, Darius never let her buy no new clothes. She was about so tall," Bulldog said, holding up his hand just below McKenzie's ear. "She don't look like she got enough to eat. Just a scrawny little thing."

McKenzie nodded. "Her hair—what color was it?" She was almost certain that Kaydie was the wife Bulldog had guarded.

"I don't know. Not as dark as his," Bulldog said, pointing at Zach.

"The color of honey?" McKenzie asked.

Bulldog scrunched his nose, making him look even more like his namesake, and McKenzie could understand why Kaydie feared him. "I s'pose so," he said.

"Then it was Kaydie!" McKenzie held her hand over her mouth. "You're sure you don't know which way they were headed? It's so important that I find my sister."

"Darius said he wanted to go farther west," Bulldog said, narrowing his eyes. "That's all I know for sure. Didn't say how far west, or which part of the West, or nothin' like that. I think he knew the law was catchin' up with 'im. There's been a lot of folks lookin' for 'im lately. But, like I said, if you'd a' come by last week, you might've caught up with them."

"We're much obliged for your help regarding Kaydie and for helping me in the saloon," Zach said.

"You shouldn't have been in there," Bulldog said. "'Specially with her." He nodded toward McKenzie.

Zach nodded. "I reckon I agree with you on that," he said. "We'll be on our way, then." Zach tipped his hat at Bulldog, and he and McKenzie walked back toward the wagon.

"Are you all right, Zach?" McKenzie asked. He'd really taken a beating, but she couldn't help feeling proud of his ability to stand up for himself—and for her.

"I will be. It's nothing time won't heal. I doubt they even have a doctor here." Zach's eyes searched the hopeless town.

McKenzie wished she were more like Rosemary. She would know what to do and not be afraid of the sight of blood and bruises. Still, McKenzie would do whatever she could in tending to his wounds—wounds that had been inflicted upon him because he had helped her. She felt guilty about the sacrifice Zach had made for the sake of finding Kaydie. Never had anyone done something like that for her.

For the first time, McKenzie realized she cared for Zach, not merely because of what she could get from him, but because she was attracted to him—his character, his integrity, his selfless compassion, and his wisdom. And that thought frightened her a hundred times as much as entering a rowdy saloon.

CHAPTER TWENTY-SEVEN

*T*he idea came to her just as she heard the rooster crow one morning. She smiled to herself. Yes, it was time to make some changes to the interior of the house where she would be staying for a while. She leaped from her bed, excited at the prospect of asking if Rosemary would accompany her to town.

McKenzie pulled her dress over her head and sat down at the small desk in her room. Zach had given her a mirror the previous week so that she would have an easier time fixing her hair. Although it wasn't a big mirror, and it had no frame, it was sufficient. Studying her reflection, McKenzie marveled at the fact that she'd been in Pine Haven for two months already. The time had passed so quickly, and so much had changed. Never would she have imagined that she'd come to enjoy living in the town she had initially detested. McKenzie leaned closer to the mirror. Her eyes seemed brighter and her smile more genuine. As a matter of fact, she realized for the first time that everything about her felt more authentic—her personality, her associations with others, and her concern for them.

With the passing of time, McKenzie had made many additions in her life. She'd learned more of how the ranch operated and had become a better assistant to Rosemary. In reality, she had even come to like and admire Rosemary, something she never would have dreamed possible after her first night at the ranch.

McKenzie had made new friends and already attended two meetings of the quilting circle, where she'd been inspired to undertake her current plan. Zach would be more surprised than he'd ever been when he discovered her strategy for making the interior of the house appealing to the eyes. No more windows covered by dowdy, mismatched blankets. No more empty walls. No more main room devoid of books. She thought of her parents' home, where the parlor walls were lined with bookcases filled with tomes of all genres, including some of McKenzie's favorites, to which she'd devoted a fair amount of time as a child. If Davey were to enjoy reading when he was older—and McKenzie hoped he would—she needed to provide him with some books and a place to store them. She also needed to begin reading to him on a regular basis until he learned to read for himself.

Thinking of books and bookcases made McKenzie suddenly remember something she wanted to do before she went into town. She reached for a pencil and paper and began writing a letter to her mother.

Dearest Mother,

I hope this letter finds you well. Things are going much better here. I am enjoying meeting new people and have found friends in many of the women in town. Even Lucille, whom I once thought to be a busybody, has become very dear to me. I have even joined a quilting circle, and, although I have been only twice, such experiences have given me a fresh outlook on Pine Haven and what it has to offer. I am also learning how to cook. Please don't think of me as being improper. I'm actually enjoying the ability to concoct different dishes—with Rosemary's help, of course! Rosemary helps around the ranch. She is the closest thing to a best friend I have here. Never have I met a more capable and patient woman! I endeavor to become just like she is.

I hesitate to tell you this, Mother, but I must let you know that Pine Haven is not as bad as I once thought it to be. Please don't fret about the conditions here, or about my welfare. Even the ranch, as outlandish as I once considered it, has potential.

Zach and I traveled to Canfield Falls a few weeks ago in an attempt to locate Kaydie. Although we were unsuccessful, we did learn that she has been spotted, and for that, I give our Lord praise. It's not known where she has gone, only that she and Darius have traveled farther west. Zach and I have placed advertisements in several Montana Territory newspapers in hopes of finding a lead. We will also be traveling to some other nearby towns once the busy ranching season is completed. I will keep you updated.

I was wondering if you would agree to ask Nellie to ship several of my early readers. Davey, Zach's son, will be learning to read soon, and I would like him to have the same opportunity I had to delight in using his imagination while reading. Because of Pine Haven's small size and limited resources, such opportunities are not readily available. What a grand thing it would be for him to read the same books I read at his age! I hope someday you will have the opportunity to meet Davey. He is a precious little boy with so much energy. He has truly stolen my heart. Next week, he will be five years old, and I hope to give him a harmonica I purchased in Boston before my trip.

This letter is much longer than I first anticipated it would be, so I had best say farewell for now. Please let Father know that I am fine. Would you also please say hello to Nellie, Biddie, and Helen for me?

Most sincerely,
McKenzie

Hesitating three times before placing the letter in an envelope, McKenzie finally decided to seal it. Yes, her mother would be shocked, but it was necessary to let her know that things had taken a turn for the better. She also wanted to update her on Kaydie, as well as ask about the books for Davey. *Davey....* McKenzie thought of the youngster who had found a place in her heart. How would she tell him that she wasn't staying in Pine Haven when the time came for her to leave? As quickly as the disturbing thought entered her mind, she dismissed it. The day was too fresh and full of possibilities to settle on unwelcome thoughts. Besides, she had work to do.

❧

Zach finished hitching up the wagon for McKenzie and Rosemary to leave for town. "You seem quiet today," Asa said, breaking Zach's concentration.

"I was just thinking about McKenzie."

"Oh? Anything bothering you?" Asa asked.

Zach sighed. "Do you think she will ever love me the way Rosemary loves you?"

Asa chuckled. "You could have asked Rosemary yesterday, and I'm not sure she would have said she loved me then." He tugged at his beard. "I had promised to take her on a picnic after church and then forgot and went fishing, instead. I praise the Lord I married a forgiving woman!"

Zach nodded. "But, still, she does love you, Asa, even if you are forgetful at times."

"Ah, that she does, and McKenzie will grow to love you in that way, as well. Remember, Zach, it's in the Lord's hands."

"I know that, Asa, but it's been so difficult for her to become accustomed to the way things are in Pine Haven. I had no idea the adjustments would be so hard."

"Ah, you thought she would come to Pine Haven, marry you, and the two of you would live in wedded bliss for the next fifty years. Is that it?" Asa put his hand on Zach's shoulder.

"Something like that," Zach said.

"I believe she at least likes you. That's a start."

"I'm being serious, Asa," Zach said.

"And I am, as well. Give her time. She's been here all of two months. True love doesn't happen in a day. Your courtship with her was not as most courtships go. You married her without even really knowing her."

"I wonder if that was a mistake," Zach said. "Maybe I should have suggested she live in town while we courted so we could know each other better before the wedding."

"Ah. Ecclesiastes tells us, '*To every thing there is a season, and a time to every purpose under the heaven.*' No use in living in the past. What is, is, and you need to make the most of it. Lord willing, you will have the rest of your entire lives to get to know each other, and, trust me, it will take that long. You will delight many times throughout those years learning new things about McKenzie—her likes and dislikes. Why, I just learned that my Rosemary hates cherries. I have been married to her for a long time yet never knew this. I brought her back a basketful after the fishing trip I took yesterday, and she informed me that cherries did not top her list of things she liked to eat. Granted, it could have been because I'd forgotten about the picnic, but, ah, well.

"Give McKenzie time, Zach. You have been the kind of husband who makes our Lord proud. You have been giving and loving. You have put her needs first and have been patient with her as she's adjusted to a new home and new friends. You have shared your life, your home, your son, and, most important, your quiet times with God with her."

"You're right, Asa," Zach said, thankful for his friend's wisdom. "I need to be patient."

"Patient and ever prayerful. Remember, First Thessalonians tells us to 'pray without ceasing.' I still pray for my marriage every day."

"Thank you, Asa."

"I am always here for you, Zach—you know that. Anytime I can offer my wise counsel, I would be happy to do so," Asa said with a hint of sarcasm.

"And wise counsel it is," Zach agreed.

"Now, tell me, where are the womenfolk going today?"

"McKenzie mentioned that she and Rosemary were going to town to fetch some supplies, and they're going to take Davey with them."

"Ah. You see there? This is the first time McKenzie has wanted to do that. Sure, she's gone to town to attend a meeting of the quilting circle or a church service, but to fetch supplies? See, Zach, you be patient. Your McKenzie is adjusting just fine to her new way of life. I need to finish some chores now, but don't you worry. Things will work out fine." With a wave of his hand, Asa turned and left the barn.

"I suppose he's right," Zach said to no one in particular. Still, there was an unsettled feeling within him that things wouldn't turn out as well as Asa was confident they would.

CHAPTER TWENTY-EIGHT

$\mathcal{D}$avey!" McKenzie called. "Davey! It's time to go to town!"

"I'm coming, Ma!" Davey ran out from behind the barn and came hurtling toward the wagon.

McKenzie watched Davey as he ran toward her. Only ten minutes ago, his clothes had been clean and his hair combed. Now, mud from last night's rain covered the knees of his trousers, and his hair was in complete disarray. In Boston, his appearance would never be proper for public presentation. McKenzie shook her head and smiled in spite of herself. Davey wasn't in Boston any more than she was, and it was unlikely that anyone in Pine Haven would think the less of him for the condition of his pants and hair. "Davey, where have you been?" McKenzie asked, putting her hands on her hips.

"I have somethin' for you, Ma," he said, keeping one hand behind his back. "Close your eyes."

McKenzie noticed Zach watching from the doorway of the barn before she closed her eyes and held out her hands and felt something lightweight settle in her palm.

"You can open your eyes now," Davey said.

McKenzie opened her eyes and saw a delicate, wild daisy, white with a yellow center. "It's for you, Ma. I picked it myself."

Davey's thoughtfulness stirred her heart, and she fought to keep the tears away. "Davey, this is very sweet of you." She reached for him and hugged him tight.

Davey returned the hug and placed a kiss on McKenzie's cheek. "Do you like it, Ma?"

"No, Davey—I love it," McKenzie said.

"That's why I was keeping you and Rosemary waiting. It was 'cause I had somethin' real important to do. I had to go through a lot of mud to get that flower. There were other ones, but this one was the best."

"Thank you, Davey. I shall treasure it."

"It's kinda like you could have any son, but you picked me, right?" Davey pulled away from her and stared up into her eyes.

McKenzie crouched down to Davey's height. She hadn't given much thought to the truth of his statement before. "You're absolutely right, Davey. I did pick you. I am the most blessed mother in the world to have you. You're very sweet, thoughtful, and handsome."

Davey laughed. "As handsome as Pa?"

McKenzie could feel her face turn red; she could tell that Zach was still watching and probably listening, too. "Almost as handsome as your Pa," she whispered in Davey's ear.

Davey giggled. "Do you have any other children, Ma?"

McKenzie shook her head. "You're my only child, Davey. But, I do have a nephew named Nate in Boston. He will be nine years old next month. I hope you will meet him someday."

"Maybe I will. Does he live on a ranch, too?"

McKenzie chuckled and shook her head. "No, he lives in the city—actually, at a special school he attends, just for boys. It's called a boarding school."

"He doesn't live with his ma and pa?" Davey sounded close to tears, and McKenzie thought of the contrast between Davey and Nate's upbringings. Davey had a father who loved him and allowed him the freedom to be a little boy. Nate had parents who loved him, too, but seemed bent on molding him into a businessman by the age of ten. They were far too busy with their own lives to be bothered with the needs of his. "I will tell you all about Nate someday, but, right now, we need to go to town."

"Yes, ma'am," Davey said, then climbed into the back of the wagon.

McKenzie rose from her crouched position and locked eyes with Zach. She wondered what he was thinking. So often, his quiet demeanor left her curious about the thoughts that filled his mind—thoughts he seldom expressed. "We'll be back soon," McKenzie called with a wave.

"Have fun!" he called back, returning her gesture.

She couldn't wait to see the look on his face when her surprise was revealed.

"Good morning," Lucille greeted McKenzie, Rosemary, and Davey when they entered Granger Mercantile.

"Good morning, Lucille. How are you today?" McKenzie asked.

"Doing very well. What can I do for you ladies—and gentleman?"

Davey smiled at her remark, then set off toward the toy section, where he usually entertained himself while McKenzie and Rosemary made their selections.

"We're looking for some fabric for curtains," McKenzie replied.

Rosemary leaned closer to McKenzie. "Have you thought about my suggestion?" she whispered in her ear.

McKenzie nodded. "Oh, and we'll need some calico for dresses," she added.

Lucille arched an eyebrow. "Dresses for whom?"

McKenzie should have known she'd ask. "Rosemary made the thoughtful suggestion that I sew some new dresses for myself. The frocks I brought from Boston aren't exactly suitable for daily life in Pine Haven." She looked down at her pleated velvet dress. Had Rosemary made that suggestion two months ago, McKenzie would have had the mind to let her know just how she felt about it. Now, however, having lived on the ranch and partaken of the day-to-day work, McKenzie saw the wisdom in Rosemary's idea. "Now, Rosemary," McKenzie said in a whisper to avoid Lucille's attentive ears, "I insist on purchasing some fabric for a new dress for you, as well."

"Oh, that's not necessary, McKenzie," Rosemary whispered.

"I insist, and it's not polite to decline an insistence," McKenzie said. "Now, please pick which print you like best."

Rosemary looked shocked. She was probably wondering if this was the same McKenzie who, just a few weeks ago, had arrived from Boston and immediately treated her as a servant and acted ungrateful with Zach. *Thank You, Lord*, McKenzie silently prayed, *for changing my heart.*

"Now, just what are you two whispering about?" Lucille asked. "You know I can't bear to be left out."

"This print looks lovely. May we have six yards of it, please?" McKenzie asked, hoping to divert her attention.

"That is a lovely print. It'll look enchanting with your coloring," Lucille said, carrying the bolt of fabric to the counter, where she began to measure it.

"This one, too," McKenzie said. "And we'll also take some of this for the curtains. Twelve yards should be enough for now. Rosemary?"

"Six yards of this, as well, Lucille," Rosemary said, albeit hesitantly, holding up a bolt of lavender fabric with tiny yellow flowers.

"Will this be on Zach's charge account? Oh, forgive me—I should say, the Sawyer family account?" Lucille asked.

"Yes, thank you," McKenzie said.

Lucille nodded as she tallied the purchases. Then, she looked at McKenzie and cleared her throat. "I probably shouldn't tell you this, and I've tried with all my might to keep it from you up until now, but…."

McKenzie eyed Lucille warily. As much as she liked the woman, she knew that not every word that escaped the lipsticked lips of Lucille Granger was to the benefit of her listeners.

"I'm…well, I'm the one who suggested that Zach place an advertisement for a mail-order bride in the first place. I suppose I can tell you this now, since things seem to be going so well. I wasn't going to say a word if the two of you disliked each other, or if you weren't suitable for our Zach, but…." Lucille flicked her wrist. "Since the two of you seem so compatible, I insist on taking a bit of the glory for arranging your marriage."

"Now, honestly, Lucille," Rosemary said, rolling her eyes.

"Well, it seems only fitting. I helped him write that first letter, too. Not that any of that matters now, mind you, since the marriage vows have been declared. Nevertheless, I do deserve some of the credit for the happy union."

McKenzie began to laugh. Had she ever met anyone as forthright as Lucille in all her life? Pine Haven would lack much of its charm if it weren't for the woman who insisted on receiving credit for arranging the marriage of the town's most eligible bachelor.

"Is that funny?" Lucille asked.

"It's just that...." McKenzie began to speak but found herself giggling too hard to complete her sentence. Before long, Rosemary and Lucille joined in the laughter, and tears soon ran down the women's cheeks.

"Grandpa Asa was right when he said women sound like a bunch of hens when they laugh," Davey said, approaching the group of women.

"Grandpa Asa said that, did he?" Rosemary asked. "Well, we'll just have to have a little chat with him about that!" She began to laugh again, making no attempt to control the fresh tears that streamed down her face.

"Before I forget," Lucille said, turning to McKenzie, "your canvases came in yesterday."

"Wonderful!" McKenzie exclaimed. She hadn't been sure if her request would be shipped in time for her plan to take shape.

Lucille reached under the counter and produced three one-foot squares of canvas. "Here are the frames, also," she said, adding three wooden frames to the pile.

After Fred had loaded their purchases in the wagon—with Davey's help, of course—McKenzie, Rosemary, and Davey began their return home to the ranch, Lucille's glory-seeking not far from their minds.

"Ma?" Davey said when they were halfway home. "Will you bake me a birthday cake for my birthday in four days?"

McKenzie turned to look at Davey. His face was bright with expectation.

"I would like a chocolate cake with some of those pretty bits of crushed candy on it, like the one I saw in Lucille's store."

"I don't know, Davey...." McKenzie had never made a cake before. What if it tasted terrible? What if she burned it? Her own mother had never made her a birthday cake.

"Please, Ma?" Davey pleaded, pressing his chubby hands together.

Rosemary leaned closer to McKenzie. "I would be happy to assist you in making Davey the best birthday cake ever," she said quietly.

"I've never made a cake before, Rosemary," McKenzie whispered.

"I know that, but you've made other things. As a matter of fact, your biscuits are right delicious, if I do say so, myself." Rosemary winked at McKenzie.

"You promise to help me?" McKenzie asked.

"I promise, but I'm sure you'll have no trouble."

"Please, Ma?" Davey begged again.

"All right then, Davey, but I must insist on one minor change to your plans," said McKenzie.

"What's that?" Davey asked.

"I must insist that you let me put something on the top of the cake along with the bits of crushed candy that I brought from Boston, special just for you." McKenzie thought of the swirly sucker that had traveled hundreds of miles with her.

"Really? Thank you, Ma!" Davey reached over and wrapped his arms around McKenzie's neck. "You're the best!"

McKenzie smiled to herself. Thankfully, she had no one to compete with in the area of being Davey's mother. It scared her to think about how she'd fall short in comparison to someone else if she did.

McKenzie spent the next three days sewing curtains for the house. Hiding the evidence whenever Zach ventured into the house was proving to be a chore, but she knew surprising him would be worth it. Putting her entire heart into each seam, McKenzie pieced together pieces of fabric for each window. Soon, the house would look nothing like it had when she'd first seen it. After that chore was completed, she would focus on sewing her new dresses from the patterns Rosemary had given her to use.

Later, McKenzie hung the final curtain, and then asked Asa to hang the three pieces of canvas, complete with frames, on the wall above the fireplace in the main room. "Zach will be mighty surprised with your idea, McKenzie," Asa said.

"I do hope so." McKenzie eyed the frames and smiled. "Thank you for hanging those, Asa. Would you do me one last favor?"

"Sure."

"Would you mind asking Zach and Davey to come into the house?"

"I'm on my way," Asa said, grinning.

McKenzie heard two sets of footsteps on the porch and watched as Zach and Davey entered the house. She rubbed her hands together in anticipation and hoped Zach would accept the changes gracefully.

Zach squinted as he surveyed the interior of the house. Was something different? Then, it occurred to him: the windows were no longer covered with mismatched, holey blankets. McKenzie must have sewn the new curtains, which hung on each window. The effect was a big improvement. He tilted his head sideways and glanced at the frames hanging above the fireplace. A portrait had been drawn on each canvas.

"I drew them pictures, Pa," Davey said, pointing to the frames.

Zach stepped up to the wall to get a closer look at the portraits. Sure enough, Davey's little-boy artistry had captured the likenesses of himself, Zach, and McKenzie in separate pictures. "You did a fine job, Davey," Zach said. His eyes misted at the hand-drawn portraits with eyes of different sizes and missing noses. Because it was only drawings of faces and no bodies, Davey had captured the very essence of an up-close caricature. He'd drawn short hair sticking up in every direction on both himself and Zach. One of Zach's ears looked more like a square than a circle. On McKenzie's portrait, Davey had etched long squiggles, which extended to the edges of the canvas. Zach didn't think he'd ever seen Davey draw anything before. "I'm proud of you, Davey. You did the work of a true artist."

"Really? Thanks, Pa!" Davey reached up and wrapped his arms around Zach's waist. "But, it wasn't my idea." Davey bit his lower lip. "It was Ma's idea."

Zach turned to face McKenzie. "I like your idea for the portraits, McKenzie," he said. "They're very…unique."

"I was thinking of how we have paintings of our entire family, including grandparents and great-grandparents, hanging above the fireplace in our parlor. It was such a hassle to have those paintings done. We had to sit so still. I was only about fourteen at the time, and it seemed as though the artist would never be done. He didn't have the best of dispositions, either. I recall that he wanted nothing more than to be done with the job and pocket the handsome price Father paid him." McKenzie paused. "We have our very own artist-in-residence here on the Sawyer Ranch, so I thought we'd take advantage of his fine artistic ability and have him provide his artwork for above our fireplace," she said. The thought had done more than given the bare walls decoration—it had also brought a piece of the home she missed to Pine Haven.

Zach reached for McKenzie's hand. She'd said "our fireplace," and it gave him hope for their future. She'd never made mention of anything as being theirs before, although he considered everything he'd owned before knowing her as shared property. "The curtains are beautiful, McKenzie. They must have been a lot of work."

McKenzie smiled. "I do enjoy sewing, although I can't say as I have ever sewed curtains before."

"Did you make them for every window in the house?"

"I did. You should see the ones upstairs—I saved my favorite fabric for those," McKenzie said.

"I'd like to see them," Zach said. He followed McKenzie upstairs.

"May I go back outside and play now?" Davey called after them.

"Sure, son. Go ahead. Thanks again for the nice portaits," Zach called down before Davey ran out through the front door.

McKenzie led Zach through first Davey's room, then her room, then finally Zach's room. "What do you think?" she asked.

"I think you're an amazing woman, my sweet McKenzie Sawyer," Zach said.

McKenzie gulped. She'd not yet heard him ever call her by her full married name. The sound of it both delighted and scared her. "Thank you," she said in a feeble voice.

Zach put his arms around her waist and pulled her to him. "I wondered for the past few days what you were up to in here. Every time I'd come in the house, you'd act so secretive and scurry to hide what I now know was the fabric."

"I couldn't let you see your surprise until I was done," McKenzie said, her legs feeling weak.

"I like my surprise very much, McKenzie," Zach said. "The curtains are beautiful, and the portraits were a nice thought."

"Davey was so excited to help me with those."

"He really adores you," Zach said.

"I adore him, too. It'll be hard when—" McKenzie caught herself from speaking the very thing that had been on her mind more and more in recent days. She knew it was only a matter of time before someone answered the ads about Kaydie.

"It'll be hard when what?" Zach asked.

McKenzie didn't want to lie, but she knew of no other way around the question. "It'll be hard when Davey gets older. I love the age he is right now."

"I think we'll enjoy every stage of his life," Zach said, "although I have to agree with you—the age he is right now has been especially enjoyable."

McKenzie nodded, grateful that Zach didn't suspect anything. "When we were in town the other day, I asked Mr. Victor whether he'd heard anything about Kaydie, but there still had been no news," she said.

"There will be, McKenzie. I know we'll find her. And, when we do, you know that she may stay here as long as she wants."

McKenzie wondered if Zach could feel the quick beating of her heart, standing as close to her as he was. He would let Kaydie stay at the ranch? McKenzie hadn't thought about where Kaydie would stay once they'd found her, since it would be a short time—just until they had scheduled a return trip to Boston. "Thank you, Zach. I appreciate that," she said.

"McKenzie?"

"Yes?"

Zach hesitated, looking pensive, then finally said, "McKenzie, I love you."

McKenzie sucked in her breath. How could he love her? He barely knew her. He certainly wouldn't love her if he knew what she needed to do once they found Kaydie.

"You don't have to repeat that to me, McKenzie, if you aren't ready yet. I know that love takes time to grow. I just wanted you to know the way I feel about you." Zach paused for a moment. "I—I wasn't sure how things would work out when we first met. We're quite different. But I have been praying that the Lord would unite us in love, even before you stepped off that stagecoach in Pine Haven."

McKenzie stared into Zach's eyes, only a few inches from her own. She wanted to tell him she loved him, too, but the words were too hard to speak. Plus, she wasn't sure if she did love him—yet. She did love the way he cared for her, the way he brought the Word of God to life when they spent their evenings together on the front porch, the way he was a wonderful father to Davey, and the way he treated the hired help as family more than employees. She loved the way he rolled his shoulders upward when he felt tense. She loved his blue eyes and the way his hair fell to one side. But loving *him*? She wasn't sure she did—or should. After all, she'd been trying not to, so as to make her inevitable departure as easy as possible for everyone.

"I've never been in love before, McKenzie," Zach went on. "I always wondered how it felt. Now I know. I love to watch you when you're deep in thought, when you twirl that beautiful hair of yours around your finger. I love it when you learn something new in the Bible and your eyes light up. I love how you sewed new curtains and talked Davey into drawing portraits, how you're fixing up our home so that it feels like it's just as much yours as it is mine. I love to watch you with Davey—your love for him is remarkable. I love how you fit right in here at the ranch now. I love you, McKenzie, and I would consider it an honor to be able to grow old with you."

McKenzie couldn't find the words to respond to Zach. She thought of Louis, and how what she felt for Zach was so different from what she'd felt for him. "I thought I was in love once," she said quietly. "His name is Louis, and he's a prestigious doctor in Boston. I thought we would marry someday, but he married my best friend, Pearl, instead."

"I'm sorry he broke your heart, McKenzie," Zach said. "But, if he hadn't, you wouldn't be here with me now. And I'm not sorry about that."

McKenzie nodded. "I suppose you're right." She sighed.

"Do you still love him, McKenzie?" Zach asked. He sounded apprehensive.

"No, Zach, I don't. I'm not sure I ever really did. You see, I have this habit of daydreaming, and I used to envision my life with Louis. I would imagine the large, diamond wedding ring, the fancy house, and the charity work I would do, since we would have servants, and I wouldn't have to do any work at home. I was angry at Pearl for taking the man I thought I loved."

"I'm sorry I can't give you large diamond rings or servants, McKenzie," Zach said. I can't give you a fancy house and carriage rides. I'll never be a doctor; I'd rather work the land than do anything else, even if it means I'll never be wealthy. I can't give you all those things, but I can give you my love."

"I don't want those things anymore—not really," McKenzie said, and she meant it. "I like the ring that you gave me. I didn't at first, but I like it now. It was your mother's, and I know how important she was to you. To know that you would entrust me with something so valuable to you...." McKenzie paused. Although she'd become comfortable with Zach over the past month, it was still difficult for her to bare her soul to him, especially when she knew doing so would make her departure more painful. "I don't care about carriages, either. I know that you fixed that hole in the road on my second day here, so the trip to town by wagon is not nearly as uncomfortable as it was." McKenzie smiled at Zach. "I think that, with some creative touches, this house will be just fine. And I'm glad you're not a doctor. I don't imagine Louis spends much time at home, as he's constantly called upon to treat patients at the hospital. Thinking I was in love with him was an idea—a daydream."

"I'm glad, McKenzie. Because I don't want to have to compete with another man."

"You don't have to, Zach." She looked up at Zach and yearned for him to kiss her. There was something about the tenderness in his lips that lent proof to his words. She felt safe and secure in his arms, protected from anything that might threaten the love that was beginning to blossom within her. Protected from everything except the decision she had made before she'd ever entered into Zach's life.

McKenzie's heart grew heavy at the thought of walking away from this new life—and from Zach. But she knew it must be done. She could no more stay in Pine Haven for the rest of her life than Zach could survive in Boston society. One thing was certain: she could not walk away from the life she knew in Boston, not when she had finally found Kaydie. They both belonged in a world that was a long train ride away. They belonged to a lifestyle so different from the one McKenzie was beginning to embrace. She was scared to admit it, but she had changed—in her thoughts, in her actions, and in her priorities. The thought of leaving and the thought of staying troubled her equally. Never had she felt more comfortable and accepted than she had since coming to Pine Haven. But nowhere did she belong more than in Boston.

Zach took his hands from McKenzie's waist and reached up to cup her face. Leaning even closer, he kissed her with what felt like all the love in his heart. Oh, how she longed to let herself love him! What was she to do?

CHAPTER TWENTY-NINE

As often happened when Darius was about to rob a bank, or whenever the law was about to finally close in on him, Kaydie Kraemer felt anxiety spread through her from head to toe. As he did every time he was about to execute his plan, Darius gave strict instructions to Kaydie, this time as they stood near a clump of trees half a mile outside of town.

"Now, Kaydie, you wait in town and act like nothing is happening. I'm going to get the loot and ride to that shack we stayed in last night. You wait awhile, and then drive the wagon out there. Make sure no one is following you. If someone follows you, head back to town. Once you get to the shack, we'll leave." Darius flung his head back, making his curly, brown hair to bounce above his collar.

Kaydie nodded at Darius and stared at him, as if to memorize his face. Something inside her felt more unsettled than usual, though she couldn't identify why. Darius's hair was slicked from his forehead, calling attention to his prominent nose and his beady eyes. This made it easier to affix his bandanna behind his head, which was important, since he was well-known in some parts of the West for his robbery schemes. His black shirt, thinning from overuse, revealed strong shoulders, yet his developing potbelly protruded over the waistband of his trousers to such an extent that suspenders were necessary to hold his pants up. Kaydie thought of the man Darius once was—a handsome man with short hair and a fit body. He'd since let his appearance suffer for the sake of changing his features to throw off law enforcement agents and vigilantes who studied artists' renditions on wanted posters.

"I mean it, Kaydie. Don't do anything to call attention to us."

"I won't, Darius," Kaydie promised. She wished he would have let her stay at the shack this time. She wasn't feeling well, and it seemed safer there. Instead, he'd insisted that she follow him to a town known as Wheeler. So great was her fear of Darius that she did whatever he demanded; even though it made her heart race with dread, it was a better alternative than disobeying Darius and suffering the consequences. He'd threatened to kill her more times than she could count, and her hopes of ever escaping from his clutches had been washed away, just like the promises made on their wedding day.

If Kaydie managed to make a getaway, she wouldn't get far—she had no money for travel expenses. And even if she somehow found a way to get to Boston for free, he had convinced her that her family had disowned her and would never welcome her back into the Worthington home. For a while, she'd hoped that her sister McKenzie would do something to rescue her, but it seemed that Darius was right. No such effort had been made, and Kaydie was beginning to believe that she would be in her loveless marriage and lawless life forever.

Darius pulled his bandanna over his face and fingered two guns, one holstered on each side in the gun belt around his waist. "This one should be easy," he snarled. "I staked it out yesterday, and there was only one teller. Talk about foolish!" Darius snickered, shaking his head. "But their foolishness is my gain." He mounted his horse and rode off toward the town. Kaydie waited until she could no longer see him, then set off in the same direction in the wagon.

After Kaydie parked the wagon across the street from the bank, she sat down on a bench nearby. People bustled up and down the street, and several of them nodded at her. She thought that this was one of the largest towns they'd encountered so far. She pulled her bonnet more tightly around her face, then reached down and gently rubbed her stomach. By now, she was confident that her suspicions were correct. She was pregnant. She'd lain awake many a night and pondered how she could or would care for a child under Darius's oppression. It was likely that if he discovered her condition, he would be less than thrilled. She'd learned in her years of marriage to Darius that he cared only about himself, and that his selfishness and self-centeredness would preclude him from ever loving the baby growing within her.

Kaydie straightened her posture and focused her gaze across the street at the bank. By now, Darius would have demanded that the hapless teller lock the door and open the safe. She knew by heart his methods and his plan of attack. She'd lost count of the number of times she'd accompanied him on his "jobs." In a minute, Darius would flee through the front door, climb on his horse, and leave Wheeler behind. In his clutches would be the loot that he so desperately craved—and so quickly spent on liquor and gambling. So little was saved for the necessities of life, such as food. Kaydie imagined that by nightfall, they would be in another town, where Darius would be celebrating yet another victory with round after round of brandy and bourbon.

"Hello, dear," said an elderly woman, who sat down beside Kaydie.

"Hello," Kaydie answered, knowing her voice was barely audible. She suddenly realized how thirsty she was. She would do anything for a glass of Nellie's lemonade to quench her dry throat on this late-August day.

"Are you all alone?" the woman asked.

"Yes," Kaydie said. She rationalized that her response was not a lie in entirety—she was alone in the world, even though she had a husband. She could hardly count Darius as someone who satisfied her loneliness.

"I was just thinking about having a nice, cold glass of water. Would you like some?"

"Umm, no, thank you," Kaydie answered, knowing that she wasn't supposed to be talking to strangers. If Darius saw her, he'd unleash his wrath.

"Are you sure?" the woman asked. "I see that you are with child. You must drink plenty of water and get extra nourishment."

Kaydie was stunned. How did the woman know about her condition? Kaydie turned her head to stare at her. She had the whitest yet most beautiful hair Kaydie had ever seen. A delicate, gold chain with a beautiful cross suspended from it encircled her neck, and she wore a simple, sensible brown dress. She was petite, like Kaydie, and had the greenest eyes—a true green, like the color of the Montana meadows in early spring. Fine wrinkles etched her face, and they deepened as she smiled and gently pressed Kaydie's arm. "I really don't care for any water, but thank you, anyway," Kaydie said.

"All right, then; I'll get one for myself and be right back." The woman left and returned a moment later with two cups of water. "I thought you might change your mind. It's quite a hot day."

Kaydie couldn't resist the cold water, and she held out her hand to accept the cup. As she bent her head and took a sip, Kaydie thought it tasted even better than Nellie's lemonade, and she knew it would soothe her parched throat. As she leaned down to take another sip, she heard a loud bang and almost spilled the water all over her lap. Her head jerked up, and she watched as Darius fell from his horse and landed on the hard earth. Trailing him was a man wearing a sheriff's badge, his gun still smoking.

Kaydie gasped and jumped up from the bench, tossing her cup of water to the side as she ran into the middle of the street, where people had begun to gather around the fallen body. The sheriff had pulled the mask away from Darius's face, and Kaydie fell to her knees at his side, staring into his lifeless eyes. "D-Darius?" she stammered. For a minute, her heart seemed to stop.

"Ma'am, do you know this man?" the sheriff asked her.

"He's—he's m-my husband," Kaydie said, not even thinking of the implications that might come to someone who revealed her identity as a bank robber's wife.

"He just tried to rob the bank. I'm afraid he's dead."

"Dead?" Kaydie asked.

"I'm afraid so, ma'am. He brandished his weapon, and I was obligated to shoot."

"I'm free, then?" Kaydie said.

"Free?" The sheriff stared at her. "Were you involved in the attempted robbery, ma'am?"

"N-no, I wasn't. I—I mean, am I free to live my life now?" Kaydie glanced up into the faces of strangers and suddenly felt uneasy. Where would she go? Who could she turn to? Would her life be better now, or worse?

"Yes, you're free to live your life now," the sheriff said, patting Kaydie gently on the back.

"Thank you," Kaydie said. No tears fell from her eyes; only a sigh of relief welled up within her.

"Do you have anywhere to go? Any family in the area?" the sheriff asked her.

Before she could answer, a woman's voice said, "She's staying with me for the time being, Sheriff."

Kaydie turned to see the petite, white-haired woman who had offered her a drink of water. She didn't know who she was; she knew only that, because of an incident that happened less than five minutes ago, she would no longer be in bondage to a man she'd grown to despise. She would no longer have to suffer his relentless acts of cruelty. She would be free to raise her baby without fearing the brutality of a man who saw her as more of a slave than a wife. "Thank you," she whispered to the woman.

The sheriff helped Kaydie to her feet. "We'll see that your husband gets a proper burial, ma'am," he said.

"All right," Kaydie said. She still couldn't believe how drastically her life had changed in an instant. The woman took her hand, and Kaydie let herself be led away. She turned around one last time to glance at Darius's lifeless body, as if to be sure she was free. Blood was still spurting from his wound, and one of his hands was clenched in a fist; the other hand held a gun. He'd undoubtedly believed he could draw faster than the sheriff. Darius had chosen one too many banks to rob. His due had come. And, in that due coming to him, freedom had come to Kaydie—both physical and emotional. Yet, for the first time, Kaydie did not know what lay ahead for her.

However, she decided that not knowing what lay ahead of her was better than thinking she knew and being wrong, as she'd been when she'd married Darius.

CHAPTER THIRTY

*H*appy birthday, dear Davey, happy birthday to you!" sang the chorus of voices to the youngest member of the Sawyer household.

"Blow out the candles, Davey," McKenzie urged him. This birthday party was turning out to be a bigger thrill to her than to the birthday boy, it seemed.

Davey leaned over the chocolate cake and blew out the five candles that topped it, bringing applause from the adults around him. "Is that lollipop mine?" Davey asked.

"That's the surprise I was telling you would be on the top of your cake, in addition to the bits of crushed candy," McKenzie said.

"It's all mine?" Davey asked. His eyes grew big as he focused on the five-inch-in-diameter lollipop with concentric swirls of yellow, purple, green, and blue.

"All yours," McKenzie answered, beaming. "It's a special one—you'll never see the likes of that type of lollipop in Granger's Mercantile. It came all the way from Boston."

McKenzie watched as Davey pulled the lollipop out of the top of the cake and eagerly peeled off the wrapper. If she had already found Kaydie, she would have missed seeing Davey's joy at receiving something as simple as a lollipop. If she had already found Kaydie, she would have missed the loving hug between Zach and Davey when Zach presented Davey with a fishing rod. If she had already found Kaydie and headed back to Boston, she would have missed out on this camaraderie with Zach, Davey, Rosemary, Asa, and Jonah. Although she still hoped to find her sister as soon as possible, McKenzie realized that she wouldn't have wanted to miss this occasion for anything. Such warm celebrations were few and far between, in her experience.

"One more gift, Davey," McKenzie said. She pulled a small present wrapped in brown paper from its hiding place under the table and handed it to Davey.

Davey tore off the paper. "What is it?"

"It's a harmonica," McKenzie said.

"I used to have one of those," Asa said. "Back when I was a boy, my father bought me one."

"Can you show me how to use it?" Davey asked.

Asa nodded and began to play the instrument. Davey squealed with delight. "It takes a lot of practice," said Asa, "but you'll get the hang of it." He handed it back to Davey.

Before his audience, Davey lifted the harmonica and began to play it as Asa had shown him. "I'm gonna play this all my life," he said. "Thanks, Ma!" He slid off his chair and ran to McKenzie, his arms outstretched.

"You're welcome, Davey. You know, I saw that at a toy store in Boston long before I ever met you. I'm so pleased you like it." McKenzie kissed Davey on the forehead. Had she been told nearly three months ago that she would have felt so blessed in Pine Haven at a birthday party for a five-year-old boy, she wouldn't have believed it. Not for one second.

That night, McKenzie joined Zach on the porch for their evening Bible study. Zach had mentioned that, before long, the weather would turn cold, and their time with the Lord would be spent inside by the fireplace. McKenzie wasn't sure she would still be in Pine Haven when winter made its appearance. Still, she thought that studying God's Word by the orange glow of the fire, with Zach next to her, sounded wonderful.

"Your cake was a big success," Zach said, interrupting McKenzie's thoughts.

McKenzie smiled. "Thank the Lord for that. When Davey asked me, I wasn't sure I would be able to make good on such a request."

"Cooking isn't as bad as you once thought, is it?" Zach asked.

"Not really. I'm still trying to master some meals, but, thankfully, Rosemary has a lot of patience."

"I'm glad the two of you are getting along," Zach said. "I love coming inside and hearing the sound of your laughter."

"I really like Rosemary. At first, I didn't. I even decided I would never like her. But, she has been so patient with me and my shortcomings. I like to think of her as my best friend. That was something I was determined never to have again after Pearl's betrayal, but God apparently had different plans."

Zach opened his Bible. "I love the place in Proverbs where it says, '*Trust in the* LORD *with all thine heart; and lean not unto thine own understanding. In all thy ways acknowledge him, and he shall direct thy paths.*' It reminds me of what you just said about Rosemary. God knew all along that the two of you would become friends, and that your life would change when you came to Pine Haven—that you would change. He directs our paths in life when we trust in Him and allow Him to work things out according to His will."

McKenzie flipped through the pages of her own Bible. She'd grown more confident in her ability to locate the books that God had so graciously provided to His children. She found the verses Zach had read and reread them to herself. "But what if He stops directing my paths?" She thought of how it could be a month or even a year before she returned to Boston, but she ultimately would return to her home.

"That's something we needn't worry about, McKenzie." Zach thumbed through his Bible again. "In Philippians, we are told that *'he which hath begun a good work in you will perform it until the day of Jesus Christ.'* God isn't going to leave you alone and never help you again, McKenzie. Once you place your trust in Him, He's there for you forever, constantly molding you to become more like Christ. I recall a verse my pa once recited to me when it seemed as though I was continually making the same mistake over and over again. It's Isaiah sixty-four, verse eight: *'But now, O LORD, thou art our father; we are the clay, and thou our potter; and we all are the work of thy hand.'* He's not finished with either of us yet, McKenzie."

"Thank you, Zach." McKenzie thought of how much she'd learned from Zach—and how much more she still had to learn. Had he not been so patient with her and had he not persuaded her to learn alongside of him, she might never have known the treasures that were found within a book she had never read before.

Such a thought surprised McKenzie, but then again, so many things in Pine Haven had been a surprise to her. McKenzie had never imagined she'd begin to have feelings for the man she'd married. She'd never anticipated she'd come to enjoy reading the Bible each night with Zach and learning more about the Lord. The friends McKenzie had made in Pine Haven were another thing that had surprised her, especially the friendships she'd formed with Rosemary and the quilting ladies....

❧

"All right, girls, we haven't much time," said Marie Kinion, clapping her hands together in an attempt to organize the women of the quilting circle. Marie took great pride in heading up secret missions. Many folks in Pine Haven teased her repeatedly that she, rather than her husband, should have been the sheriff.

"McKenzie, you and Rosemary finish stitching the top piece onto the quilt. Wilma, you'll be the lookout. Keep an eye on Lucille and let us know when she starts walking this way. Myrt, you arrange the goodie plate and pour the cups of tea. Eliza and Diane, you put the chairs in a circle. Put Lucille's chair out in front, since she'll be the guest of honor."

Wilma Waterson took her job very seriously. As Lucille's closest friend, she wanted nothing more than for this plan to go off without a hitch. Bending her knees, she crouched low and walked to the front window. Carefully bringing her head up level with the windowpane, she glanced across the street. Making sure that her eyes and the top of her gray head were the only things showing, Wilma watched Lucille's movements closely.

"Is she coming yet?" McKenzie asked. Never had she pictured herself getting excited about scheming up a surprise for Lucille Granger, but keeping a secret from the town busybody was no easy feat, and she was as anxious as everyone else to see her reaction.

Wilma squinted. "No, she's still talking to Zach outside of the mercantile."

"These might be helpful," said Myrtle, pulling from her patchwork purse a pair of opera glasses made from mother of pearl and brass.

"I'm impressed, Myrt," said Rosemary, looking up from her stitching. "Where did you find such a fine pair of binoculars?"

Myrtle smiled. "I got these when I was a young woman in Connecticut. Many times, Mother and Father would take us to the opera house, but we couldn't afford the best seats in the house. So, these opera glasses came in handy." Myrtle handed them to Wilma.

She held the ornate binoculars to her eyes and peered through them. "Everything far away looks so close!" she exclaimed. "We must never allow Lucille to get her hands on these. Why, she'd be spying on unsuspecting people miles away!"

The group giggled at Wilma's remark. "Yes, Myrt, you must keep those glasses away from our beloved Lucille."

Myrtle nodded in agreement.

"Is Lucille any closer?" Marie asked.

"No," answered Wilma, "but it looks as though she's attempting to get away from Zach, judging by her gestures in this direction and the look of impatience on her face."

"Thank goodness for Zach," Rosemary sighed. "He was so kind to agree to be a part of our plan."

McKenzie smiled to remember how amazed she'd been when several of the quilting ladies had cornered Zach after church one Sunday and asked him to help, and he'd agreed. Such a gesture on Zach's part had added to McKenzie's growing admiration of him.

"You couldn't pay my husband to initiate a conversation with Lucille, much less deliberately prolong it," declared Marie.

"I know what you mean," said Rosemary. "Asa is a wonderful husband, but he, too, has his limits as far as what he will do to humor me."

"You are fortunate to have a husband like Zach," Diane told McKenzie with a smile. "Men like him don't grow on every tree."

"Especially not on the aspens and evergreens in Pine Haven," chortled Marie.

"Oh, no! She almost got away from Zach again," Wilma alerted them.

"Y'all are making me so nervous," said Eliza. "It's like we're all spies in the army or somethin'."

Marie laughed. "I hardly think spying on Lucille is like spying on the enemy during a war."

"Still," said Eliza, "here we are, tryin' to finish up a quilt for Lucille, and we're watchin' her every move. Perhaps we should enlist in the United States Army."

"Oh, no!" Wilma gasped. "She got away from Zach, and she's coming this way!"

"Women of the esteemed Quilting Circle of the Town of Pine Haven, do not panic!" said Marie, even as she fanned herself.

"She's getting closer!" exclaimed Wilma, her voice a panicked whisper.

"All right. Rosemary and McKenzie, would you take that quilt into the other room and finish sewing on that last piece?" Marie asked. "The rest of us will pretend that nothing out of the ordinary is going on. We'll do our best to distract Lucille while you two finish up."

Several moments later, the front doorknob jiggled. They had locked it and had forgotten to unlatch it in the frenzy caused by Lucille's approach. A knock sounded next. "Hello?" came Lucille's voice as she knocked again.

"Oh! Hello, Lucille," said Marie, opening the door.

"Well, I'll be!" exclaimed Lucille. She pushed her way past Marie and into the room. "Why on earth was the door locked?"

"Sorry about that," said Marie, avoiding the question.

"I suppose I'm the last one here?" asked Lucille. "I hope I didn't miss any juicy gossip!"

"No, no, don't worry," Myrtle assured her. "Come, Lucille; sit down." She led Lucille to the chair they'd chosen for her in the circle.

"You won't believe why I was late," Lucille said with a dramatic sigh. She waited for all eyes to focus on her before continuing. "By the way, where's McKenzie?"

"I'm right here, Lucille," McKenzie said, and she and Rosemary emerged from the other room.

"What I am about to say about my reason for my delay has everything to do with you," said Lucille.

"How is that?" asked McKenzie.

"I am late because of that husband of yours. Here I am, going to be on time, as I always am, to the quilting circle. I finish my chores at the mercantile, then head out to walk across the street. But, as I am minding my own business and preparing to cross the street, from out of nowhere comes Zach." Lucille pursed her lips together and paused for a moment. "Anyway, Zach begins talking to me about some things he needs to buy at the mercantile. I said to him, I said, 'Now, Zach, you just go right on into the mercantile, and Fred will help you with whatever you need.'" Lucille sighed. "I know I'm the one most folks want to come to for help in the mercantile, and that Fred sometimes doesn't provide the same level of excellent service that I do, but surely Fred could have helped Zach just this once."

McKenzie nudged Rosemary and gave her a knowing look. The other women put on looks of surprise and shock that Zach should have distracted Lucille and caused her to be late to the quilting circle.

"So, then, Zach starts talking about his horse and how it hasn't been feeling well lately. I told him, I said, 'Now, Zachary Sawyer, I am sorry about your horse's health condition, but I don't have the time to discuss such matters with you right now.' But Zach didn't listen. That is so out of character for him. He is usually such a good listener. But not this time. He just kept talking and talking and talking. I lost track of what he was talking about after a while. I started to grow nervous at the thought of being late and tried to escape."

Lucille's breath came in gasps, as if she were a prisoner of war giving an account of an escape from an enemy camp. "Twice he caught me by the arm and said he had something else important to tell me. Then, he would go on and on and on about nothing." Lucille stopped to catch her breath. "Finally, I said to him, I said, 'Now, Zach, unless you have some good gossip that I may share with my quilting ladies, I must go.' He finally released me and allowed me to come over here. I tell you, I am exhausted beyond words from all of his chatter!"

"I'm so sorry you had to go through that," said Eliza. "Be thankful it wasn't my Billy Lee holdin' y'all hostage with his words. You'd a'still been over there listenin'."

"Oh, mercy, am I thankful for that!" declared Lucille. "So, I do want to apologize for being late, but the truth is that it really was not my fault. I suppose I could make it up to you by telling you I just heard firsthand that Gretchen Edwards is expecting another child."

Unable to contain her laughter any longer, McKenzie began to giggle. Poor Lucille. She had no clue that her friends had wanted her to be late and that they had asked Zach for his assistance. Rosemary began to laugh, too, followed by the other women.

Lucille's eyes grew large. "Why is everybody laughing? Is it really humorous that Gretchen is expecting again? Yes, she and her husband have seven daughters already, but I fail to see the humor in adding another baby to their brood." She glanced from one woman to the next with a look of befuddlement. "By the way," she said, speaking loudly over the gregarious laughter, "why am I all alone in this chair here, and everyone else is in the circle?"

"Go ahead and tell her, Wilma," urged Diane.

"Lucille, you're sitting there because you are our guest of honor," Wilma announced.

"Your guest of honor?" asked Lucille, beaming with a slight flush to her cheeks. "I was wondering why there were tea and cookies."

"Yes, we have something special for you to show our appreciation," added Rosemary. "McKenzie, would you like to help me carry it?"

Lucille held her hand to her chest. "Something special for me?"

"Yes, Lucille. Now, go on and close your eyes," said Eliza. "And no peekin'."

Lucille did as she was told. McKenzie and Rosemary left to retrieve the quilt. "Keep your eyes closed and hold out your hands," said McKenzie as she and Rosemary laid the quilt over Lucille's arms.

"You can open them now," said Myrtle.

Lucille opened her eyes. "Oh, it's lovely!" she exclaimed. "I love the colors and the pattern!"

"Unfold it all the way," suggested Diane.

Lucille unfolded the green, orange, and yellow block quilt and exposed the last piece, which McKenzie and Rosemary had stitched so quickly. With tears in her eyes, she read aloud the words embroidered in a multicolored arc: "Lucille's Love Connections: Finding True Love for the Eligible Bachelors of Pine Haven."

"We asked Zach to distract you on purpose, Lucille, so we could finish the quilt," McKenzie confessed. She felt a seed of *pride sprout within her to be married to the man who had helped to make the surprise possible.*

"Oh, dear," said Lucille. "And here I was, complaining about being late and blaming Zach. He sure had me fooled! Why, my first inclination was to let him know how I don't appreciate being tricked, but now I'm having second thoughts. McKenzie, I don't think you know what a gem you have in Zach."

"Speakin' of Zach, McKenzie, how is married life treating y'all?" asked Eliza.

Before McKenzie could stop the words, they came tumbling from her mouth, sounding more plaintive than grateful. "Zach gave me a foal as a wedding present."

"Oh, my! A foal?" asked Eliza. "What a grand idea! I love to ride horses and all." She paused. "'Course, Billy Lee forgot to give me a wedding gift."

"I don't even think Orville realized it was proper etiquette," said Diane. "But that was more than two decades ago, and he's such a sweet man that I don't hold that against him."

"I love my husband, but he didn't give me something as special as a foal for a wedding gift," said Myrtle.

"Fred gave me a cactus plant," spouted Lucille. "He said he bought it from some traveling salesman passing through town—you know, those snake-oil salesmen who peddle everything from tonics and potions to useless and unneeded items? The salesman said it came all the way from Mexico. Balderdash, I say! I must admit, a cactus plant was not what I was expecting. Fred said he thought I would like it. Nothing could be further from the truth! And that ornery plant—hard to kill since it was as hardy as they come. I couldn't even give it away and ended up suffering with the ownership of it for years." Lucille waved her hands in the air in dramatic fashion. "So, you are fortunate, McKenzie, to have received a foal for a wedding gift."

"With a shortage of worthy men in this town, you are particularly blessed to have married Zach," added Marie.

Lucille nodded. "I fully agree. If I'd have been a few years younger and unmarried, I would have chased Zach until I caught him. As it is, I'm old enough to be his mother, and...and I ended up marrying Fred." Lucille sighed. "Alas, you can't change history. However, I must say, this quilt is delightful and so appropriate, since I'm the one who arranged the happy marriage between Zach and McKenzie."

"We thought you could hang it on the wall in the mercantile to advertise your services," suggested Rosemary.

"That's a lovely idea. Simply lovely." Lucille held the quilt to her chest. "After all, I do feel proud that I was so successful in arranging Zach and McKenzie's wedding."

"Yes, and many more weddings to come, we're sure," said Diane.

McKenzie listened to the exchange between the women. Gazing at the quilt she'd helped sew, she read the words over again: "Lucille's Love Connections: Finding True Love for the Eligible Bachelors of Pine Haven." A deep ache began to settle in her heart. Everyone at the quilting circle, as well as many of the townsfolk, had deemed Lucille's matchmaking between Zach and McKenzie a great success. But none of them knew that McKenzie had responded to the ad with every intent to marry Zach, rescue her sister, and take her back to Boston. None of them knew how she'd determined not to be attracted to Zach—and how the love blossoming between them had thrown a wrench in her plan. How could she have known that her quest to find Kaydie would lead her instead to a desirable, handsome, godly husband?

Thoughts of her sister brought McKenzie back to the present. "I sure wish we would hear something about Kaydie," she said. "I pray every night that the Lord will bring her back to us. I pray that she is safe—and that she's still alive." McKenzie's voice caught on the last word. What if McKenzie was too late, and Kaydie was dead?

"We will hear something, McKenzie; I'm sure of it. The advertisement is bound to do some good. It's in a lot of papers across the Territory, and a lot of people read those papers. Someone has to know her whereabouts."

"What if she's no longer in the Montana Territory?" McKenzie could envision Darius dragging Kaydie to California or Texas.

"Trust the Lord that we will find her, McKenzie. He loves Kaydie even more than you do." Zach reached for McKenzie's hand. "I pray every night, too. I know how important your sister is to you. We have to remember that the Lord sometimes works in ways we might never have expected. It could be that way with Kaydie. We may find her where we least expect to."

"You're right, Zach." McKenzie sat back in her chair and gazed up at the stars. Somewhere, whether it was in Montana Territory or in Nebraska, whether in Missouri or the Oklahoma Territory, Kaydie was under the same sky. *Please, Lord, bring us back together,* she prayed. *And, Lord, please help me when I must say good-bye to this man who has captured my heart.*

Three days later, McKenzie was awakened early in the morning by Davey, crying outside her bedroom door. She jumped out of bed. "Davey, what's wrong?" she asked, flinging open the door.

"It's Duke. He's—he's d-dead," Davey sobbed, burying his face in McKenzie's nightgown.

"What?" McKenzie couldn't fathom the thought of Davey's beloved pet not being around anymore. "Are you sure?"

"Yes…Pa—Pa s-said so."

"How did it happen?" McKenzie asked. She got down on her knees and held Davey's head in her hands. Seeing him so sad made her feel as if her heart might break.

"We—we don't know. Pa says maybe—maybe 'cause he's old, or maybe he—he ate something he shouldn't have. Ma, I want him back!" Davey wailed uncontrollably.

"Oh, Davey, I'm so sorry." McKenzie began to cry with him. She would miss the dog who'd guarded the ranch so faithfully and had provided hours of playtime with Davey. She held Davey in a tight embrace, trying to console him.

"Davey?" came Zach's voice. McKenzie looked up to see him standing at the top of the stairs.

"I want Duke back, Pa!" Davey wiped his nose with the back of his hand. His little body shook, and McKenzie sat on the floor and held him in her lap.

❧

Zach hung his head. This was a part of fatherhood he hadn't prepared for in the least. He walked over and sat down with McKenzie and Davey. "I know you want Duke back, son, but he's not coming back. He was a good dog, and we loved him dearly, but he was old."

"But he can't die. I loved him all my life," Davey wailed.

"I know, son." Zach knew of nothing else to say to ease the pain in his son's heart. He prayed for words of consolation. "He'll need to be buried. Would you help me do that?"

"No! I don't want him buried!" Davey clung to McKenzie and continued to cry.

"Then, would you help me make a cross to put on his grave?" Zach asked. As much as he'd loved Duke, he knew it was nowhere near the love his son felt for the retriever.

Davey nodded. "Yes, but I don't want to see him dead again."

"You won't have to. I'll ask Asa or Jonah to help me bury him. But I would like your help in making the cross."

"All right," Davey said. He climbed from McKenzie's lap into Zach's and wrapped his arms around Zach's neck, burying his teary face in his shirt. "I wish he wouldn't have died."

"We all wish that, Davey."

"Wait a minute," McKenzie said. She slowly rose to her feet and disappeared into her room. "Davey, I have something for you," she said when she returned moments later and sat back down again.

Davey sniffled and turned his head toward her. "What is it?"

"It's a ball. I thought you might like it. Children in Boston throw these back and forth and play games with them. I know it won't bring Duke back, but maybe it'll help you feel a little bit better."

"Thank you," Davey said gloomily, reaching for the ball. "I hope nothing ever happens to you or Pa."

"That's not something for you to worry about, son," Zach said. "God is in control, and He has His hand of protection on our family."

McKenzie watched as Zach got to his feet and picked Davey up in his arms, then carried him down the stairs. She sat for a minute longer on the hardwood floor, trying to swallow the lump in her throat. Someday, she would leave the ranch. Someday, she would leave Zach and Davey behind. If Davey expressed so much sadness over the loss of a dog, his grief over losing her would be unbearable. McKenzie swallowed hard. The grief of leaving Zach and Davey would be unbearable for her, too.

CHAPTER THIRTY-ONE

*T*hat night, Kaydie told the story of her predicament to Ethel, the woman who had so graciously offered her a place to stay. She began with how she'd fallen in love with Darius when he was visiting Boston and how he'd made promises to her. She told of Darius's dragging her to the Montana Territory, where he'd begun treating her badly and made her feel like a prisoner in her own marriage. She told of how he'd robbed banks to make a living and was a fugitive from the law, and how she'd been trapped and powerless to do anything about the situation. Tears filled Kaydie's eyes as she explained how she'd hoped that her sister, McKenzie, had received the few letters she'd been able to send to Boston. Under Darius's ever-watchful eye, it had been no easy task to mail the missives that were Kaydie's only connection to the family she longed for. Of her family members, McKenzie was the one she loved and missed the most, and she hoped that her sister still cared for her.

Ethel did her best to comfort Kaydie. Over the next several days, she made sure Kaydie got plenty of rest, healthy food, and prayer, along with a few heaping doses of God's

Word. It was Ethel's nature to help those who needed to be rescued, just as she, herself, had needed to be rescued a time or two. She took Kaydie to the doctor, who confirmed that she was four months pregnant and said the baby and Kaydie both appeared to be healthy. Without Ethel's intervention, Kaydie thought, she wouldn't have made it through this time of solitude and uncertainty.

The following week, Kaydie walked with Ethel to the mercantile in Wheeler. As Ethel gathered the items on her list, Kaydie reached for the copy of the *Wheeler Gazette* that she'd set aside and found a seat by the door, then began leafing through the thin newspaper. The front page included an article about Darius's foiled bank robbery and his subsequent death. Kaydie read it through, without emotion:

> A man identified as Darius Kraemer attempted to rob the Wheeler Town Bank on Tuesday, August 18. As he exited the bank, he pulled out a weapon and threatened Sheriff Lionel Powell, who outdrew him and fired the fatal shot.
>
> There has been a reward for information leading to the arrest of Darius Kraemer, age 23, for more than two years. He has allegedly robbed several banks throughout the Montana Territory, causing combined losses of approximately $4,000.

Thankful that she'd suffered no repercussions because of her link to the outlaw, Kaydie turned the other two pages of the *Gazette*. An advertisement on the last page caught her eye:

> Looking for one Kaydie Worthington Kraemer, last known residence: Canfield Falls in the Montana Territory. If you have any information about her whereabouts, please contact Zach or McKenzie Worthington Sawyer at the Sawyer Ranch in

Pine Haven. Your assistance is greatly appreciated.

Kaydie blinked her eyes and reread the advertisement
three times. Finally, the information sunk in, and she nearly
dropped the paper in a mixture of shock and delight. Tears
fell from her eyes, smearing the ink on the page. Kaydie
wiped the damp spots on the new dress Ethel had given her.

"Whatever is the matter, dear?" Ethel asked. She'd just
paid for her purchases and was coming toward the door.

"She's looking for me," Kaydie said, tears filling her eyes.

Ethel shifted her bag of goods, then ushered Kaydie out
of the store and sat her down on a bench outside.

"Who's looking for you, dear?" Ethel asked.

"M-my s-sister, McKenzie. She's—she's looking for me,"
Kaydie stuttered through her tears.

"That's a good thing, right?" Ethel said, smiling warmly.

"Yes, it's a v-very good thing," Kaydie sputtered, her voice
choked from crying and laughing at the same time.

"Praise God!" Ethel said, lifting her hands skyward.
"Where is your sister now? How can we get you to her?"

"She's in a town called Pine Haven. Oh, Ethel, I can't
believe this! I wondered for so long whether she'd received
the letters I'd mailed. I wondered if she had disowned me, as
the rest of my family probably has, for eloping with Darius.
And now, to think…." Kaydie clutched the newspaper to her
chest. "I think she might even have married someone in Pine
Haven. Can you believe that? My sister, McKenzie, long bent
on marrying a wealthy Bostonian and climbing the ranks
of high society, may have married someone in Pine Haven!"
Kaydie unfolded the *Wheeler Gazette* and showed Ethel the
advertisement. "It says here to contact Zach or McKenzie
Worthington Sawyer. Oh, Ethel, I can't wait to see her again!"

Ethel scanned the advertisement. "Well, I'll be! I'm so happy for you, Kaydie. Now, let's make plans to get you home."

❧

"This is all I have to pay my fare," Kaydie said, removing the thin, gold band from her left ring finger.

"That will do just fine, won't it?" Ethel asked her sons, Abe and Amos, whom Kaydie had just met.

"That'll do, Ma," Amos answered with a nod.

"Fine, then. When will you be able to take her to Pine Haven?" Ethel asked.

Abe scratched his head. "I think we'll be taking the stage-coach that way next Wednesday."

"Is that the soonest?" Ethel asked. "This girl has been needing to find her sister for quite some time."

"That's only a week away, Ma. It's the best we can do. Now, if she wants to go to Nevada City or Elkhorn, instead, it would be sooner," Amos explained. "But, as for Pine Haven, it won't be until next Wednesday."

Ethel sighed. "Well, then, I guess we'll be satisfied with next Wednesday. We'll make sure Kaydie is all packed and ready to go first thing Wednesday morning." Ethel turned to Kaydie and placed her hand gently on her shoulder. "Kaydie, my sons will take good care of you. I've traveled with them many times when they've had an extra seat in the stagecoach."

"It's a long trip, but we haven't had any trouble in the past several years," Abe said.

"That's good," said Ethel. "She's been through so much already."

"We'll take good care of her, Ma. Don't worry," Amos said, preparing to leave. He turned around and looked at Kaydie. "We'll see you next Wednesday, ma'am."

Kaydie nodded. Finally, after years of waiting, worrying, and wondering, after a life of unhappiness and abuse, Kaydie Worthington Kraemer was going home.

CHAPTER THIRTY-TWO

*T*he hot days of August gave way to the first day of September with no noticeable shift in weather. Zach, Asa, and Jonah finished working in the fields early. "I think I'll take McKenzie on a picnic," Zach said, lifting his hat and wiping the sweat from his brow.

"That sounds like a good idea," said Jonah. "Summer's coming to an end. Might as well enjoy the last days of nice weather before fall."

Asa nodded. "Rosemary and I would be happy to keep an eye on Davey."

"Thanks, Asa. I think I'll take you up on your offer, if you don't mind," said Zach.

"It seems she's becoming accustomed to ranch life," Jonah noted. "I know for quite a while there, some of us were a bit concerned."

Zach laughed. "You think you two were a bit concerned?"

"Ah, but the Lord always answers prayers in His time," Asa said.

"Speaking of McKenzie, Lucille mentioned to me the other day that she would be happy to arrange a mail-order bride for you, Jonah," Zach said, winking.

"Now, don't you and Lucille go getting any ideas," Jonah said. "I'm perfectly content with my life. I've never much cared to be married, anyhow."

Asa elbowed Jonah in the ribs. "Ah, my boy, but you don't know what you're missing. It's nice not to be alone."

"Right now, being alone is fine with me," Jonah said. "The last thing I want is the stress of finding a wife. I'll be satisfied being a bachelor my entire life, if that's the Lord's will for me."

An hour later, after Zach had saddled the horses, he helped McKenzie mount Sugar and then climbed up on Cinnamon. "I'm not too sure about this, Zach," McKenzie said. She'd been thrilled when Zach had suggested a picnic but not when she found out they would be riding horses to reach their destination. "Are you sure we can't just take the wagon?"

"I'm sure, McKenzie. The wagon is too large to fit on the narrow paths, and we could go only as far as the ridge, about half a mile away. Besides, you'll see much more scenery this way."

"I think you're forgetting what happened the first time I rode a horse," McKenzie said.

"Oh, I haven't forgotten," Zach said, grinning.

McKenzie felt precarious as she sat in the saddle, not unlike the first time she'd tried….

As if giving her a foal as a wedding gift wasn't bad enough, now Zach wanted her to ride a horse? Of all the outlandish propositions he could make! McKenzie glared at the man who had recently become her husband. Why on earth was it necessary that she learn to ride a horse? Being a passenger in horse-drawn carriages, and even wagons, was much more to her liking.

McKenzie stared at the horse Zach had prepared for her. Her name was Sugar, and she was the mother of the foal he'd given to McKenzie, whom Davey had named Starlight. According to Zach, Sugar was the gentlest horse on the farm; he'd chosen to teach Davey to ride on her. Sugar and Cinnamon, Zach's favorite horse, were often a team, whether pulling the plow during planting season or leading the wagon to town.

"Let me help you," Zach offered.

McKenzie narrowed her eyes at him. Why was he always being so helpful? Did she look inept? "I can mount this horse perfectly fine by myself, thank you very much," she said, placing one foot in the stirrup. So much for riding sidesaddle. What would her mother think of her unladylike horsemanship? At least McKenzie was wearing her favorite dress—and her fanciest one, too—red velvet with lace trimmings. She was certain that a more elegant woman had never graced Sawyer Ranch with her presence. McKenzie swung her other leg over the horse and situated herself in the saddle, feeling rather pleased.

"Now, with your heel, gently tap Sugar's flank," Zach told her as he hoisted himself onto Cinnamon's back.

McKenzie rolled her eyes. She could figure out how to make a horse go! Her intelligence insulted, she gave Sugar a good kick. The horse responded by taking off at a gallop, gaining speed with every stride.

"Zach! Help!" McKenzie screamed as the horse began to run.

"Hang on, McKenzie!" Zach shouted, following her on Cinnamon.

"Zach!" McKenzie screamed again. She turned to see if Zach was coming to her rescue. When she saw the amused look on his *face, she became even angrier. "Zach! Help me!" In that second, McKenzie lost her grip on the reins, and she tumbled backward off the horse, performing an acrobatic maneuver that the Boston Circus Company would surely applaud.*

"McKenzie, are you all right?" Zach asked, slowing Cinnamon to a stop beside McKenzie, who lay motionless on the ground. "McKenzie?"

"Zach?" McKenzie finally managed.

"McKenzie, thank God. I thought you…."

McKenzie felt her head throbbing, and, with effort, she tried to sit up.

"Here, let me help you," Zach said, scrambling down from his horse.

"I need no more of your help, thank you kindly. Now look what happened! Of all the preposterous suggestions! I can't believe I allowed you to talk me into riding that horse," McKenzie muttered with irritation.

"McKenzie, I'm sorry. Next time, tap Sugar gently in the flank. You confused her—"

"I confused a horse?" McKenzie couldn't believe what she was hearing. Her headache was spreading to every recess of her head, and she closed her eyes tight. "How can a person confuse a horse?"

"Never mind, McKenzie. Let's get you back to the house." Zach proceeded to pick her up and carry her toward the house.

"Put me down!" McKenzie shrieked. "I can walk myself."

"I don't think that's such a grand idea," Zach said.

"I mean it, Zach, put me down!" When Zach finally lowered her to her feet, McKenzie attempted, with wobbly legs, to walk toward the house. Glad to be free of Zach's grasp, she brushed off her dress as best she could. It was then that she spied a rip in the side of her prized garment. "My dress! It's ruined!" she cried.

"McKenzie, that can be fixed. We just need to make sure you're all right. You hit your head mighty hard back there," Zach said, grasping her elbow.

"Let me go, Zach Sawyer. I can walk by myself!" However, the next step McKenzie took was her last for the time being. She stumbled into Zach's arms....

✑

"McKenzie?" Zach said, interrupting her reminiscing. "We should probably start toward the river. It'll take a little while to get there."

"Pardon?" McKenzie looked over at Zach. "Oh! Sorry, Zach. I was just thinking back to that first time I tried to ride a horse."

"I know that wasn't a good experience for you, McKenzie. I am truly sorry I ever made you try before you were ready."

"I just don't want to fall off again," McKenzie said.

"You won't."

"How can you be so sure? This is only my second time riding."

"Remember to nudge her gently—not with a big kick, but gently," Zach said.

"All right—I'm ready." McKenzie carefully nudged Sugar. In response, the horse began walking slowly alongside Cinnamon.

"We'll just take it easy," Zach said. He held the reins in one hand and the basket of lunch McKenzie had prepared in the other. "You've come a long way since that first horse-riding adventure," he said, winking at McKenzie.

"Now, Zach Sawyer, you listen here," McKenzie said in the most uppity tone she could manage. "I'll have you know that in the past few months, I have become an expert horse rider. As a matter of fact, many a time, while you were sleeping in the deep of night, I sneaked out of the house and practiced riding Sugar, unbeknownst to you."

"Oh, really?" Zach grinned. "No wonder you're riding with such poise!"

McKenzie giggled. "Actually, I'm terrified of falling off!"

"You'll be fine, McKenzie. Besides, it can't be any worse than last time."

"No, there's probably no horse riding adventure that could compare to that," McKenzie sighed. "I'm sorry, Zach, for being so unkind during those first days at the ranch. I should have been more grateful when you gave me Starlight and less rude when you offered to teach me to ride."

"I forgive you, McKenzie," Zach said. "Those early weeks were a mite rough, but God has answered my prayers in ways above and beyond what I could have ever expected. Please forgive me, McKenzie, for not doing more to make you feel more at ease."

"But, you did make me feel at ease. You were kind and patient with me. I'll never forget when I discovered you'd filled in that hole in the road so it wouldn't rattle me when I traveled into town. Thank you."

"I want to make you happy, my sweet McKenzie. I want to grow old with you and enjoy the life we share."

McKenzie turned her head away from Zach so he wouldn't see the tear trickling down her cheek. Was it a tear of remorse at the way she had first acted? Perhaps. A tear of regret for not being honest with Zach about her intentions? Perhaps. A tear of sadness that she would have to leave someday soon? Definitely. But, what other choice did she have? She'd written to her parents and promised to bring Kaydie back home again. To stay in Pine Haven, as much as she wanted to, would defy all that her parents were counting on.

"McKenzie, let's stop here for a minute." Zach turned Cinnamon around facing the opposite direction. He climbed down from his horse and helped McKenzie get down. "Isn't this an amazing view?" he asked.

McKenzie took in the panorama from the high ridge they'd climbed, far above the ranch. Pine trees surrounded them, and the songs of birds filled the air. "The ranch looks so small from here," McKenzie said.

"That it does," Zach agreed. "I can just barely make out our house, the barn, the cattle, Rosemary and Asa's house, Jonah's bunkhouse, and the fences."

"I didn't realize how high we'd climbed. It is beautiful up here," McKenzie said.

"I used to come up here once in a while with Davey. He and I would ride Cinnamon and collect leaves up here from the aspen trees. Every time I'm up here, I am astonished at the view. Look at what the Lord has blessed us with, my sweet McKenzie. That entire area down there is our ranch."

Our ranch. The words echoed in McKenzie's mind, and she realized that Zach had never called the ranch, or anything else, just "his." No, he had always been quick to share with her the blessings God had given him: Our ranch. Our home. Our family.

Zach reached for McKenzie's hand. "I love you, McKenzie," he said, leaning forward to kiss her.

As she returned his kiss, McKenzie was struck by the fact that even though he kissed her more frequently, she hadn't grown accustomed to the flutter in her stomach—the flutter she had experienced the first time they'd kissed, during their wedding. She reveled in his strong protective arms around her and the love she could feel in his kiss. She knew that she would never find a man who could compare with Zach in love, godliness, character, and integrity.

"I suppose we should continue on toward the river," Zach said, pulling gently away from her. He reached up and stroked her cheek.

McKenzie nodded and allowed Zach to once again help her mount Sugar.

The river water was clear and blue. In some places, it swirled calmly, while in others, it cascaded in mighty rapids. McKenzie and Zach ate their lunch by the riverside, where they took in the sights and sounds of the forest. "I'm sure thankful that I have someone to share raising Davey with," Zach said.

"He is such a precious boy," McKenzie said. "He won my heart from the beginning."

"Mine, too. My first day as his father seems so long ago."

"It probably seems like he's been your son always," McKenzie said. She knew she was beginning to feel as though Davey had always been hers.

"It does seem like that," Zach mused. "I was concerned about him after Duke died. That was a good idea of yours to give him that ball. I think it took his mind off of his sadness, even if for only a short time."

"I didn't know what to do. He was so distraught, and I just wanted to hold Davey and comfort him, let him know everything would be all right."

"You're a fine ma, McKenzie," Zach said.

McKenzie had never thought she would hear those words. Her own mother, though she loved her, wasn't a role model McKenzie desired to emulate with Davey. Her mother lacked compassion when things went awry and mercy when it was desperately needed. "I think Davey has really taken to Waddles," McKenzie said, allowing her mind to shift to the topic of Davey's new dog.

"I think so, too. I couldn't believe it when Wayne Waterson told me his dog had just had pups. It was perfect timing. I didn't even have to explain to Davey that I knew Waddles wouldn't be able to take the place of Duke."

"The other day, I looked out the window and saw Davey teaching Waddles how to play fetch with the ball," McKenzie said, giggling. "Poor Waddles had no idea what Davey was trying to teach him."

"Waddles will learn in time. I guess Jonah has really been helping Davey to train Waddles and teach him some tricks. For years, Jonah had a dog that could do all kinds of things— fetch, sit, shake paws, you name it." Zach paused. "That was a great meal, McKenzie. You're becoming quite the cook."

McKenzie felt herself blush. "I don't know about that, Zach. I still have so much to learn."

"You've got all the time in the world. We both know Rosemary has the patience of Job."

"That she does," McKenzie agreed. "If you think my first attempt at horseback riding was trying, talk to her about my debut in the kitchen. I'm sure she never met a more hopeless cook than I, and yet she put up with my mistakes and withheld the criticism I surely deserved. It seems I've found a cherished friend in Rosemary."

"I think she favors you in the same way," Zach said.

After a few minutes of companionable silence, Zach announced, "I'm going for a swim. The river is beckoning. Care to join me?"

"I think I'll pass," McKenzie said. Although she no longer wore her fancy dresses, except to church or for other social occasions, the thought of getting her prairie dress wet and possibly ruined didn't hold much enticement for her.

"You don't know what you're missing. We won't have many more summer days like this one," Zach said, then took off his hat and ran to the water without awaiting McKenzie's response.

McKenzie placed the remnants of their lunch in the picnic basket, then leaned back on the rock she was seated upon, watching Zach in the water. She felt so relaxed, so at peace. She stretched out her legs and was reveling in the warmth of the sun on her face when she suddenly felt a cold, wet spray on her arm. She opened her eyes to see Zach standing in the water with a sly grin on his face. "Zach Sawyer!" she admonished him with mock severity.

"If you won't get in, I'll bring the river to you," Zach declared, splashing her again.

McKenzie scooted away from the river's edge, out of range. "How about now?" she asked.

Zach walked closer to the bank, and, with one gigantic swoop of his arms, sent a tidal wave of water toward McKenzie.

"That's it, Zach Sawyer!" McKenzie yelled, but she couldn't help giggling. "It's time for a water war!" She jumped up from her place on the bank and, not caring about her prairie dress, jumped into the water. Tripping over a polished rock in the river, she tumbled and fell, immersing completely in the water.

"McKenzie? Are you all right?" Zach waded over to McKenzie as she reemerged and held out his hand.

"I don't know, Zach," McKenzie answered, feigning worry.

"We can get out now, if you want," Zach said.

Without warning, McKenzie reached into the water and splashed Zach with all her might, then gave a triumphant laugh.

"Of all the nasty tricks!" Zach exclaimed. He splashed her back, and they continued trading heaps of water until Zach wrapped his arms around her. "Truce?" he asked.

"Truce," McKenzie agreed. There wasn't a dry spot on either of them.

Zach kissed her, then tenderly pushed back several strands of hair, which had escaped from her braid. McKenzie reached up and smoothed Zach's hair to one side, though a few stray pieces remained plastered to his damp forehead. Zach closed his eyes at her touch. Who would have guessed that they would grow so close so quickly?

❧

An hour later, McKenzie and Zach were riding back to the ranch, taking their time and laughing about their water war. McKenzie couldn't recall when she'd had so much fun—especially in one day!

When they got back to the ranch, they stabled the horses in the barn, and Zach took McKenzie's hand as they walked toward the house. "I enjoyed being with you, McKenzie," he said, slowing to a stop and leaning down to give her a kiss.

"I enjoyed spending time with you, too, Zach," McKenzie said, tilting her head upward to receive Zach's kiss. As she did, she noticed a wagon on the road, approaching the ranch. Who could be coming to visit them? Reverend Eugene and Myrtle? Lucille and Fred Granger?

When their kiss ended, Zach followed her gaze. "It looks as though we have company," he said, nodding his head toward the road. The wagon continued to make its way slowly toward the house, crossing under the Sawyer Ranch arch.

"Who could that be?" McKenzie asked.

"I'm not sure. I don't recognize the driver," Zach said.

As the wagon came closer, McKenzie couldn't believe what she saw. "It can't be!" she exclaimed.

"What is it?" Zach asked.

"Why, it's my mother and our driver, Lawrence!"

CHAPTER THIRTY-THREE

*W*hat? Your mother? From Boston?"

"Yes—I can't believe it!" McKenzie tried to sound excited, but she couldn't help feeling extremely nervous about why her mother had come and what she'd have to say. "I can't wait for her to meet you!" McKenzie exclaimed, keeping up the façade of delight. She took Zach's hand and led him toward the wagon, which had stopped just in front of the house.

McKenzie watched as Lawrence climbed down from the wagon, then helped her mother get out. "Mother! What an unexpected surprise," McKenzie said.

"Ugh! What a detestable ride," her mother lamented as she smoothed her skirts before giving McKenzie an appraisal and then embracing her briefly.

"What brings you here, Mother?" McKenzie asked, her apprehension mounting. "Is Father all right?"

"Yes, your father is fine," her mother said flatly.

The awkward silence that followed prompted McKenzie to make an attempt at conversation, starting with introductions. "Mother...uh, this is Zach...my husband. Zach, this is my mother, Florence Worthington, and our butler and chauffeur, Lawrence."

"Pleased to meet you, ma'am," Zach said in a reverential tone, extending his hand to her mother.

"Yes, indeed," McKenzie's mother said, sounding less than convinced. She didn't shake his hand, either.

Put off, Zach let his hand fall at his side. He'd pictured someone not unlike the woman standing before him when McKenzie had talked about her mother, but he'd expected her to be a bit more eager to meet her son-in-law for the first time. After all, he'd been enthusiastic about meeting her someday, as well as meeting McKenzie's father, who evidently hadn't made the trip.

"We've come to take you home, McKenzie," Florence announced.

Take her home? But she is home! Zach thought.

"Mother...?" McKenzie looked nervous.

"You don't have to pretend, McKenzie. He won't be able to hurt you anymore," Florence said, glaring at Zach. What had he done?

"W-what do you mean, Mother?" McKenzie stammered.

Just then, Davey skipped up to the group. "Ma, is this your mother?" he asked McKenzie.

"Yes," McKenzie said, shooting a quick glance at her mother, who looked enraged.

"'Ma'? How can you ask what do I mean, McKenzie? Surely, you remember the letter you sent to your father and me."

McKenzie gasped.

What letter? Zach wondered.

"That means you're my grandma!" Davey ran toward Florence and gave her a big hug.

"Boy, stop that this instant!" Florence said, pushing him away.

Zach fought the urge to yell at her in Davey's defense.

"But, you're my grandma! Don't grandmas give hugs? Grandma Rosemary does," Davey said, his lower lip trembling, as if he were about to cry.

"I am not your real grandma. I don't even know you. Now, get away from me, boy. You'll soil my dress with your filthy little hands."

Zach pulled Davey to him in a protective embrace. "Davey, why don't you go inside and play? I'll be in shortly," he said, trying to ignore the pained look in his son's eyes.

"Okay," Davey said, then trudged inside.

Without as much as a word of apology for how she'd hurt Davey, Florence continued her tirade. "Now, McKenzie, we are going to return you to Boston while the weather still holds. Go pack your things. We'll leave first thing in the morning."

"But, Mother—"

"No arguing, McKenzie." Florence held up her hand, as if to dismiss her daughter, then turned to Zach. "And you, Mr. Sawyer! How dare you make demands on my daughter? How dare you make her live in this sorry excuse of a home?" She nodded toward the house. "How dare you treat her with anything less than the respect and privileges she deserves? You are a pitiful excuse for a husband. She deserves much better than the likes of you, and had it not been for her determination to rescue her sister, she would not be here. As it is, McKenzie has had to deal with the likes of you for far too long. You are an abusive and hateful man, and the sooner I remove my daughter from you, the better."

Florence paused long enough to catch her breath. "My husband told me to let it go, like we did with Kaydie—whom she married was her decision, and if she was being provided for, she was no longer our responsibility. But, I will not allow my daughter to be mistreated and lowered like this. I can't help Kaydie, but I can help McKenzie. I won't stand to have another daughter stolen from me."

"I'm not sure I understand, ma'am," Zach said, deeply confused and hurt. Wasn't McKenzie here with her parents' blessing? Hadn't she come to make a life for herself because they could no longer afford to support her?

"You're not sure you understand?" Florence fumed. "Are you an imbecile?"

"Mother, please," McKenzie interjected, but Florence cut her off.

"Hush, McKenzie. Believe me, I wouldn't be here if I hadn't convinced your father to let me come for you. You are his favorite daughter, you know, and the thought of you living in these conditions was unbearable to him. So, he allowed me to come here, accompanied by Lawrence. I see now that I should have come sooner."

"But, Mother, you don't understand—"

"I understand perfectly. Your marriage charade with this boorish stranger is about to end. You said it would be temporary, and the time has come to make good on your plan. Just look at you, dressed like some peasant girl! What type of frock is that? And your hair! Why, it looks a wreck! Your father didn't work as hard as he did to give you a life of ease just so you could throw it away for an impoverished existence. If marriage is what you want, we'll find you a suitable match in Boston—a man with a social status and upbringing more befitting to yours."

McKenzie stared down at the ground and kicked a small pebble. "Mother, we were having a picnic, and we went swimming in the river afterward." Her voice wavered slightly.

"Of all the unscrupulous things! Swimming in the river? Have you no common sense, McKenzie? Have you no recollection of the things your Father and I taught you? Or has this miserable husband of yours made you forget all proper training and etiquette?"

"Mother, please. I wanted to go swimming—"

Florence put her hand up in front of McKenzie. "Please. I don't want to hear it." She reached up and straightened her hat. "Now, then, have you found Kaydie?" The question sounded like an afterthought.

"No, Mother, I haven't found her yet, but Zach and I were able to find out some information recently in Canfield Falls," McKenzie said, looking dejected rather than jubilant at the progress they'd made. After a moment, she reached for Zach's hand. "This has all been a big misunderstanding, Zach."

Zach couldn't take McKenzie's hand until he'd figured out what was going on. He was stunned. What had Florence meant by calling their marriage a charade? A temporary situation? What had prompted her to accuse him of mistreating her daughter? "What did you say in your letter, McKenzie?" he asked, his voice devoid of emotion.

❧

"Zach, I can explain…" McKenzie began, but then she stopped, not sure of what to say. How could she tell him that she'd meant for their marriage to last only as long as it took her to find Kaydie?

When a minute or two of silence had passed, Zach gave a disgusted sigh and then looked at her mother. "You're welcome to stay here for the night. There are no hotels in town."

"That's a shame," she said. "I guess we have no other choice, though."

"Lawrence can stay in Davey's room, and you can stay in the spare room, Mother," said McKenzie. Perhaps, if she was able to stay in her and Zach's room for the first time, she'd be able to explain to him the reason for the unexpected chaos, even if it took all night to do so.

"I'll stay in the barn tonight," Zach offered.

"Zach…." McKenzie again reached for his hand, and again, Zach pulled away. She could see the tears in his eyes— tears that she'd convinced herself she'd never see. Her heart felt heavy, and tears stung her own eyes. "Zach…."

"How could you, McKenzie?" Zach asked, then lowered his voice so that only McKenzie would hear him. "I loved you." With that, he turned and, with long strides, set off toward the fields. Never had his heart felt so broken, and never had he been so hurt and angry at the same time.

Zach tried everything in his power to shoulder McKenzie's disloyalty without the outward appearance of tears. But the betrayal was too much for him to bear. The promise of marriage he had made would now be broken. He tried to convince himself that he didn't care, that it was for the best, since McKenzie had married him only to use him. But it was hopeless. He did care. He loved McKenzie. Davey loved McKenzie. And, now, they both stood to lose her forever. His anger burned at how she'd manipulated him into believing she cared and wanted to marry him because she had feelings for him. "This is no small thing, Pa!" Zach shouted when he was alone in the middle of the field. "No small thing at all!"

⤖

After she'd shown her mother and Lawrence to their rooms, McKenzie ran to the barn. If her mother wouldn't listen to her, if Zach wouldn't listen to her, then she knew who would. "Jonah, will you please saddle Sugar for me?" she asked.

Jonah looked up from his task. "Are you all right, McKenzie?"

"Yes—I mean, no. Jonah, please, could you just saddle the horse? And could you keep an eye on Davey, too? He was inside, but I think he's out back, now, playing with his frogs."

"Yes, ma'am."

McKenzie watched as he prepared Sugar's saddle. "Here you are, McKenzie," he said, handing over the reins. "May I ask where you're going?"

Without answering, McKenzie put her foot in the stirrup and climbed into the saddle. Nudging Sugar gently in the flank, as Zach had instructed her, she rode Sugar out of the barn and toward Rosemary and Asa's. As she neared the house, she nudged Sugar to go a little faster and hung tightly to the reins as the horse began to canter.

When she arrived at the house, she dismounted and tethered Sugar to a tree in the yard. "Rosemary!" McKenzie called, walking toward the open front door.

A moment later, Rosemary emerged with a towel in her hand. "Whatever is the matter, dear?" she asked. "It'll be dark soon. What are you doing out and about by yourself?"

"Rosemary, c-can I p-please—please s-speak—w-with you?" McKenzie struggled with the words and tried desperately not to cry. Like her heart, her language was broken.

"Yes—please, come inside." Rosemary led McKenzie inside the house. "Asa is still in the field, so we are alone. Please, tell me what's going on." She pulled out two chairs at the kitchen table, and she and McKenzie sat down.

McKenzie flung her arms around the older woman, who returned her embrace. "Now, now," Rosemary said, patting McKenzie's head. "Is Zach all right?"

When McKenzie nodded, Rosemary continued, "Is Davey all right?"

"Yes, they're fine—at least, they aren't hurt or sick. Oh, Rosemary, I've made such a mess of things!"

"Whatever do you mean, McKenzie?"

"With Zach—I—I—"

"Now, slow down. Everything is going to be fine."

"But it's not going to be fine. It'll never be fine again." McKenzie let out a moan and buried her head in Rosemary's shoulder.

"Please, try to explain it to me, so I can help you," Rosemary said as she smoothed McKenzie's hair with her fingers.

"You won't be able to help, Rosemary. Nothing will help. You see, I—I sent this letter to my parents in Boston. I wrote it when I first arrived here, right after the wedding. I was so lonely and miserable then. It was the day Zach gave me a foal for my wedding present. I was so frustrated because things were not going the way I wanted them to."

"Tell me what the letter said," Rosemary urged her gently.

McKenzie thought about the letter and tried to recall the exact words that had prompted her mother's trip to Pine Haven—and provoked her fury. "I—I wrote that I was miserable, and that Zach failed to treat me kindly and made me live in a poverty-stricken state." McKenzie began to sob. "I—I wrote that he made ridiculous demands on me...."

Rosemary drew in her breath but continued to listen quietly.

"You see," McKenzie continued, "the reason I married Zach was to get help finding my sister, Kaydie. She's married to this horrid man named Darius, who mistreats her. When my mother read my letter, she must have feared that Zach was like Darius, and she decided to come and get me. She's here now, and she wants to take me back to Boston tomorrow. Oh, Rosemary!"

"Let me make sure I understand," Rosemary said calmly. "You married Zach so that you would have somewhere to stay and someone to help you find your sister?"

"Yes. Isn't that awful? I didn't see how appalling it was then, but I see it now." Another sob racked McKenzie's body. "Anyway, I hated it when I first came here. I didn't even like you, Rosemary. Remember that first night, when I treated you like a servant? And then I vowed I would never, ever like you."

"Now, now, McKenzie. I forgave you before you even apologized over what happened at dinner. How were you to know? Besides, I wasn't too fond of you at first, either."

McKenzie suddenly sat up in her chair. "I'm so sorry, Rosemary. I'm getting tears all over your dress."

Rosemary pulled up a corner of her apron and dabbed gently at McKenzie's tear-streaked cheeks. "It doesn't matter to me at all that you're getting tears on my dress. I am here for you, McKenzie. Pour out your heart, if it helps."

McKenzie didn't know what to say. Rosemary had every right to hate her after what she had done. Zach was as dear to her and Asa as a son, and the thought of someone knowingly hurting him would undoubtedly hurt them, as well.

McKenzie stared at Rosemary. Her own mother had never comforted her in the way Rosemary vowed to do. When she'd been upset as a child, she'd always run to Nellie, and then to Kaydie, when she'd gotten older. Kaydie hadn't been around when Louis had broken her heart, and so Nellie had sat patiently and listened to McKenzie as she'd spouted her sadness. Yet, her comfort and care had scarcely been as genuine as Rosemary's. Nellie had never hugged her or reassured her; she'd merely listened out of duty, since she was paid to do so. "Rosemary, you don't realize how awful I have been," McKenzie moaned.

"You deceived and betrayed Zach, and that was wrong of you; he didn't deserve that. But you've changed, McKenzie. You've changed since you wrote that letter to your parents. You must make your mother see that."

"But—but she won't listen to a word I say. Besides, Zach will never forgive me for what I have done." McKenzie relived in her mind the terrible moments when she had first introduced Zach to her mother. "Mother wouldn't even shake Zach's hand or give Davey a hug when she met them."

"There, there," Rosemary said in a soothing voice.

"Zach—he sees marriage as a vow, an unbreakable promise between two people. He sees it as having trust, not deceit," McKenzie whimpered. She could still see the tears in his eyes— tears she had never seen in a man, let alone a man she loved.

"Zach also knows that issues will arise in a marriage, and that God is faithful to see husbands and wives through those issues."

"But how could he forgive me for this, Rosemary? It was all a lie—at least, that's how it started, until I fell in love with him. I'm not sure how I expected my plan to turn out, but it seems as awful as could be! And, since I complained about Zach, my mother thinks he's a monster, like my sister's husband, Darius. Yet nothing could be further from the truth!"

"Then, you must make that truth known to her," said Rosemary.

"But she won't listen. I kept trying to tell her. Then, I saw the hurt in Zach's eyes, and I knew things would never be the same. He was crying, Rosemary. I've never seen him cry."

"His heart was broken beyond measure because he loves you, McKenzie. Surely, you can understand his pain."

"He told me he *loved* me, implying that the feeling is past," McKenzie said dejectedly.

"He said that out of hurt," said Rosemary, grasping McKenzie's hand. "We all say things we don't mean when we are hurt. You have to believe that God can heal your marriage, but you have to want Him to do so."

"I do want that, Rosemary. I never thought I would say this, but I want to be married to Zach. I want to live here in Pine Haven. I know that sounds odd, but it's true. I would be a fool to leave him."

"Yes, you would," Rosemary said. She paused for a moment. "You see, when Zach loves, he loves deeply."

"I know," said McKenzie. "And he's the last person I would ever want to hurt. I have come to love Zach with all my heart, but it took the thought of actually leaving him to make me realize that."

"Let's pray that you will have the chance to tell him, and that he believes you," Rosemary said, then bowed her head and began to pray aloud.

CHAPTER THIRTY-FOUR

*H*ave you seen McKenzie?" Zach asked Jonah. He'd just come back to the barn after a long walk to clear his head.

"She asked me to saddle Sugar and keep an eye on Davey. Then, she rode off. I'm not sure where," Jonah said. "She seemed pretty upset."

Zach stared at the floor. "I reckon she was," he said, his voice barely audible, even to himself.

"You know, Zach, it's none of my business, and I don't want to pry, but is everything all right?"

Zach sighed. "No, Jonah, it's not. McKenzie came here to be my wife under false pretenses. She wanted to locate her missing sister, and she needed a place to stay, someone to help her, and financial resources for her operation. I can't believe it took me so long to put two and two together and figure that was why she answered my advertisement for a mail-order bride. It's not every day a woman of her class and social standing would leave all of that behind to move to the Montana Territory. But I was blind. I thought—" Zach stopped himself. It didn't matter what he thought. What was done was done. McKenzie didn't love him, and their marriage had been a cruel joke. Once the town found out, there would be no shortage of pity for him—pity he neither wanted nor felt he could handle.

"I don't understand," Jonah said.

"McKenzie wasn't looking for a husband any more than you're looking for a wife. She wants to find her sister, and it seems she'll do whatever it takes to accomplish that goal—even get married. From what I understand, when she first arrived here, she wrote to tell her parents about the 'horrible conditions' here. She complained that I was treating her unkindly and making unreasonable demands on her, and that's why her mother decided to travel here. Mrs. Worthington had no shortage of words to let me know just how she felt about a man who would treat her daughter the way I was supposedly treating McKenzie."

"I'm sorry, Zach," Jonah said. "You know, I'm not an expert about marriage, and I'm especially not an expert about women. You know my background. After my ma left, my pa filled my head with all the negative parts of marriage; all he did was complain. But, I will tell you something, Zach. What you and McKenzie share—I'm not talking about when she first arrived here; she was different then. But now, she's changed; you have to admit that."

"I know she has, or seems to have," Zach said. "But, like her desire to get married in the first place, it could all be just a farce."

"I don't think so, Zach. She would have to be a mighty fine actress to be able to hide her true feelings. I've seen the way she looks at you. I've heard how highly she speaks of you to others. It's not a farce, Zach. It's the real thing."

Zach stared at the man who had worked for him for the past three years. In that time, Jonah had become like a brother to him. "You really think so?" he asked.

"I do. Like I said, I don't know much about marriage. I don't even like the thought of getting married, myself. But, when I see you and McKenzie together, I see something like…something like what Asa and Rosemary have."

"We're far from what Asa and Rosemary have," Zach said. "Especially now."

"Look—here comes Asa," said Jonah. "He's got a lot of experience when it comes to matters like this."

Zach turned to see Asa coming through the barn door. "Asa, have you seen McKenzie?" he asked him.

"She's with Rosemary. Davey and I were just over there. I took Davey home and put him to bed, and then I saw a light on out here and thought maybe you could use another friend to talk to."

Zach nodded. "That I do. I'm glad McKenzie is all right. Jonah said she rode off pretty upset, and he didn't know where she'd gone."

"She's all right physically, but, emotionally? That's a different story," Asa said. "I didn't stick around to find out all the details, and I didn't want Davey to hear them, anyhow, so we rode back. I reckon she'll be on her way shortly."

"She fooled me into thinking she wanted to marry me for who I was, not what I could do for her," Zach said.

Asa nodded. "So I heard."

"What should I do, Asa?"

"I told him you had a lot of experience in matters like this," Jonah put in.

"Ah, yes. Years of experience. But, I will never know it all." Asa chuckled. "If you think this is the only fight you will ever have with your wife, you are sorely mistaken. There are many more to come. It's only natural when two totally different people join in marriage."

"But she's going back to Boston once she finds her sister, if not sooner," Zach said. "That was her intent in the first place. Our marriage was to be a temporary arrangement."

"Ah, that may have been her intent in the beginning; perhaps her plans have changed. I may be wrong, of course, but, from what I can tell, it seems that her feelings for you are very different now from what they once were."

"I don't know, Asa. Even if she's changed her mind about me, how can I ever forgive her? She lied to me. She manipulated me into marrying her with a promise of forever, when she had no intentions of keeping her end of the deal. Not only that, but she also hurt Davey. That's unpardonable. I'm not sure I could let her remain a part of our lives, even if she wanted to."

"Unpardonable, you say?" Asa asked, arching his eyebrows. "Do you think God would call what she did unpardonable?"

"No, probably not, Asa. But I don't really feel up to a lecture right now," Zach said.

"Few people ever want a lecture, Zach. I'm going to give you one anyway."

Zach sighed. "She never cared about me, never loved me, never meant to stay. She married me only to use my help in finding Kaydie. And, she told lies about me."

Jonah snickered. "You really want that lecture, don't you?"

"Zach, the Lord forgives us of all sins when we repent," said Asa. "He doesn't pick and choose and say, 'You know what? That sin was just too bad. Sorry. Can't forgive you for that one.' No, He forgives us for every sin. He also tells us in the gospel of Matthew, *'For if ye forgive men their trespasses, your heavenly Father will also forgive you.'* He then tells us, *'But if ye forgive not men their trespasses, neither will your Father forgive your trespasses.'* The Lord not only wants you to forgive McKenzie, but He also wants you to forgive her completely, thoroughly, and more than once." Asa paused and put his hand on Zach's shoulder. "Also in Matthew, Jesus commands us to forgive someone *'seventy times seven'* times. That's a lot of times."

"You're right, Asa," Zach said with a groan. "I just don't feel like I'm in the forgiving mood right now. I have a broken heart that might never heal."

"Ah, you have been wronged, no doubt about that. What McKenzie did was unthinkable. She betrayed your trust and defamed your character, and I'll not excuse her for a minute for what she has done. However, I will tell you one thing. The woman you chose to marry—the woman you made a vow to love, honor, and cherish through good times and bad—is at my house, crying with no end in sight at the way she has hurt you. You must ask the Holy Spirit to equip you with a forgiving heart. Surrender to Him. When you do, He will restore your marriage and help you both to grow. Trust me on this, Zach. I have had my share of arguments with Rosemary. There was a time in our early years of marriage when she was so angry with me that she loaded all her belongings in the wagon and drove to town. I feared she would never come back, and so I went after her. It was hard, because I was hurt and angry, too, but I humbled myself and asked her to forgive me, even as I forgave her. I didn't want to lose her any more than you want to lose McKenzie."

Asa paused and looked at Zach. "The last thing I came in here to do was lecture you. But I have seen with my own eyes the changes that McKenzie has undergone. As Rosemary always says, 'The Lord is the changer of hearts.' And she's right. McKenzie is not the woman you first married. She is by no means perfect, yet, none of us is. But you made a vow to her before God. Are you going to turn your back on your vows at the first sign of trouble?"

"You're right, Asa," Zach said. "My pa said never to make a big deal out of the small things, so I didn't. But this is a big thing."

"Yes, it is," Asa said. "And you have every right to be hurt and disappointed. But don't you go nursing that broken heart too long. If you do, you might miss out on the gift the Lord has given you in McKenzie."

"I just learned more than I ever wanted to know about marriage," Jonah said, shaking his head.

"Ah, I'm glad you listened. Then, someday, when you get married and have an argument, I won't have to repeat myself," Asa said with a chuckle, then turned to Zach. "Let me pray with you, and then we all had better get some sleep," he suggested. "Things always have a way of looking better in the morning. Pray that God will give you the courage to have a talk with McKenzie and work things out."

Zach nodded and bowed his head while Asa led him and Jonah in prayer. Again, he'd been reminded of the blessing he had in friendship with Asa and Jonah. Now, if only his heart could be reminded of the blessing of his wife.

CHAPTER THIRTY-FIVE

"I can't believe you have to make your own meals. Where are the servants?" McKenzie's mother asked her the next morning, when she came downstairs and found her daughter making breakfast preparations in the kitchen.

The last thing McKenzie felt like doing was arguing with her mother and justifying her lifestyle. She had left Rosemary and Asa's late in the night, and sleep had eluded her at every turn.

"Rosemary helps most mornings," McKenzie said, "but this is my home now, and one of my responsibilities is to prepare the meals." She figured she wouldn't need to prepare much of a meal, as it was unlikely that Zach would join them. She'd asked Rosemary if Davey could spend the day with her, and Jonah had agreed to take him over there earlier that morning, where he said he'd eat breakfast. So, the only people she needed to feed were Lawrence, her mother, and herself. Had it been left up to her, she would have declined food altogether for lack of interest and absence of appetite.

"Who drew those horrible little pictures hanging on the wall?" her mother asked, eyeing the portraits Davey had drawn.

"'Those aren't horrible little pictures, Mother; they're precious portraits of our family, drawn by Davey. He's five." McKenzie found it difficult to hide her anger.

"Oh," her mother said. "Well, he could use some art lessons, that's certain. Surely, you are not going to leave them hanging there for guests to see?"

"Yes, Mother—yes, I am," McKenzie said. She busied herself at the stove, praying that God would give her the ability to prepare a decent meal and endure her mother's criticism in the meantime.

"Well, I pity you for having to live in such a humble abode," her mother said. "The curtains are rather slipshod, and the walls look so bare. It's quite a confining house, too. But, I suppose that's a good thing, since there aren't enough furnishings to fill a larger space."

"Mother, would you please refrain from making unkind comments about my home?" McKenzie asked.

"Your home?" her mother screeched. "You would claim this as your home? What on earth for?"

"Because it is my home, and I'm proud of it. Zach built most of it himself. I sewed the 'slipshod' curtains, and Zach built this table and the rocking chairs by the fireplace. His good friend, Will, made the desk upstairs and helped Zach construct the staircase. Asa and Jonah helped with the front porch, and Zach designed and built the fireplace. I would say that this house was built with love."

"Pish posh!" her mother exclaimed. "A house built with love? What love? Anyone can build a sorry excuse for a home, with or without love. Why, in Boston, only people suffering from poverty would ever lower themselves to live in such a modest dwelling. Tell me, don't you miss your home in Boston? The ornate woodwork? The crystal chandeliers? The plentiful bookcases?"

"As a matter of fact, I sent you a letter not long ago asking if you would please mail me some of my early readers for Davey when he begins to read. It won't be long now. He'll start school next year."

Her mother gasped. "You would want that boy to have your books? Well, I never!"

"Yes, Mother, I would like Davey to have my books. I love him very much—as if he were my own son."

"Well, I have yet to receive the letter to which you allude."

"I'm sure you haven't. It was just recently that I sent it. If you had read it, you would have understood that I no longer view my life here as a jail sentence." McKenzie checked the biscuits in the oven. It was unlikely that her mother would eat food prepared by her, anyway. Still, she announced, "Breakfast is just about ready," hoping a change in subject would pacify the atmosphere a little.

"If you're making breakfast on my account, I'll decline," said her mother. "I'm not hungry in the least."

"You might be hungry later, and what about Lawrence?" McKenzie asked.

"Lawrence has gone for a walk, and I'm not hungry."

"Fine, then," McKenzie said. She turned toward the oven and refused to let the tears fall. Instead, she pretended that what had occurred in the past twelve hours hadn't really happened. For a minute, she willed her creative mind to take her back to a time when husbands and mothers weren't an issue. But her attempts to stay there were futile.

"We'll leave here as soon as Lawrence returns. Are you packed?" her mother asked, interrupting McKenzie's thoughts.

"I'm not going back to Boston with you, Mother," McKenzie said, taking the biscuits from the oven and setting them on top of the stove.

"What do you mean, you're not going back to Boston with me?" her mother asked. "You wrote to tell me that your life was miserable. Surely, you don't desire to stay! Zach is powerless to keep you here. If necessary, I'll have Lawrence fetch the town sheriff."

"I'm not returning to Boston because I am not really miserable."

"What? But you said—"

"Yes, I said I was miserable, but that is no longer the case. I tried to tell you this, Mother, but you wouldn't listen."

"Well, I'm listening now. You need to make your choice, McKenzie. I won't be coming back again to rescue you. Either you leave with me today, or you stay here forever."

"If Zach will have me, I'm going to stay." McKenzie wondered if reconciliation with Zach were truly possible. After all the pain she'd caused him, she doubted it.

"If Zach will have you? Whatever are you talking about?"

"Mother, I'm sorry you traveled all the way out here. You really needn't have," said McKenzie. "Now, Zach knows the truth about my awful motives for marrying him in the first place, and he's been deeply hurt. I hope I can convince him that my heart has changed."

"When I received your letter, I knew something needed to be done to remedy the situation. You must understand, McKenzie, that I am only trying to protect you."

"I'm so thankful for that, Mother. But, the truth is, I never should have written that letter. I was in a miserable state of mind when I wrote it, and, at the time, I wanted nothing more than to return to Boston. The things I wrote were not all true."

"So, you lied?" Her mother looked aghast. "I thought your father and I brought you up better than that."

"You did, Mother. They weren't complete lies, more like exaggerations of the truth. Zach never made any 'ridiculous demands' on me; I was simply averse to doing basic household chores. I claimed he treated me unkindly because I was angry at him for giving me a foal for my wedding present, when what I really wanted was a fancy armoire. I wasn't really poverty-stricken, although, after years spent living in our home in Boston, Zach's home felt like a rather crude structure. Those things I said in the letter—they weren't valid or fair. Zach has never been unkind to me. He's never made cruel demands or treated me harshly. He's never reacted to my selfishness in the way I deserved."

"So, are you telling me that Zach is not a cruel, abusive husband?"

"Exactly, Mother. He's the most godly, sensitive, kind, and thoughtful man I've ever met."

"I can't imagine how you can think that about someone who lives in such primitive conditions. What could he possibly have to offer you, McKenzie?"

"It's not about what he has to offer me, Mother. You see, I've changed over the past three months. I'm a different person now from when I first set foot in the town of Pine Haven."

"Well, from what I can see, the changes you have made are far from positive. Your appearance is unkempt, your manners lacking, and your common sense nil."

"I'm talking about changes in character, personality... and faith. I've come to realize that it isn't about me and my own comfort. Zach has taught me so much, Mother. We spend almost every evening together, just he and I, sitting on the front porch, discussing our days, and reading God's Word. Can you believe it? I always thought that the Bible was just a dusty, old book that we had to carry to church because everyone else did. But, when I began to open it regularly and study its pages, I found such treasures, such richness—truths I could apply to my own life, including the mundane, everyday aspects. For example, did you know that the Bible has a lot to say about marriage?"

"I'm not sure what all this gibberish about the Bible means, McKenzie. We raised you in a Christian home. You went to church with us every Sunday from the time you were an infant."

"I know that, Mother, and I'm not placing blame. But we went to church—or, at least, I went to church—for purely social reasons. Sure, I heard some of what the reverend preached, but I never remembered it after I walked out the door after the service. Here, Reverend Eugene has a way of exploring the truths of the Bible that has stuck with me, day after day, in every facet of my life."

"That's all fine and well, McKenzie. I appreciate that you have grown closer to the Lord. We all have some distance to travel in that arena. Still, what about your appearance, your manners, your common sense? You act as though you are in love with this man you married for convenience's sake."

"I am in love with him, Mother. I don't know exactly when it happened, but it did. I want to spend the rest of my life with him. I want to live here with him and wake up each morning with the anticipation of seeing him across the table at breakfast. I want to spend every evening with him on the porch. I want to be Davey's mother."

"Now you're talking nonsense. How could you possibly be in love with a man you found through a newspaper advertisement? You hardly know him."

"I know him well enough to be convinced that he is the one God had planned for me to marry. I don't care anymore about marrying someone like Louis—some wealthy doctor or lawyer or banker. Money doesn't hold the same sense of security or sway over me that it once did. To me, love is much more important."

"Obviously, money no longer matters to you at all," her mother said, glancing about the room. "You do realize, don't you, that Zach can never provide for you in the way a man from a wealthy family could? You'll miss out on social events, charitable balls, tea parties, carriage rides in the moonlight, elegant dresses and expensive jewelry, a large home with the most modern of conveniences...the list goes on and on. Are you willing to trade all that for this?" She made a sweeping gesture with her arm. "Are you willing to disgrace the good Worthington name for the sake of what you believe to be love?"

"I am, Mother. But I won't disgrace the Worthington name. I would be a fool to leave Zach. He loves me and cares for me. He has taught me so much about God, love, and life. I don't need the social events and tea parties in Boston. I have potlucks after church and the quilting circle here. The women of Pine Haven befriended and accepted me more readily than any woman ever has before. Besides, I don't need carriage rides in the moonlight. I have horseback rides in the mountains—the loveliest surroundings you could imagine. I don't need elegant dresses and expensive jewelry. Instead, I have these functional calico dresses and Zach's mother's wedding ring. A large home with the most modern of conveniences—why, Mother? I have a home that Zach is willing to share with me, a home that I may decorate in any fashion I desire in order to make it my home, too. I have everything I could ever want here, Mother. It took me so long to see it. I fought it every day, thinking that I was too important, too superior and well-bred, to live here. I was too proud to marry a poor rancher." McKenzie paused. "But I have the Lord and His unconditional love, Zach and his boundless devotion, the close friendship of those I've met in Pine Haven, and a son who calls me Ma. What more could I want?"

"Oh, yes, that little urchin of a boy who calls you Ma." McKenzie's mother rolled her eyes. "He's not even yours. How could you ever truly love him?"

"I don't know, Mother. I used to think I couldn't, but, now, I know differently. He won my heart on the day we met, and I look forward to working together with Zach to raise him into the kind of man that would make God proud."

"I simply cannot comprehend what love has to do with any of this," her mother said. "All I hear you talk about is those who love you and those whom you love. I didn't love your father when we were first married, and I doubt he loved me. It was just understood that, for the sake of social standing and money, our families would blend. The most logical choice was for me to marry your father to increase that wealth and ensure that it would continue for future generations. Granted, I grew to love your father in a friendly sort of way as the years passed, and I'd never trade him for another husband. But this love you speak of is so foreign to me—and to most people living in the real world, McKenzie. I'm afraid you have your head in the clouds, and when you wake up to reality, it will not be pleasant."

"It's the kind of love you can have only when you realize the kind of love the Lord has for you," McKenzie said. "I don't really understand it completely yet, but it's more than just a feeling. It's deeper than that. Right now, Zach is angry with me, and I'm not sure whether he will be able to forgive me. He might even send me away." McKenzie bit her lip. "And—and I couldn't bear that."

"I suppose I don't understand why you think you need Zach's forgiveness," her mother said, frowning. "Surely, you've done nothing wrong."

"On the contrary, Mother, I have maligned his character and caused him much pain. I led him to believe that I married him for love—or, at least, a commitment that would lead to that—when nothing could have been further from the truth."

"Well, it appears you're not going to be accompanying me back to Boston, and that this has been a wasted trip." Her mother sighed dramatically. "I suppose I shall go pack my things so that when Lawrence returns, we can leave and catch the stagecoach to the train depot."

"Mother, you needn't leave so soon. Please, stay and visit for a few days." McKenzie studied her mother's face as she considered her proposition, noticing that she appeared older and more fatigued than when last she'd seen her. Wrinkles that McKenzie had never noticed before had begun to take up residence in her mother's soft, polished cheeks, and her tall, slender frame appeared more fragile than McKenzie remembered. She suddenly felt herself soften toward her mother. "Mother, I know you were only trying to help me escape from a bad situation. I honestly appreciate that, but there is no bad situation from which I need to be rescued. Please, stay for several more days, and let me prove to you that the words I have spoken to you are true. Stay and come to know the people and places that now mean so much to me."

After a moment's hesitation, her mother shook her head. "I see no reason why I should. Never before have you and I had so significant a disagreement. No, McKenzie, I believe it's time I return to where I belong. If you insist on confining yourself to this unsophisticated culture, so be it. However, I'll not stay longer, no matter how short the visit." She sighed.

"Perhaps I should do what I can to find Kaydie while I'm in the Montana Territory."

"Mother, we have placed advertisements in numerous territorial newspapers. Kaydie or someone who knows her is bound to see one of those advertisements and alert her. Until then, there is nothing more we can do. Zach and I were told in Canfield Falls that Kaydie and Darius had traveled somewhere further west. Given the vastness of the area, there is no way we can locate her by merely traveling from town to remote town." McKenzie took a step closer to her mother. Regardless of their differences, she loved her mother and always would. McKenzie would honor and respect her opinion, no matter how difficult a task that would prove. However, she wished things could be different between them. She longed to share the same love and camaraderie with her mother that she shared with Rosemary.

"Mother," McKenzie persisted, "please, stay."

She reached for her hands, but her mother took a step back and kept them at her sides, closed her eyes, as if suffering a headache, and then opened them again. "This is not the reunion I had envisioned with you, McKenzie. I had anticipated that you would gratefully follow me back home, that you would appreciate the sacrifice I made by traveling far from the comforts of civilization for the sake of your welfare. What will I tell your father when I come home without you?"

"Tell him what I have told you. He will understand in time, just as I know you will." McKenzie stepped closer and reached down, taking her mother's hands in hers.

This time, her mother didn't pull away but rather gripped her daughter's hands. "It seems just yesterday that you were a baby, McKenzie. There was so much potential within you. Your father always said that if you had been a boy, you would have been the best lawyer in the city. You could have joined him in his practice, and—" She stopped and swallowed audibly.

"Mother, I am not throwing my life away by making this decision. On the contrary, I feel that this is where I am meant to be. Besides, I plan to make plenty of visits to Boston. I would love for Father to meet Zach and Davey. I have told Davey all about the candy stores there, and he can't wait to set foot inside one." McKenzie smiled as she imagined the look on Davey's face when he saw the shelves lined with every type of candy imaginable. "Zach was born in Chicago, and he spent a good part of his life there. I'm sure he would enjoy seeing a city again. I intend to make a family trip to Boston once we find Kaydie, provided Zach is in agreement. And I'm sure he will be."

McKenzie grasped her mother's hands tighter. "And this is not good-bye. You will always be my mother, and I will always care about you and love you. Just because we have different opinions doesn't mean we have to discard our family ties." McKenzie silently thanked God that the anger she'd harbored only a few minutes ago had subsided.

"Well, if you put it that way…" her mother said. "I'll never agree with your choice to stay here, and I'll never understand your reasoning. But, as you say, our differing opinions don't necessitate discarding our family ties."

McKenzie nodded. "There is just one matter I need to fix. I must find some way to repair my marriage and seek Zach's forgiveness. I'm not sure that will ever happen, but I hope it does." McKenzie blinked away the tears that were pooling in her eyes. "I only hope he does forgive me, Mother. I have never felt for anyone else what I feel for Zach." Her voice shook as she spoke the words.

Would Zach understand why she'd lied? Would he find it in his heart to pardon her lapse in judgment? What if he didn't? What if he sent her away on the stagecoach with her mother? What if he told her he no longer loved her? Concerns crowded McKenzie's mind and became almost unbearable. Finally, unable to contain herself any longer, McKenzie began to sob. Never had she cried so much in her life. Never had she had so much to lose.

"Now, now," her mother said. "If his love for you is as strong as you say it is, he will forgive you and want to remain married to you." In an uncharacteristic move, she reached over and patted McKenzie tentatively on the back.

McKenzie responded by leaning closer to her mother and putting her arms around her. "I know that I may get tears on you, Mother, and that—"

"Shh. That's quite enough," her mother said. She returned the embrace, and McKenzie could tell that it was awkward and ungraceful, but it comforted, just the same.

"Mother, I love you," McKenzie said, looking up at the woman who held her.

Her mother remained silent for a moment, then whispered, "I—I love you, too."

"Thank you, Mother. Thank you for saying that." McKenzie buried her face in her mother's dress.

"I'm so sorry I didn't say it long ago, McKenzie." Her mother sighed. "I have so many regrets."

"Instead of having regrets, Mother, make changes. Pray that God will show you how. That's what I had to do. And, you know what? It works. He works."

"I would like to start over with you, McKenzie. I may have lost one daughter already." She sniffled. "I hope Kaydie is all right, but...."

"I know that she's all right. I have faith that God has kept her safe. Zach also has faith that she is safe. We will find her, Mother, and everything will be fine."

"I hope so," her mother said. "I truly do."

With her finger, McKenzie twirled one of the tendrils that had come loose from her braid. "Mother, I wish so that things had turned out differently. I wish that you had come for the purpose of visiting me and meeting the man I love."

"I'm not sure I can understand or accept all you are telling me," her mother said with a sigh. "But, you are my daughter, and so I will stay a few more days, if it is important to you that I do so. Perhaps, then, I can better comprehend why Zach, the boy, and this town mean so much to you."

"Thank you, Mother," McKenzie said. She knew that it would take time for her mother to realize what was really important in life, just as it had for her. But McKenzie rejoiced in the baby steps her mother had taken in the past few minutes.

❧

Zach stood on the porch for quite some time, listening to the conversation between McKenzie and her mother. He knew it wasn't right to eavesdrop, but his feet wouldn't move. He hadn't heard the entire conversation, but he had heard enough to know that although things were different, and it would take some time, everything was going to be all right. God was still in control. He also knew that McKenzie wasn't the only one who needed forgiveness.

CHAPTER THIRTY-SIX

*M*cKenzie, can we talk?" Zach asked. So much had already happened that morning that he wasn't sure if he could handle more, but he knew that the sooner he and McKenzie sorted things out, the better.

"Yes," McKenzie said. She followed him to the barn, where he began saddling the horses.

"I hope you don't mind going for a ride again," he said.

McKenzie shook her head. "I'm beginning to enjoy riding—when I don't fall off," she said, smiling feebly.

Zach and McKenzie rode in silence until they came to the ridge overlooking the ranch. There, they stopped Cinnamon and Sugar and dismounted. When the horses had been tethered, Zach motioned for McKenzie to join him in the shade of an aspen tree.

"So, your mother has agreed to stay for a few days? She certainly seems to have a new outlook on ranch life," Zach said.

"She wanted to start fresh and get acquainted with you and Davey." McKenzie shifted her weight, looking somewhat unsure of what to say or do.

Zach removed his hat and squinted down at the ranch. "It's a nice day, isn't it?" He felt equally unsure of where to start or how to repair the damage that had been done to their relationship. All morning, since overhearing McKenzie's conversation with her mother, he had prayed for the right words to say. He'd prayed that God would guide him and bridle his tongue so that nothing unnecessary would be uttered.

"McKenzie—"

"Zach—"

When they realized they'd both spoken at the same time, they laughed. "You go first," Zach said.

"I want to apologize, Zach. I—I didn't want to like you, let alone fall in love with you. I didn't want to like it here, and I for sure didn't want to be Davey's mother. When I first arrived in Pine Haven, all I could think about after meeting you was how ridiculous this plan was, how obliging you were, and how pathetic my surroundings appeared." McKenzie paused. "I came with one purpose, and one purpose only: to find Kaydie, whatever the cost. To do that, I needed support and assistance, and I decided to inure myself to the pain of anyone who might get hurt along the way. In the midst of my manipulative plan, while I was using you and looking forward to the day I'd leave this place, I fell in love with you. I—I never expected that to happen." Softly, she began to sob.

Zach put his arm around McKenzie and pulled her to him. "McKenzie, it will be all right."

"No, Zach. I was so wrong. How could I have used you the way I did? How could I have lied about your integrity? You have been nothing but kind and generous to me, while I've been so...." McKenzie sniffled and looked up at him. "I pray that you can find it in your heart to forgive me."

"I forgive you, McKenzie," Zach said, surprised by how effortless it felt. "I didn't want to forgive you at first. I was so hurt that you could even do such a thing. I took seriously every promise I made to you, and I thought that you made the same promises in sincerity. I just felt like a dupe when I found out the true reason you'd married me. Somehow, I failed to see how unlikely it would be for someone like you to seek out someone like me."

"Oh, Zach. It was such a ludicrous idea to begin with, and then, when you continued to correspond with me, I was stunned. It all began to happen so quickly, and everything seemed to be falling into place. When I arrived here, I tried to keep my distance, tried to stop myself from returning your affection, but it didn't work." McKenzie's lip quivered, and she rubbed her teary eyes with her knuckles.

Zach placed a finger gently on McKenzie's mouth. "You don't have to say any more, my sweet McKenzie. I was wrong not to want to forgive you, especially given all the times I've needed the Lord to forgive me. I ask you to forgive me, as well, for not immediately showing you the same mercy and grace I have continually received from God."

"Of course, I forgive you, Zach."

"Then, it's settled. You know, Asa told me we would have many more fights during our marriage. My pa always told me not to make a fuss over the small things. I guess I have a lot to learn." Zach paused. "In order for our marriage to be one of trust, we have to feel we can talk honestly with each other at all times, about anything."

"I agree with you, Zach. No more secrets." McKenzie paused for a moment, searching his eyes. "It's not too late, then?"

"Too late for what?"

"Too late for us? For our marriage?"

Zach placed his hands tenderly on both sides of McKenzie's face. "No, it's not too late. Not if you'll have me. I can't promise you the things you are accustomed to—the material wealth you've known your entire life—but I do promise you one thing. I promise to love you always."

"I told my mother I don't want to return to Boston. I want to stay here—to be your wife, to be Davey's mother, to begin our future together."

"May nothing ever come between us," Zach said. He kissed her then with all the love that was in his heart at that moment—and all the love that was to come.

CHAPTER THIRTY-SEVEN

Kaydie sat back in her seat on the stagecoach and watched the passing scenery out the window. The trip had already been a long one, and it wasn't over yet. Her anxiousness at the possibility of seeing her sister again made the journey seem even lengthier. Questions filled her mind: What if McKenzie was no longer in Pine Haven? What if she was still angry at Kaydie for eloping with Darius? For McKenzie was Kaydie's closest sister and best friend, but she'd had no shortage of words to inform Kaydie of her low opinion of Darius and her disapproval of his moving Kaydie so far from her family. Still, McKenzie had placed the advertisement, which Kaydie never would have seen had it not been for the Lord's perfect timing and His bringing Ethel into her life.

What if neither McKenzie nor their parents would allow her to stay with them until she found some way to support herself and her baby? Kaydie shuddered at the thought of being alone with no home, no food, and no way to provide for her baby.

Who was this Zach Sawyer McKenzie had married, and how had she met him? If he had a ranch in the Montana

Territory, he was about as opposite as could be from what Kaydie thought to be McKenzie's ideal. She remembered how infatuated her sister had been with Dr. Louis Clarence III. Whatever had become of that relationship?

Kaydie patted her stomach. "We'll find out soon enough the answers to these questions, little one," she whispered. Thankfully, only a couple of other passengers had occupied the stagecoach for a small portion of the four-day journey; it had relieved Kaydie of having to answer too many questions. She was also relieved that the succession of mornings spent vomiting seemed to have ended. Kaydie knew for certain that she would not have been able to endure the bumpy ride on the uneven roads had she still been experiencing nausea.

One of the stagecoach drivers, Ethel's son, Amos, had informed her that, unless something went wrong, they had less than two hours of travel time left. To Kaydie, that meant less than three hours until she would be reunited with McKenzie. *Thank You, Lord*, she silently prayed, thinking of the eloquent examples Ethel had set for her. *Thank You for rescuing me and my baby. Thank You, too, Lord, that Abe and Amos have been so charitable toward me. And please bless their mother, Ethel. Had it not been for her, I might not be traveling to see McKenzie.*

❧

"I'll be back in time for supper," Jonah said, pulling his hat over his head. Zach needed some supplies in town, and Jonah had offered to make the trip.

"Would you please ask Mr. Victor if he has received any news on Kaydie's whereabouts?" McKenzie asked.

"Will do, ma'am," Jonah said. He walked to the barn, hitched the horses to the wagon, and set off toward Pine Haven.

During the trip, Jonah marveled at how the trees were already preparing for the coming season of autumn. He rather liked the changes in seasons, even if the winters here were longer than the winters he had known growing up in Mississippi. Given his choice, he'd much rather be where he was now. It was the simple fact that Mississippi held too many memories—memories that Jonah was better off forgetting. The best choice Jonah had ever made had been to leave his father miles behind. After all, the man had cursed the day Jonah was born. While he never gave much thought to his father, Jonah did think often of his mother, who left when he was very young. Was she still alive? Did she ever think of him? Why hadn't she taken him with her? Jonah knew firsthand that his father was not an easy man to live with, but why had she turned her back on her young son, as well? To his knowledge, Jonah hadn't done anything to prompt her to leave her family. Still, such memories made him wary of ever starting a family of his own. He would be content merely to watch as other families grew around him.

Of course, Jonah was pleased that Zach and McKenzie had reconciled. He had wanted so badly for their marriage to work. He wouldn't have wanted to watch as McKenzie left behind not only Zach, but also Davey, for it would have been like reliving a painful episode from his own past.

Jonah mused that it had been of great benefit when McKenzie's mother had returned to Boston last week. Although he could tell Mrs. Worthington was trying to resolve her differences with her daughter, he also thought that it would be a long time before complete peace prevailed between mother and daughter. As a spectator, he'd detected some lasting irritation on the parts of both women. Still, as he'd overheard McKenzie say to Zach, "It was a start in the right direction."

In Pine Haven, Jonah whistled as he loaded the supplies for Zach into the back of the wagon. Then, he went to the post office to see Mr. Victor.

He was surprised to see an unfamiliar woman standing there, facing the wall. A faded, blue bonnet hung down her back, and stands of wavy, blonde hair had escaped the confines of her braid. The profile of her face, while thin, was more beautiful than any Jonah had ever seen. When the woman turned around, her eyes met Jonah's, and she immediately turned back to face the wall, hunching her shoulders slightly.

Chastising himself for apparently having made the woman uncomfortable, Jonah strode up to the counter and cleared his throat. "Uh, Mr. Victor?"

"Yes?" Mr. Victor's voice carried from among the rows of shelves behind the counter.

"Uh, you have a customer."

"Well, hello there, Jonah," said Mr. Victor, coming to stand at the counter. "What brings you to town today?"

"Zach needed some supplies, and I offered to pick them up."

"Very well. What can I do for you?"

Jonah glanced over his shoulder in the direction of the woman. "She was here first," he said.

"Pardon?"

"That woman over there—she was here first. I reckon she might need some help."

Mr. Victor craned his neck to see where Jonah had indicated. "Oh! I apologize, miss. I didn't notice you come in. Can I help you with something?"

The woman shuffled warily up to the counter, her eyes darting back and forth between the two men. "I—I'm looking for the Sawyer Ranch," she said.

Jonah sucked in his breath. What were the odds of finding this beautiful woman in the post office and then learning that she was seeking the very place where he lived and worked?

"The Sawyer Ranch?" Mr. Victor asked. He looked from Kaydie to Jonah. "Jonah lives there; perhaps he'd be obliged to take you there."

The woman gulped and looked, wide-eyed, at Jonah.

Suddenly, it hit him. Could this be McKenzie's sister? Jonah decided not to say anything just yet, for fear that she'd be suspicious of him and run away. "I do live there. I work for Zach Sawyer," Jonah said, removing his hat and holding out his hand. "Jonah Dickenson. Pleased to make your acquaintance."

Kaydie took a step backward and eyed the handsome man with suspicion. His hair was the color of copper, his eyes a deep shade of gray. His deep voice carried the hint of a Southern accent. He was clean-shaven, and he had a stocky build, although he wasn't tall. The man didn't appear to be someone untrustworthy. Still, Kaydie had made inaccurate assumptions before, and she no longer trusted her own judgment, especially on first impressions.

"I reckon I could take you to the ranch," he said. "I just need to ask Mr. Victor a question, and then we can be on our way."

Kaydie touched her stomach and thought of how she needed to protect not only herself but also her baby. She had always been timid; now, she was even more so.

"Do you...do you know McKenzie?" Kaydie asked Jonah.

Jonah's eyes widened. "McKenzie? McKenzie Sawyer?" he asked.

"Everyone knows McKenzie," said Mr. Victor.

"Her maiden name was Worthington," Kaydie said.

"I believe that was her maiden name. She used to live in Boston?" Jonah asked.

"Yes!" Kaydie covered her mouth with her hand at her outburst of excitement. "Does she have curly, strawberry blonde hair, and is she tall?" she asked in a quieter voice.

"I believe so," said Jonah. "Yes, yes, she is tall for a woman."

"I'm Kaydie Kraemer. I believe my sister may be looking for me." Kaydie's heart raced within her chest. How many nights had she dreamed about this moment?

"Kaydie? Well, I'll be!" Jonah scratched his head. "I was just going to ask Mr. Victor if he'd had any news about the posting McKenzie had placed on the wall over there."

"You're Kaydie?" Mr. Victor asked.

"Yes—I'm McKenzie's sister!" Kaydie glanced around at the walls and spied the posting. She read it and gasped. "Please, can you take me to her?"

"I reckon I can do that," Jonah said, smiling wryly. "Do you have any belongings with you?"

"Only this one bag," Kaydie said, pointing to the dingy, brown knapsack that held her sole possessions.

Jonah picked up the bag. "Follow me, ma'am," he said. "Let's get you to your sister."

Kaydie thanked Mr. Victor and followed Jonah to the wagon. He helped her into the seat, and it was all she could do to keep from grabbing the reins and whipping the horses into a full-tilt gallop. Her long-awaited reunion with McKenzie was finally here!

❧

McKenzie was outside tending the garden when she saw the wagon coming back up the drive. For a second, she thought for certain her eyes were failing her—it looked like there was a petite woman seated next to Jonah. As the wagon grew closer, McKenzie gasped when the two figures came into focus. Could it be? *Thank You, Lord!* she prayed and ran toward the wagon.

"Kaydie?"

"McKenzie!"

With Jonah's assistance, Kaydie climbed from the wagon and practically fell into McKenzie's welcoming arms.

McKenzie clutched her younger sister tightly and felt tears that had been withheld for years begin to fall. "Kaydie, I wasn't sure if you were…." Her sentence went unfinished at the horrifying thought that Kaydie might not have returned to her alive.

Kaydie pulled back from McKenzie's embrace and stared through tear-filled eyes at her older sister. "Oh, McKenzie, how I have longed for this. Let me look at you closely now." Kaydie stood back and gazed at McKenzie. "Oh, I never thought this moment would come! I—I have m-missed missed you—s-so much," she stammered.

"I have missed you, too, Kaydie. We have so much catching up to do."

"I would say so," Kaydie said, beaming. "I never would have pictured you as a ranch wife. That in itself is enough of a surprise to last me the rest of my days."

McKenzie shrugged. "I never thought I would be a ranch wife, either, but, as my sweet friend Rosemary says, 'The Lord is the changer of hearts,' and He sure has changed mine." She put her arm around her sister. "Come in the house. I'll make us some tea."

Together, the two women walked across the yard and into the house. There would scarcely be enough daylight hours to share all that had transpired during their years apart. What was more, there would be no way to offer near enough praises to the One who had brought them together.

CHAPTER THIRTY-EIGHT

$\mathcal{K}$aydie sat down at the dinner table, taking care to keep some distance between herself and Jonah Dickenson, who was seated on her left. She tried to subtly scoot her chair closer to Davey, seated on her right. Kaydie still knew very little about Jonah since her arrival in Pine Haven three days ago, but his closeness made her nervous. Even his attempts to make polite conversation with her made her uneasy, although she had no facts on which to base her judgment of him.

McKenzie placed a basket of bread on the table and then took her seat next to Zach. "I'll lead us in a word of prayer," said Zach, folding his hands.

"Dear heavenly Father, we thank You for this day, and for bringing Kaydie to us. We pray for her healing, and for the health and safety of her baby. Thank You for the food we are about to eat, and bless the hands that prepared it. In Jesus' name, amen."

"Amen," Kaydie said, then breathed a sigh of relief. She had explained what had happened to Darius and told McKenzie about her condition, and she was thankful not to feel any shame, even among people she'd met just recently.

That evening, McKenzie joined Zach for what would be their last evening on the front porch for several months to come. Beginning the next day, their evenings of reading their Bibles would be spent inside the house, by the fireplace. McKenzie shuddered to think how she had almost put a permanent end to their evening ritual—and to their marriage. She had come dangerously close to tossing aside the love that had grown between them, but, thankfully, God had opened her eyes, convicted her conscience, and reconciled her to Zach.

"What are you thinking, my sweet McKenzie?" Zach asked, reaching for her hand.

"I was just thinking about reading our Bibles together in front of the fireplace during the winter months, and how grateful I am that I'll have the opportunity to do just that."

Zach smiled. "These past several months have been interesting, haven't they?"

"That they have," McKenzie agreed. "Speaking of interesting happenings, I'm concerned about Kaydie. Did you see her this evening at dinner? Zach, I can tell she has changed so much. Not that such changes aren't to be expected, in light of what Kaydie has been through, but I do hope she'll be all right."

"I did notice that she seemed a bit withdrawn and also that she seemed uncomfortable sitting next to Jonah," Zach said.

"I noticed that, as well. I'll have to reassure her that Jonah is a kind man of unquestionable integrity."

Zach nodded. "It's going to be rough for her for a while, McKenzie, but the Lord has brought her this far, and I know that He will continue to guide her away from all those past hurts and into the life He has planned for her." Zach paused. "Let's pray for Kaydie."

They bowed their heads, and Zach began, "Dear Lord, You know the pain Kaydie has in her heart. We look to You, Lord, our Healer and Comforter, to mend the hurts Kaydie has experienced. Please use us, Lord, to accomplish Your purposes in her life. Help us to see when she needs us and to be there for her. In Jesus' name, amen."

"Thank you, Zach. You always have a way of reassuring me," McKenzie said.

"It's part of my job as your dutiful husband," Zach teased. "By the way, how would you like to go riding tomorrow? The leaves are beginning to change color, and they are quite a sight to see, especially up toward the mountains."

"I'll have to think about that," said McKenzie, winking. "I'm only now becoming accustomed to riding horses."

"Actually, you're adjusting quite well. Before you know it, you'll be entering the horse race at the Founder's Day Celebration next year."

"I'll have you know, Zachary Joseph Sawyer, that I don't intend to enter any horse races—not now, and not ever," McKenzie scoffed.

"Not even if Starlight is ready to ride by then?" Zach asked.

"Not even if Starlight is ready to ride," McKenzie confirmed. "However, I might be convinced to join you on many a ride through the mountains next year on my beautiful new horse."

"And to think you didn't much care for Starlight when I first gave her to you as a foal," Zach teased.

"Things have changed—for the better, I might add," said McKenzie. She leaned over and planted a kiss on her husband's lips. "I love you, Zach."

"And I love you, McKenzie," Zach answered, drawing her close.

McKenzie thought of how she had come to Pine Haven with the hopes of rescuing Kaydie and how, thankfully, God had made that a reality.

She also thought of how she'd met Zach with the intention of changing and molding him into the man she was supposed to marry. Instead, she was the one whose heart was changed. For that, she would be forever grateful.

ABOUT THE AUTHOR

Penny Zeller is the author of four books and numerous magazine articles in national and regional publications. She is also the author of the humor blog "A Day in the Life of a Mom, Wife, and Author" (www.pennyzeller. wordpress.com). She is an active volunteer in her community, serving as a women's Bible study small-group leader and co-organizing a women's prayer group. Her passion is to use the gift of the written word that God has given her to glorify Him and to benefit His kingdom. When she's not writing, Penny enjoys spending time with her family and camping, hiking, canoeing, and playing volleyball. She and her husband, Lon, reside in Wyoming with their two children. Penny loves to hear from her readers at her Web site, www.pennyzeller.com.

Coming in 2011…

Kaydie

Book Two in the Montana Skies Series
by Penny Zeller

CHAPTER ONE

*N*o, Darius, I'm not going with you!" Kaydie Kraemer winced in pain as her husband, Darius, grabbed her arm and pulled her out the door of her sister's house toward his waiting horse. She tried to pull her arm loose from his tight grasp, but her efforts were futile.

Darius then reached around and grabbed her other arm, squeezing it so hard that Kaydie could already see the bruises he would leave behind. "You don't have a choice, Kaydie. You're my wife, remember?"

"No, Darius. I'm staying here. I don't want to be married to you anymore." Kaydie fought back her tears, hating that they would be sign of weakness to her husband.

"You don't have a choice," he snarled. "Now, you can either come willingly, or I can carry you. Which will it be? Because I ain't leavin' without you." He turned his head to the side and spit on the front porch.

"I thought—I thought you were dead," Kaydie stammered.

Darius threw back his head with an evil laugh, which caused the nostrils on his prominent nose to flare in and out. His mouth was open wide, revealing more missing teeth than Kaydie remembered. His stringy brown curls bounced from his collar, and he removed a hand from Kaydie only long enough to slick back the few strands of greasy hair that had fallen over his forehead. He squinted his narrowed eyes, which were already too small for his large face, making them appear even smaller. "I had you fooled, didn't I? You're a foolish woman, Kaydie. Ain't no way I'm gonna die and let you go free! When you said 'I do,' it meant that you were bound to me forever!" He gritted his teeth and gripped her arm even tighter.

"No, Darius! No!"

Kaydie's eyes popped open, and she stared into the darkness. She could hear her heart thumping in her ears, a sound loud enough to rival cannon fire. She placed her hand over her heart and felt it thudding wildly. Sweat poured down her neck; her hands were damp with moisture, and her forehead was covered in beads of perspiration. *It was just a nightmare,* she told herself, still breathless with terror. The vision had seemed so real.

Her heart continued to pound as she reached with her other hand and rubbed her belly. "I think it was only a nightmare, little one." Sitting up, she swung her legs over the side of the bed and stood to her feet. Groping in the dark, she made her way to the window and looked outside. The moon and the stars were the only things she could see. Darius and his horse were nowhere in sight.

"Thank You, Lord, that it was just a dream," Kaydie whispered, then turned around and went back to her bed. Burying her face in her pillow, she whimpered softly, not wanting to wake McKenzie, Zach, and Davey. "Thank You, God, that Darius is not coming back," she prayed, her voice muffled by the pillow. "Thank You that You are my *'refuge and strength, a very present help in trouble.'*"

You are safe here, My child, she felt the Lord say to her.

"I know, Lord, but I don't feel safe—not with the memory of Darius," she whispered. Turning over on her back, she gazed up at the ceiling, and the words of Psalm 91 filled her heart: *"He shall cover thee with his feathers, and under his wings shalt thou trust: his truth shall be thy shield and buckler. Thou shalt not be afraid for the terror by night; nor for the arrow that flieth by day; nor for the pestilence that walketh in darkness; nor for the destruction that wasteth at noonday. A thousand shall fall at thy side, and ten thousand at thy right hand; but it shall not come nigh thee."*

Tears of joy slid down Kaydie's face and onto the pillow. "We're going to be all right, little one," she whispered to the baby within her. "We're going to be all right, because the Lord will keep us safe." She gently rubbed her belly again, thankful that God had been there when her husband had been tormenting her and had delivered her from him.

Darius was dead, and he wasn't coming back to take her away. Kaydie had been there. She'd seen it happen. Now, here she was, staying with her beloved sister McKenzie, McKenzie's husband, Zach Sawyer, and their young son, Davey. Never would Kaydie have guessed that McKenzie would move to the Montana Territory and marry a rancher. For one thing, McKenzie despised hard work; for another, she'd had her eyes on a wealthy doctor from Boston for years. Yet, from everything Kaydie had seen in her first month at the Sawyer Ranch, McKenzie was happy and wouldn't trade her life there for anything.

McKenzie had told her that God had changed her heart. Kaydie smiled at the memory because He had changed her heart, as well. She had learned about the Lord from Ethel, the woman who had taken her in after Darius's death and given her a steady dose of God's Word. That solid foundation had stayed with Kaydie, and she yearned daily to know more and more about her Creator. Yes, she had grown up knowing there was a God, but she hadn't truly experienced Him until she'd met Ethel.

Kaydie turned from one side to the other, unable to fall asleep. In a few short hours, it would be dawn, and she would join the Sawyer family and their hired help at the kitchen table for breakfast. The day she'd met each of the members of McKenzie's new family filled her mind, and she recalled asking McKenzie in private about each one of them. Fearful of placing herself and her unborn baby in danger again, Kaydie felt it necessary to find out as much as she could about the people with whom she would be living as long as she stayed with her sister. She felt safe around Zach—and, of course, precious Davey. The others she wasn't so sure about, especially the hired man named Jonah, who had driven her from Pine Haven to the Sawyer Ranch the day she'd found McKenzie....

❧

"Thank you, McKenzie, for taking me in like this," Kaydie said as she sat with her sister on the front porch, sipping tea. The late September air was chilly, but the fresh breeze felt good.

"I wouldn't have it any other way," McKenzie said. She leaned over and put her arm around her sister. "I have missed you something horrible, Kaydie. I thought for a while that I might never see you again."

"I thought the same thing, myself," said Kaydie. "I never dreamed you would go to all the trouble to find me. I hoped that you would, but I knew better than to count on it."

"It happened thanks only to the Lord," McKenzie said. "Montana Territory is a huge place. I could not have imagined how big it was until I arrived here, and I've seen barely a fraction of it. To have found you within its borders is a miracle, indeed."

"Yes, it is," Kaydie agreed. "I must have thanked the Lord more times than I can count for rescuing me through you."

"And I must have thanked the Lord more times than I can count for rescuing you and bringing you to me," McKenzie said with a giggle.

Kaydie giggled then, too, something she hadn't done for a long time. Oh, how she had missed her sister! "I think you were the only one in our family who didn't give up on me," she said.

"Well, Mother did come out here to take me back to Boston—"

"Thank you, McKenzie."

"You are more than welcome. Besides, I couldn't let 'my baby' stay lost somewhere in the uncivilized Montana Territory forever!"

Kaydie giggled again. "Oh, yes. I remember when you called me your baby when we were little. I think Mother feared you would call me that as long as you lived!"

"Mother feared a lot of things," said McKenzie. "However, I don't think she ever counted on my falling in love with a rancher and leaving our home in Boston to become a wife on the wild frontier!"

Kaydie smiled and shook her head. "No, I don't believe she did, or her worst fear would have come true."

"I think the worst thing, though, would have been for Peyton to have done the same thing we did—follow a man to the ends of the earth and forsake our privileged upbringing."

"Oh, Peyton never would have done such a thing." Kaydie rolled her eyes. "Perhaps she isn't our true sister. She's so different from us."

"She's our true sister, just completely unique. I pray for her daily that she will someday find true joy."

"It would take not being married to Maxwell for that to happen," Kaydie said. She thought of her oldest sister's uppity, prudish husband. "Speaking of husbands, Zach seems like a good one," she said, choosing to change the subject to something more positive.

"He is. I'm blessed beyond belief, Kaydie. It took me so long to see the gem that he is. Someday, I'll have to share the entire story with you. To think that I could have missed out on him because of my own pride and stubbornness...." She shivered.

"I'm happy for you, McKenzie."

"Someday, God will give you a love like that, Kaydie."

"Oh, I think the days of courtship and marriage are over for me. I have my little one to think about now."

"I know marriage is the furthest thing from your mind right now, Kaydie, especially in light of the horrid circumstances in which you found yourself while married to Darius. Still, I have faith that someday God will bless you with the husband He's planned for you all along."

"I suppose I might reconsider marriage—when I'm forty-five," Kaydie said, laughing. But she wasn't kidding. Never again would she trust a man, especially with her heart. She now had not only herself to consider, but also—and more important—her baby. How many times had she thanked the Lord that her baby hadn't been born while Darius was alive? She shuddered at the realization that her survival—and her baby's survival—would have been unlikely, at best, if she had remained with Darius. No, never again would Kaydie be so foolish as to fall in love. Things like true love happened only to others, like McKenzie, not to her. Such a thought might have in the past bothered her, but not now. She was content in the thought of being a mother and reuniting with the sister she loved.

"I will tell you whose marriage is a wonderful model: Asa and Rosemary's," McKenzie said. "They both have taught me so much about a marriage that's centered on God, and they've been married pretty close to forever."

"Yes, it was so nice to meet them yesterday," Kaydie said. "They seemed quite friendly and charitable."

"They are. I wasn't fond of Rosemary at first, and I didn't really know Asa, since he works with Zach outside most of the time, but once I became acquainted with them, I realized the treasures they are. They have both taught me so much—especially Rosemary. She's like the mother we never had. No offense to Mother, for I know she tried the best she knew how to raise us, but Rosemary…she's different. She has always been so accepting of me, even when I didn't accept her. She taught me how to cook and stitch and how to survive in a home so different from anything I have ever known. She and Asa are like grandparents to Davey, and I believe Zach has all but adopted them as a second set of parents, even though he speaks very well of his parents, who, as I told you, are deceased."

"I think I shall like Rosemary, too," Kaydie said. "And Asa does seem like a good father figure."

"That he is. His Irish accent makes him unique in these parts. I think Rosemary confided to me once that was one of the things that drew her to him when they began courting so many years ago."

"They live just down the road, right?" Kaydie asked.

"Yes, they do. It's nice having them so close. We'll visit Rosemary soon. I know you'll come to love her as much as I do." McKenzie paused. "And then there's Jonah Dickenson, the other hired man. He's a hard worker, always willing to help. He lives alone in the bunkhouse."

"He makes me nervous," Kaydie admitted.

"Jonah?" McKenzie asked. "Why do you say that?"

"When he brought me here from town yesterday, there was just something about him…I can't place my finger on it, exactly, but it was odd."

"I'm not sure what it could be, Kaydie. He's never been anything but polite, and Zach doesn't know what he would do without him. I think the two of them have become brothers, in a way. When Davey's father, Will, died, I think Jonah slipped into the spot he'd had in Zach's heart."

"I think it's wonderful that Zach adopted Davey after his parents died," Kaydie said.

"Yes. A man who accepts another's child as his own is a special man, indeed. Of course, who wouldn't want Davey for a son? I loved him almost immediately."

"So, you don't think I need to be afraid of Jonah?"

"I honestly don't, Kaydie, but if he makes you uncomfortable, you are within your rights to keep your distance. If he ever does anything…." McKenzie paused. "If he ever lays a hand on you or anything else, tell Zach or me right away. Promise?"

"I promise," said Kaydie.

"But, again, I don't see any reason to fear him. He's a godly man with a heart the size of the Montana Territory. I think you'll discover that for yourself once you get to know him."

Kaydie nodded but still wasn't convinced.

CHAPTER TWO

*J*onah walked into Granger Mercantile to retrieve the supplies for Zach. He pulled out his list and eyed the requested items.

"Well, hello, Jonah," said Lucille Granger, who owned the mercantile with her husband, Fred. She waved from the counter at him.

"Hello, Lucille." Jonah removed his hat and searched the far wall of the store for the coffee Zach had requested and the tea McKenzie had asked for.

"What brings you in to town on this cold October day?"

Jonah turned to face Lucille. She always looked the same—her gray hair pulled into a tight bun on top of her head, her short, plump, apple-shaped body bulging in her gingham dress, the front of which was covered by a white apron. "I needed to pick up some supplies for the ranch."

"Anything I can help you find?" Lucille prided herself in being helpful.

"Uh, yes—actually, there is something you can help me with, Lucille. McKenzie mentioned something about some special-order fabric. She wanted me to ask you if it had arrived."

"Why, yes, it did! I had forgotten about that. I'll be right back." With short, quick strides on equally short legs, Lucille sprang through the door toward the back room. A minute later, she returned. "Here it is. Isn't it just the loveliest print you've ever seen?"

Jonah arched an eyebrow. Didn't Lucille realize that fabric prints, lovely or not, mattered nothing in the least to him, a member of the male species? He thought of her husband, Fred, to whom Lucille had been married probably for more years than Jonah had been alive. Did Lucille often ask him whether or not he found a piece of cloth to be lovely? Likely more than once, Jonah thought. "It's fine, Lucille," Jonah answered, trying to sound sincere.

"Well, it's more than fine, Jonah. This fabric came all the way from back East. It's my understanding that McKenzie wanted it so she could sew Kaydie a dress." Lucille, ever the town busybody, leaned forward over the counter as if the next thing she was to say was strictly between the two of them. "I hear that she's getting quite large in the belly."

"I wouldn't know about that, ma'am," said Jonah, feeling himself blush. Why did Lucille insist on gossiping with him as if he were some townswoman?

"Now, Jonah, you tell McKenzie that I said this is the best fabric this side of the Mississippi." Lucille unfolded the piece of cloth on the counter and repeatedly ran her chubby hand across it. "And the color, too—won't it just make Kaydie's brown eyes stand out? I mean, not everyone can wear yellow gingham. For one, it just doesn't compliment some women's features. For instance, it makes some women appear extremely pale, sallow, and unhealthy. Complexion has everything to do with choosing just the right fabric for that new dress." Lucille leaned over the counter, as if to insinuate that her conversation with Jonah was private, even though they were the only ones in the mercantile. "But with Kaydie's big, brown eyes and her long, blonde hair, it should go quite well."

Jonah shook his head and silently thanked the Lord that he wasn't a woman. Each morning, he pulled on one of the three shirts he owned, neither knowing nor caring whether it complemented his complexion. What's more, he cared little whether the fabric came from back East or from the nearby Dakota Territory. All he cared about was that the item of clothing did its job. "I have a few more things to get, Lucille," Jonah said, placing several sacks of coffee and tea on the counter. "I'll need three pounds of sugar and some kerosene."

"Of course—we have everything you need here at Granger Mercantile," Lucille said, pride raising the pitch of her voice. She retrieved the items and added them to the growing pile on the counter. "Will that be all for you today?"

"Yes. Please add it to the bill."

"Certainly," said Lucille. Reaching for a pencil, she carefully recorded the items and their prices in her journal. "You know, Jonah," she began when she had put down her pencil, "I've been giving a lot of thought to your predicament."

"My predicament?"

"Well, yes—your predicament." Lucille looked baffled that he didn't know what she was talking about.

"I wasn't aware that I had a predicament," said Jonah, bracing himself for her answer.

"*You* know," said Lucille, her eyes widening.

"I honestly don't know, Lucille. Last time I checked, I was happy and healthy."

"Now, now, you may be healthy, but you don't really believe you're happy, do you?"

Jonah looked around to be sure no one else had walked into the mercantile. Zach had so much more patience with Lucille than he did. Jonah thought she was a gossipy nuisance, albeit a good-hearted one. Of course, his friend and employer, Zach, had every reason to think highly of Lucille. She and her husband had treated him like their own son and had given him a job when he'd first come to Pine Haven. That, and Lucille was the reason Zach had found McKenzie; she'd helped him place an advertisement for a mail-order bride in several Boston newspapers. "I am happy, Lucille," Jonah insisted.

"You might think you're happy, but you're really not," Lucille stated with a decisive nod of her head. "You're not one hundred percent happy because you don't have a wife."

Jonah was taken aback. "Now, wait a minute here, Lucille. With all due respect—"

"Oh, fiddlesticks," said Lucille. "Don't even try to argue with me, Jonah Dickenson. Besides, I know what you're going to say. You may hide it well, but inside, your heart is broken, like a piece of fine china that has fallen from its high place on the hutch in the kitchen...." Lucille held her hand to her heart and closed her eyes.

Then, her eyes popped open again, wide with fervor. "But don't despair, Jonah," she said, her voice deepening in seriousness. "I can help you."

"Lucille—"

"Lucille's Love Connections, at your service." She pulled a tablet from under the counter and reached again for her pencil. In her neat, large printing, she wrote at the top of the page, "Jonah Dickenson."

"Lucille, really." Although Jonah knew Lucille, he was still shocked at how domineering she could be.

"Now, don't interrupt me. This'll do you no good. Now, let's see here. How old are you?"

Jonah sighed. "I'm twenty-five." He acquiesced to play along with Lucille's game but dreaded the outcome.

"Very well. You're twenty-five, and you have...let's see, how should we describe that hair?" Lucille reached up and patted him on the head. "Hmm. Let's say you have hair the color of a dark-orange pumpkin."

"A dark-orange pumpkin?" That was the farthest thing from a compliment Jonah had ever received. He'd always rather liked the color of his hair but never considered it to resemble an autumn squash. He'd always thought of his hair color as rust or copper. But the color of a pumpkin? Jonah shook his head. Not even close. He thought of his pa's hair, which was the color of a bright-orange pumpkin, rather than a subdued copper orange, as his hair was. His pa had a collection of freckles dotting his face, whereas Jonah had not a one.

"Well, it is kind of an orange hue," Lucille said, her tone defensive.

"Kind of orange, yes. Pumpkin-colored, no," said Jonah.

"Well, anyway, let's see those peepers," Lucille said, changing the subject as she leaned toward him and stared into his eyes.

"Lucille, really...." Jonah was beginning to feel very uncomfortable under her scrutiny.

"I think we could say that your eyes are the color of... hmm." Lucille put her hand on her chin. "What's something gray? A rock, perhaps?"

"Couldn't you just say that my eyes are gray?" Jonah suggested.

"You're so right, Jonah. You see, even though I have much experience in this matter, and I have had some formal schooling, to say that your eyes are the color of a rock is just not becoming, especially to a potential bride."

"You're writing this down to find me a wife?" Jonah asked.

"Why, yes," Lucille replied as she jotted down the information.

"I've told you before, Lucille, I don't need or want a wife."

"But I found one for Zach—a mighty good one, at that."

"Yes, and he's grateful to you, Lucille. But I'm not Zach."

"Oh, you'll thank me someday. Every man tries to argue, but in the end, they see that I was right all along. Now, let's see, here's what I've written so far: 'Kindhearted Montana Territory ranch hand, twenty-five years of age, with handsome gray eyes and hair the color of a pumpkin, seeks a wife.' How does that sound?"

Jonah knew he was in a losing battle and once again thought of Lucille's husband. Poor man, he probably never won an argument with Lucille. That likely explained why he almost always worked in the back room of the store instead of in the front with Lucille. Fewer opportunities for arguments. How could Jonah persuade Lucille that he didn't need a wife? She'd already refused to listen to him when he'd stated it plainly.

Then, an idea came to him. "Lucille?"

"Yes, Jonah?" Lucille said distractedly, her eyes still on the paper.

"I have an idea."

"Now, Jonah, if you really are opposed to seeking a mail-order bride, I have an alternate plan in mind. Do you know that new family who recently moved here, the Grouards? Well, they have a daughter—she must be close to twenty—named Gillian. I could arrange for the two of you to meet. That way, we could keep the whole affair in Pine Haven."

"No, thank you, Lucille. That's not what I was thinking of at all. Besides, I hear that there's someone else who has his eye on Gillian. No, what I'm thinking is far better than that." This time, Jonah leaned toward Lucille to privatize their conversation. He motioned at her to do the same.

"Yes?"

"I don't know, I probably shouldn't say—"

"What do you mean, you shouldn't say?" asked Lucille. The quickest way to pique her curiosity was to make her think one was privy to information yet unknown by her.

"All right, I suppose I can tell you. It's Mr. Victor."

"Mr. Victor at the telegraph office?"

"Yes, he's the one," Jonah said, trying to muffle a chuckle at the thought there might be more than one Mr. Victor in the small town of Pine Haven.

"Well, of course, I know Mr. Victor," said Lucille. "Who doesn't? He's worked in the post office forever."

"He is the one in desperate need of a wife," said Jonah, shaking his head. "Poor man, he would like to have a wife, but the years are passing him by faster than a wild pony runs from a cowboy."

Lucille looked pensive for a moment.

"I would feel horrible, Lucille, if you found a wife for me before you found one for Mr. Victor," Jonah went on. "I mean, I'm still young. I can wait. Mr. Victor…." He shrugged. "Mr. Victor isn't so young."

"Oh, poor, poor Mr. Victor," Lucille lamented. "I had forgotten about him." She shook her head. "Yes, you are right. I must find him a wife first." She tore the page she'd written about Jonah from her notebook and, at the top of the next page, wrote the words "Mr. Victor."

"Let's keep this between us, Lucille," Jonah said, meanwhile knowing that would never be the case if Lucille was involved. She was far too nosy and excited to share the newest piece of gossip to keep anything to herself.

"But of course we will," she said, patting Jonah's arm. "Whatever would I have done if you hadn't stopped by today? My goal is to use Lucille's Love Connections in the best way possible. You have made that a reality by suggesting Mr. Victor. I'm forever indebted to you."

"I best be going now, Lucille. I think a storm is coming in, but you keep me posted on the progress with Mr. Victor."

"I will, Jonah. You tell everyone at the ranch I said hello."

Jonah nodded and grabbed the box of items. He heaved a huge sigh of relief as he climbed into his wagon. Never had he been so thankful to be released from the clutches of Lucille Granger.

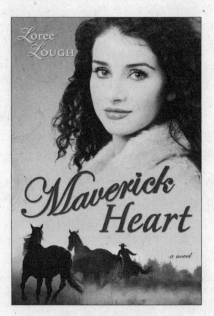

Maverick Heart
Loree Lough

When a coincidental meeting brings the tragically widowed
Levee O'Reilly and rancher Dan Neville—a confirmed
bachelor for reasons of his own—together, they're awakened to a
long-ignored desire for love and acceptance by the realization that
they might have finally found it. Can these two mavericks accept
the plans God has for their lives?

ISBN: 978-1-60374-226-9 • Trade • 400 pages

WHITAKER
HOUSE

Little Hickman Creek Series
Sharlene MacLaren

Love blossoms in surprising places in this quaint Kentucky town. In *Loving Liza Jane*, Liza Jane Merriwether, the new schoolteacher of Little Hickman Creek, finds love when she wasn't looking and learns that with God, all things are possible. In *Sarah, My Beloved*, mail-order bride Sarah Woodward feels that God led her to Little Hickman Creek for a reason and wonders if she will find true love from the hand of the ultimate Matchmaker. In *Courting Emma*, an unexpected romance softens the steely-edged beauty Emma Browning and draws her closer to God.

Loving Liza Jane ✦ ISBN: 978-0-88368-816-8 ✦ Trade ✦ 352 pages
Sarah, My Beloved ✦ ISBN: 978-0-88368-425-2 ✦ Trade ✦ 368 pages
Courting Emma ✦ ISBN: 978-1-60374-020-3 ✦ Trade ✦ 384 pages

WHITAKER
HOUSE

The Daughters of Jacob Kane Series
Sharlene MacLaren

Welcome to Sandy Shores, Michigan, where there's never a dull moment with the witty, winsome Kane sisters. In *Hannah Grace*, the feisty, strong-willed eldest Kane sister strikes up a volatile relationship with the new local sheriff, Gabriel Devlin—a relationship that turns to romance, thanks to a shy orphan boy and a little divine intervention. In *Maggie Rose*, the middle Kane sister moves to New York City to work at an orphanage, falls in love with a newspaper reporter, and discovers God's greater purpose for them. In *Abbie Ann*, Jacob Kane's youngest daughter is a busy woman with little time for frivolous matters, including romance—until a handsome, divorced shipbuilder comes to town, his young son in tow, and God changes their hearts.

Hannah Grace ✦ ISBN: 978-1-60374-074-6 ✦ Trade ✦ 432 pages
Maggie Rose ✦ ISBN: 978-1-60374-075-3 ✦ Trade ✦ 432 pages
Abbie Ann ✦ ISBN: 978-1-60374-076-0 ✦ Trade ✦ 528 pages

WHITAKER
HOUSE

Love's Rescue
Tammy Barley

To escape the Civil War, Jessica Hale flees Kentucky with her family and heads to the Nevada Territory, only to lose them in a fire set by Unionists resentful of their Southern roots. The sole survivor, Jess is "kidnapped" by cattleman Jake Bennett and taken to his ranch in the Sierra Nevada wilderness. Angry at Jake for not saving her family, she makes numerous attempts to escape and return to Carson City, but she is apprehended each time. Why are Jake and his ranch hands determined to keep her there? She ponders this, wondering what God will bring out of her pain and loss.

ISBN: 978-1-60374-108-8 ✦ Trade ✦ 368 pages

WHITAKER
HOUSE

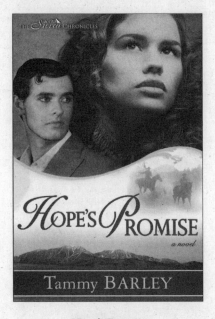

Hope's Promise
Tammy Barley

Jake Bennett is finally wed to the love of his life, Jessica Hale—but he isn't convinced she won't leave him. Life is a constant struggle for the Bennetts as they battle drought and live in fear of raids on Southerners, and he is not sure that Jess knew what she was getting herself into when she married him. Jess, however, despairs for another reason—she is unable to conceive a child. While trying to prove their unconditional love for each other, the Bennetts must stand in faith through betrayal, danger, and barrenness, trusting that God will reward their hopes for a better future.

ISBN: 978-1-60374-109-5 ♦ Trade ♦ 368 pages

WHITAKER
HOUSE

Beautiful Bandit
Loree Lough

Having escaped a gang of robbers who forced her to participate in a bank heist, Kate Wellington adopts an alias and decides to flee to Mexico. Lost and hungry, she stumbles upon the camp of a man named Josh Neville who offers to escort her across the border. But when she injures her ankle, the kindly cowboy takes "Dinah" home to his ranch to heal, instead. As the two grow closer, Josh realizes he's fallen in love, even as he learns the truth about Dinah. But does he know the whole story? And, after the truth comes out, will he put his life at risk to keep her with him?

ISBN: 978-1-60374-225-2 ✦ Trade ✦ 400 pages

WHITAKER
HOUSE